BLACK DOG

JOHN TERRY MOORE

Dreamspinner Press

Published by
DREAMSPINNER PRESS

5032 Capital Circle SW, Suite 2, PMB# 279, Tallahassee, FL 32305-7886   USA
http://www.dreamspinnerpress.com/

Black Dog
© 2014 John Terry Moore.

Cover Art
© 2014 Maria Fanning.
Cover content is for illustrative purposes only and any person depicted on the cover is a model.

ISBN: 978-1-62798-961-9
Digital ISBN: 978-1-62798-962-6
Library of Congress Control Number: 2014944017
First Edition September 2014

Printed in the United States of America
∞
This paper meets the requirements of
ANSI/NISO Z39.48-1992 (Permanence of Paper).

"It was the victim-sickness. Adrenalin howling in my head,
the black dog was my brain. Come to drown me in my breath
was energy's black hole, depression, compere of the predawn show
when, returned from a pee, you stew and welter in your death."

From "Corniche" by Les Murray

To Russell.

GLOSSARY

a good root—Old-fashioned, countrified description of the sex act.

arsehole—Asshole.

as gay as—Definitely gay.

Aussie Rules—Australian Rules football.

B&B—A bed and breakfast; mini hotel.

badgered—From "to badger," to be driven crazy.

bagging—Criticizing someone or something.

beat—A place to pick up gay sex.

black dog—Depression; a mental illness (the black dog on my shoulder).

Blind Freddie could tell—It was so obvious.

Blue Lake—Across the state border in South Australia. The Blue Lake is a
     well-known tourist attraction and very… blue.

Blundstone boots—Iconic Australian footwear.

bog—Public toilet.

bogan—Rough person, usually without principles or means of support.

boofy head—Large head like a plum pudding.

bushies—People from the country.

capsule—Like a bassinet, strapped into the seat belt harness in the car.

Caulfield Cup—The second most noticeable race of the Spring Carnival.

chook—Chicken.

chooks came home to roost—Everything happened because it was
     deserved.

clucky—Like a mother hen, broody, wanting a family.

crèche—Day care center.

cut off at the pass—Surprised.

CWA—Country Women's Association.

dob 'em in—Inform on them, tell other people.

flat out like lizards drinking—Bloody busy.

flyblown—Common problem with sheep; flies attack certain animals in warmer weather and they become infested.

gong bangers—People or persons in authority; an irreverent dig at the churches and religion, in the same category as a wanker.

Inter Dominion—Australia/New Zealand annual harness-racing competition.

It's a joke, Joyce—Old-fashioned gay-speak used where the situation or behavior is obvious.

jumping the fence—Switching orientation; gay to straight, straight to gay, etc.

Kelpie—Australian working-dog breed.

Lil/Lily Law—The police.

Melbourne Cup—World famous and most prestigious horse race. The nation stops for it.

packed to the rafters—Full up.

paddock—Field.

piss off—Leave!

pissed—Drunk.

pissed/pissed off—Upset, angry.

pissheads—Drunks.

ploughing an autumn paddock—Cultivating a field ready for sowing a crop.

poofter—Old-fashioned and derogatory term for a homosexual person.

rocked up—Arrived.

run up a dry gully—Nothing, no support, no sympathy.

schoolies week—A week of celebrations to mark the end of the final year of senior school.

sheilas—Women.

shit hits the fan—Self-explanatory; stand to one side.

slanging match—A prolonged exchange of insults.

sleepout—A shed in the back yard of a home converted to sleeping/living quarters.

spit the dummy—React negatively, with feeling.

stacking on a turn—A reaction to something unpleasant, showing displeasure.

strapper—A groom for racehorses, who also has general duties around the stables.

sulky—Light cart used behind trotters in harness racing.

talkback—Phone-in.

Tullamarine—Melbourne's main airport.

two bob each way—An old horse-racing term; also means being married and having a male lover on the side.

ute—Utility vehicle.

Watchtower—Religious magazine.

within cooee—Close, near to. Cooee is the bush person's call from one to the other.

CHAPTER 1
AWAKENING

I LOOKED across at Danny as we lay sunbaking. His cock lay straight up his bare belly, as hard as stone. I couldn't stop myself running my fingers along its length, curling them around and stroking it, the first time my hand had ever touched one other than my own.

It was longer than mine, but mine was much thicker, and it certainly had Danny's attention. By now he was gently fisting it, looking both pleased and curious all at once.

His gaze caught mine as we turned, facing each other on the warm flat rocks beside our swimming hole in the little creek, reaching orgasm in record time, yelling out as we came all over each other, reveling in the luxury of complete privacy because "our" swimming hole wasn't even known about.

Ever the leader, I found a spare towel, which had magically found its way into my bag, and I wiped him clean, his eyes following me with amusement.

It seemed, at least in my case, that what had happened was a relief in more ways than one. We'd grown up with our homes just a few minutes away from each other and had simply done everything together—school, family functions, farmwork, and now, in our immediate postpubescent life, we had finally roared over the imaginary line between wanting to and actually doing "it."

And we really liked each other—best mates, we were—and I felt a sense of wonder that I'd finally found something I now realized I'd been unconsciously looking for ever since I'd had thoughts about anything.

I knew I'd been sort of flirting with him for a while now, and he'd actually led me on. Mum said I was a master of the double entendre. Anything that wasn't remotely erotic I managed to turn into a joke with sexual overtones, and this time he'd called my bluff.

But it was worth it. In my eyes, he was stunning. I had a very good idea by now what pressed my buttons, and he was definitely it. Taller than me, dark, almost jet-black hair, a tendency toward a barrel chest—even as a fourteen-year-old—which was lightly covered in fine dark hair, a contrast to me because I had brown hair and was a little shorter.

There was common ground in one area. After constantly talking about sex, we discovered we not only had out-of-control libidos, but we both loved dicks. He loved my dick, and I loved his.

We rested close together in the warmth, listening to the wattlebirds busy with their airborne chatter in pursuit of nectar. Bruce, my twelve-month-old Kelpie, looked over his paws, and I'll swear he smiled at me.

We'd even jerked off together, but this was just so different. Neither Danny nor I mentioned the obvious—we didn't have to. We knew our relationship had changed forever as we reached for each other again. We'd watched porn on my laptop, and I decided, being the more confident and wicked one, that I'd try giving him head and see what happened.

I knew I shouldn't scrape him with my teeth and was conscious of giving him a good time as well as enjoying myself.

I must have been successful because he started moaning the instant I went down on him. After a short time, he quickly pulled out of my mouth and said "sixty-nine" so full of authority that I laughed at him. He looked at me a bit sheepishly, but I steered him in the right direction, and we found heaven on earth together.

"Are we okay?" I said to him as we packed up, our brief freedom over.

"Sure." He grinned. "Why shouldn't we be?"

"Oh, no reason." I grinned at him, but I could tell there was some turmoil behind those beautiful eyes. I put it out of my head because tomorrow was school, and we had chores at home. He had calves to feed, and I had to help my mum with her bath routine before Dad closed up at work.

Sunday trading at Prentice Farm Supplies had boomed. There were ever-increasing numbers of hobby farmers who were only around on weekends, and Dad was busily rounding them up. The weekly turnover had increased by 30 percent, he'd said. So it was now seven days a week for him, which made my home duties with Mum even more important.

Mum had multiple sclerosis, and my two young sisters, Emma and Megan, were too small to help her yet. Mum could do most things, including the cooking and housework, but she found showering or the weekly bath she enjoyed impossible to do without help. Dad had rigged up a small crane and a sling over the bath, and I actually looked forward to helping her. Any lingering embarrassment over her nudity had long gone. Mum instead turned the exercise into a weekly catch-up of harmless gossip, family news, and a one-on-one problem-solving exercise—if indeed either of us had problems that needed solving. The door was locked, not so much for Mum's privacy but to keep my sisters out so Mum and I had each other's full attention. Today she sensed something had changed, but I deliberately avoided discussion about Daniel and his family. She knew, I was sure. Her eyes told me so.

But she would never press me on it, because that just wasn't her way.

I WAS always a mature kid, I guess. Dad and Mum were well educated and people of the world, somehow lost souls in this maze of conservative thinking that was Victoria's southwest. They made sure that no topic was off the discussion list at home, particularly in areas of social interaction.

So it was relatively easy for me to work out my orientation.

Not that I was antifemale, far from it. I knew I'd simply have to try one or two just for fun, even though I knew at this early stage that it took a bloke to float my boat.

Yep, I was a gay boy for sure. I hadn't discussed it with Mum, Dad, or my sisters yet, but that would be a subject for another day. Happily for me, I knew that would be the least of my concerns as my life unfolded.

Around puberty I grew wistful, wondering why I was chosen to be this quirk of nature, one of so few within the vast majority. But since then, because I had generous access to the Internet, I reasoned there were quite a few others like me out there, so I wasn't alone. And because I grew up with parents who were just so cool and natural, I was able to answer my own questions and not get depressed.

I realized then I was quite normal, just a variation of nature's plan, and I knew I had to handle it. The alternative was unacceptable.

DANIEL, ON the other hand, came from a more traditional farming family, descended from the many Irish immigrants who had populated the district, wearing their Catholicism like a winter overcoat, locking their puritanical thoughts inside them.

Except no one gave a shit about the church these days, as my Dad and Mum correctly confirmed.

Daniel's dad, Bill Morgan, was a raw-boned, red-faced, loud bloke who drank too much on Friday nights and seemed ignorant of anything else but hard work. But he and Mrs. Morgan were always really nice to me and understood that Danny and I were the closest of friends. They encouraged the friendship, always knowing where to find their youngest son when he wasn't at home.

Over the years, Mr. Morgan had driven himself and his family hard in their mixed farming and dairying operation, and with all that hard work and focus, the family's fortunes had obviously turned for the better. With plenty of willing hands to run their assets, Danny had a much easier young life than his older brothers. Danny's brothers were not as assertive as their father but instead seemed very quiet and naïve, usually marrying the first girl they went out with. They still worked from daylight till dark seven days a week and had little exposure to the modern world outside the farm gate.

The exception was Simon, the second youngest, who was around five years older than Daniel and had escaped, living in town with his girlfriend, Julie, and working as a salesman in rural real estate. Simon was really cool, and Julie was just—lovely.

CHAPTER 2
THE ANIMALS

"PRENTICE CENTRAL" as Dad called it, the family property of over 1,200 hectares, or three thousand acres, was next door and run by my uncle Edward—"call me Ted." In fact, our house and land were once part of the original holding.

Uncle Ted and Aunt Helga had three kids, and Toby, the youngest, was about five years older than me. We were always close—really good mates—not just because we were cousins, but because Toby was one of the nicest people I've ever met. I loved him because, even though he had his own group of friends, he always took the time to stay in touch with me. He was always interested in what I was doing, and I suppose, like Dad, he was my sounding board and advice giver if I asked for it. The five years between us seemed to melt away when we were together. We'd gossip away like two old sheilas, and the family would joke about us being each other's best girlfriend.

By the time my sex adventures started with Daniel Morgan, Toby was nineteen and living in the big regional town just over an hour away, working for one of the banks and completing his accountancy degree at night school.

But he was home at least two weekends a month, and he would be at our back door within minutes of driving in the gate.

It was Toby, like Dad, who understood my love of animals before I actually knew it myself and encouraged me to think about a career involving them. Somehow I *knew* things about animals—"a connection," Dad said, laughing.

When Uncle Ted needed his stock horse to ride the fences, he rang me first because I could always catch old Jigger for him. If Uncle Ted went anywhere near his paddock, Jigger would piss off, tail over his back, leaving Uncle Ted yelling at him. The louder Uncle Ted yelled, the faster old Jigger ran—a total waste of time and energy for both of them. It was easier for me to get involved first up. I'd just talk to Jigger, and he'd hang his head over the fence and snuffle at me, drooling strings of slobber because he knew I had a carrot for him. When the bit was in his mouth and the bridle in place, only then did Jigger get his reward.

I never knew what the fuss was all about, but apparently old Jigger liked me!

The summer Danny and I finally got it all together, I started working part-time for the busiest vet in the district, Tim Rodgers.

Most fathers would have insisted their son work in the family business during the school holidays and afterward, and usually for nothing, but Dad and Uncle Ted were great parents, wanting nothing more than for their kids to find something in life they wanted to do, in an occupation where we could reach our full potential.

Tim Rodgers was a lovely man who was prepared to share his knowledge with a fifteen-year-old kid because I obviously had a natural aptitude and, more importantly, an interest in animals. The initial arrangement was that I was to spend a few days doing work experience. But at the end of the first week, I knew I had found my future career path, and Tim agreed, putting me on staff and paying me wages.

IF I ever needed confirmation of my career direction, it came the very next August as lambing got underway. The Prentice and Morgan families had shared a team of rams that year, a couple of whom had big boofy heads. Problem was their progeny were faithfully following the same genetic pathway, and there were some sudden losses of ewes and lambs as a result.

Uncle Ted asked Tim Rodgers to visit urgently because he could see the beginning of a disaster on his hands, and he didn't know how to handle it. Neither did Danny's father, so Uncle Ted invited him across as well.

Tim suggested they should gently drive the affected ewes in and put them undercover in a shearing shed, creating a maternity "hospital." Uncle Ted and Mr. Morgan looked at each other in horror, knowing they couldn't afford a vet for a temporary resident, yet not prepared to suffer any more losses of valuable breeding stock.

Tim just grinned at them and said the best little midwife in the district lived right next door—me—and that I already had a good idea what to do, but he'd retrain me that very night as soon as they yarded the sheep.

My August school holidays had actually begun that very day, and suddenly I was much busier than ever I expected to be.

I was nearly beside myself with excitement. I mean, here was a chance to prove myself and help everyone in the process.

And guess what? I had Danny as a helper!

Doctor Dean and Nurse Daniel!

Tim arrived, and as he did, about three ewes started pushing.

I caught the one that was furthest along, and Blind Freddie could have seen she had no chance unless we intervened.

The lamb presented in the correct manner with both front legs partially out but no sign of the head, which meant she was in serious trouble. Tim said he thought she'd been in labor for too long, and besides anything else, she'd probably dried out.

After he gloved me up, he pushed the lamb back against the contractions slightly and reminded me how to lubricate the canal with copious quantities of this marvelous gel. I looked up and winked at Danny, and he blushed. I could feel the head and smothered that in lube as well, as the mother gave a great cry and pushed, delivering the huge youngster at our feet. Quickly I cleared the mucus from his nose and with Tim's help gave him a little colostrum to tide him over until he got a drink from his mum. We had heaps of antibiotics, and after a time I could tell what to do when I saw the ewe struggling. It didn't take a genius to work out what stage of labor she was at and if it was just a breech or if the lamb had already died inside her.

In all we lost only about eight lambs and not a single ewe. But there were several sets of triplets, and so mothers that lost their babies ended up with a lamb anyway. I told Danny that plenty of lube solved everything, whether it was birthing ewes or horny young blokes looking for a good fuck, and, typically, he believed me. So one night when we were supposed to be sleeping and Dad was watching the ewes, Danny lost his virginity. That was the first time he ever kissed me. We were so emotionally charged at the time that we didn't even think much about what we were doing, except that it felt right.

That naughty night stripped away another layer of innocence, but it didn't seem to worry either of us because it really felt so good, and I think Danny just wanted more, much more, and who was I to deny him? I was in love. I knew it. At age fifteen, I was feeling all the highs and lows of a torrid love affair with my best friend.

Come to think of it, he had become my only friend as we spent more and more time together.

After that lambing, both families seemed to accept that Danny and I were a team—a fact that delighted me at the time and didn't seem to worry Danny one little bit. Nothing could stop Nature. Our houses were ten minutes away from each other at a leisurely walk, and around five and a half if we were horny, and that was all the time. Danny would disappear after the evening meal and bring his homework over, which we would do together. He'd say good night to everyone, make his way to the fence where he'd hang his schoolbag, and then double back in through my bedroom window, which was always open for him, of course. After a few months, Dad dumped a large rock under the window, which made access easier, making me smile and puzzling Danny.

But it didn't stop there. Many times in the middle of the night there would be a scratch at the window, and he'd be there again, a grin plastered all over his face and his shorts distended.

WE KIDS were so lucky to grow up where we did because we had animals all around us. Their lives were our lives, and we each depended on the other for our existence.

Bruce was a present to me from Uncle Ted, who took great pride in his Kelpies. He was a registered breeder, and Bruce's lineage was impeccable.

Kelpies were a laid-back, relaxed breed generally, rather like Australians, and generally were happy to go anywhere and be with anyone who had a mob of sheep or cattle to work and who fed them regularly.

Bruce was different.

A beautiful-looking creature, a long-legged black dog with some red underneath when he lost his winter coat. But he was such a stubborn bastard—just like me, Danny said—he refused to work for anyone else and was my dog alone. So much so that if he thought I was in danger of any sort, he'd get quite protective and fight for me.

I couldn't leave home without him. He'd fret and howl if he was chained or locked up when I was at school, so he came to school with me.

Danny and I usually rode our bikes the three kilometers there, and he loped alongside like a four-legged athlete, just so cool and self-assured.

Once we were there, I'd chain him up to a tree for shelter with a big pot of water beside him. Like me, our teachers were concerned when, for several days in a row, his water bowl was upset and he was dehydrated when I finished lessons for the day.

With my class teacher's acquiescence—that's different from giving permission, he said—I discreetly staked out the area and watched. Sure enough, along came bloody big Phillip Harrison, the school dickhead and resident fucking bully. As he bent down to tip Bruce's water over, I aimed my number twelve school shoe at the crack of his big fat arse and kicked it. He shrieked in fright, but that wasn't the end of his troubles. With me in plain sight, Bruce saw the kid as a threat and managed to add a few nips to the same area, while making enough noise to wake the dead.

"What did you do that for, you arsehole?" I yelled at him as he stood up, shaking the dust off his clothes and giving me a malevolent look.

"Fancy bringin' your fuckin' dog to school, you fuckin' poofter," he sneered. "Me an' me mates are just givin' you a little warnin' we don't want no fags or poofs in this school. This school is for decent people."

I suppose the worst thing I could have done, in hindsight, was to laugh at him as I did. "You are so out of your fucking tree, Harrison," I said. "Only a fucking moron talks like that these days. I could get you expelled for making sexist remarks like that, but because I'm a good and tolerant person, I wouldn't lower myself to deal with the town fucking trash."

His big pudgy mouth fell open as I poked his chest with my finger, and I looked him in the eye, smelling his foul breath. "If I ever again catch you or any of your hopeless fucking cronies taking your spiteful shit out on animals, particularly one owned by me," I whispered, "I promise you that you'll be wearing your arsehole around your throat for a collar. Now fuck off and enjoy your nice little detention." I grinned evilly as I saw my class teacher approaching.

I didn't mention Harrison's remarks to Danny because I had a feeling I was already treading a fine line there. Harrison and his mates had absolutely no evidence individually or collectively that we were gay, but they'd obviously picked up on the fact that Danny and I did everything together and rarely bothered with the various social circles that are part of every high school.

To defend ourselves on the charge of being gay guys would have drawn instant attention to the issue, and I wasn't sure how Danny would handle it.

But I also knew if I was asked a direct question, I didn't want to deny who I was, even at this early stage of my life, because it was important to stand up to cunts like Phillip Harrison and put them on notice.

Every night after Danny had gone home I lay there and worried, waiting for the rumors to start up and take over our lovely life together.

It was like living on the edge of a volcano. I had all the expert scientific knowledge about the subject but no idea when it would erupt.

CHAPTER 3
THE TIMES THEY ARE A-CHANGIN'

I RANG Dad at work and asked if he, Mum, and I could have some family time that night after dinner, to which he agreed. Then I told Danny we had some private family discussions going on and please not to come over until after nine o'clock. He looked hurt, of course, so I quietly pointed to one of our predesignated "rest areas" on the way home and blew him among the beautiful tree ferns that shielded us from the road. Bruce just sighed, turned, and sulked, which made us laugh.

We got to the Morgan driveway, and he air-kissed me good-bye.

Christ, Danny is going to have some explaining to do to his parents, sitting around over there until after nine o'clock. They'll think we've had a massive argument. And he's becoming so gay—the air kisses and the real kisses are coming thick and fast.

I TOLD Mum and Dad what the Harrison kid had said and done, including the gay slur, but begged Dad not to say anything to Danny, because I thought neither he nor his family could handle the real facts of life.

"And these are the facts of life," I said, surprising myself by being a little tearful, and told all.

"We know, dear," Mum said, and Dad just smiled.

"Yes, I know you do, guys." I smiled through a veil of tears as Dad jumped up and cuddled me. "Danny couldn't work out the rocks under my window, but I thought it was hilarious."

We all laughed at one another, and as usual my parents were light-years ahead of me.

"You're worried about your relationship with Daniel, aren't you, mate?" Dad asked, and I nodded.

"Danny isn't, umm… sophisticated enough yet to understand that we're even in a relationship. The moment someone goes public with any homophobic stuff, Danny will be distraught because his family are just so straight, and I think that would be the end of everything for us."

"You love him, don't you, darling?" Mum said, and I started bawling my eyes out.

"Y-y-yes," I stuttered.

"Then love usually finds a way," Mum said with feeling, and I couldn't help but think how much wisdom they shared between them.

"You're such a smart person, Dean, and we're so proud of you. We feel so honored that you've chosen to talk these issues over with us before anyone else. You're an old head on young shoulders, mate," Dad said, smiling.

"Wonder where I get it from," I said in a joking manner but fully meaning everything I said.

"You're sixteen years old physically, Dean, and while you're probably sixty years old in the head, one of the things that physical age does for us is to give us some perspective on things. At your age, the troubles of a love affair seem insurmountable, but I can tell you, over time it all sorts itself out like magic. But in the meantime, we should have a plan."

I looked at Dad and Mum, who had clearly thought the issues through. "There's still homophobia out there, as you've discovered today, and in a country area like this, it can be both unreasonable and dangerous. The bullies are targeting you and Daniel, yet there's not a shred of evidence to identify you as gay boys. Imagine what could happen if they *did* have some evidence," Dad said, lifting an eyebrow.

Mum looked upset and took my hand, stroking it.

I thought about my young sisters and casually wondered if they would ever need the focus on their lives that our parents had so unselfishly devoted to me.

No, growing up in the bush is still hard because I'm a boy. If I were a girl, even a lesbian, no one would give a shit.

"I want you and Daniel to be trained in the martial arts," Dad said, "so you're able to defend yourselves if you're ever physically attacked. I have an old friend in town who can give you a crash course first, then over a period of several months can develop your defensive skills to the point where no one in their right mind would take you on."

I knew I could refuse. I was going to miss some of my part-time veterinary work with Tim Rodgers, and the cash would have been really useful, but Dad made good sense. My main concern was Danny, but Dad told me not to worry, he'd talk to Mr. Morgan.

"He owes us for your efforts at lambing." Dad grinned. "He won't be a problem."

I sold the bill of goods to Danny, who was ecstatic. He naturally didn't see the bullshit I had been through at school as a future problem, but he thought being even semiskilled in martial arts was so cool. He was going to be the local Bruce Lee, so watch out, world!

So a few days later, Danny and I fronted up to this quite ordinary little weatherboard in town, and we met Linh, an Australian Vietnamese who had gone to school with Dad.

Quite apart from anything else, Linh taught Danny and me to have a deep respect for other ethnicities and other people. I watched with pride as Danny finally began to grow as a person, leapfrogging out of the immaturity of an unsophisticated country boy and appearing to be just a fraction more attuned to the greater world out there rather than just our little district.

HIGH SCHOOL morphed into college. Both were in the same location, sharing all the essential facilities. I enrolled in Chemistry, Mathematics B including Statistical Data Analysis, and Cell Biology, prerequisites for the Veterinary Science School. Danny took Basic Engineering and technical subjects.

There were decisions to be made before our last year was over. If I was accepted at Henry University, it meant I would have to transfer to the regional center and live there, hopefully with my cousin.

But for a young guy in love it was difficult, because Danny didn't want to move away from his "safe" environment. He was interested in diesel engines and thought he'd like to be apprenticed to one of the farm-machinery dealers in our local town.

We were sad about the arrangement. I offered him the alternative of working in the big town and us living together, but he seemed just tied by the family umbilical cord, and so we had to settle for weekends together.

It was around this time that I realized I hadn't seen Toby for weeks and rang his mobile. He apologized and said he'd had a lot going on in his life but hoped to be down in a few days, and he'd see me then.

Besides Mum and Dad, only my sisters knew my lifestyle secret. We had all discussed the situation, and they understood why I had to lead such a careful existence. Emma was twelve and Megan was ten, and they handled my coming-out with great class and intelligence, asking questions that were so sensible. It appeared they, too, had old heads on young shoulders.

But everyone agreed that I should include Toby in our little circle of knowledge as soon as possible.

But before I could do that, the shit hit the fan in a big way.

It was early Saturday morning, about six o'clock, and I could see Toby's car parked in the machinery shed, so obviously he had arrived sometime during the night. It was unusual because he normally drove down Saturday mornings and went back on Sunday afternoons.

Something wasn't right. I felt the hairs on the back of my neck stand up as I looked over at Prentice Central.

I was about to go across when suddenly Aunt Helga's voice rang out. I couldn't hear what she said, but somehow it didn't sound very complimentary.

The back door opened, and Toby stormed out, head down, not looking very happy, but at least he was headed in our direction.

"Hey, cuz," I said, "what's up?"

Toby looked totally stressed. His eyes were red, and he looked as if he'd just thrown his clothes on without a shower, which was so unlike my immaculate cousin.

Dad was getting ready for work and stopped in his tracks, on the same wavelength as me. "Tobes, what on earth's wrong?"

Toby turned around, looked us in the eye, and said, "I've just told Mum and Dad I'm gay, that's what's wrong!"

Dad and I looked at each other, and we nearly pissed ourselves. We laughed and laughed while poor cousin Toby looked on as if we were mad.

"Join the club," I said to Toby.

"What?"

"That's why I tried to contact you, to tell you I'm gay too."

We launched ourselves across the room at each other, laughing madly while Dad looked on with amusement.

"I must ask the obvious question, Toby," Dad said. "Why on earth did you leave it so long?"

"Because I wasn't sure what Mum and Dad would say. I've spent weeks and weeks, Uncle Allan, trying to get the courage to tell them. Three times I drove down here and went back again because I chickened out. The final straw was Mum demanding to know which girl I was sleeping with and wanting to give me the benefit of her advice. So I got in about ten o'clock last night, and Dad was in bed watching telly. I said hello to Mum and went straight into the bedroom and finally told Dad what was on my mind."

"And I know he'd be supportive," Dad said.

Toby smiled at us and nodded. "You know what he said? 'So what? So bloody what?' So we had a really good discussion and an amazing cuddle when Dad realized the bloody agony I'd put myself through. But Mum was different, as you can imagine," Toby said with some regret in his voice.

I could imagine. Auntie Helga was probably the kindest, nicest person anyone could meet. She cooked for us when Mum was sick and helped nurse her when she was really ill. And looked after we three kids as if we were her own. But there was a European stubbornness and directness with her, plus some naïveté when it came to matters like sexuality. And it wasn't good, because she didn't really know what a gay person was!

Dad's phone buzzed, and it was Uncle Ted. Knowing without asking that Toby was with us, he requested an immediate family meeting, to which Dad agreed. Dad rang his helper, who agreed to open up for him, and we all trooped across, Mum sitting the wheelchair up on its rear wheels as she expertly rolled along, much faster than we could walk.

MY OPINION of my cousin Toby as a smart guy was reinforced.

During the week he'd rung his sister Gail and his brother Brian and explained to them what was likely to happen that weekend and why, and enlisted their support. They were neither surprised that they now had a gay brother nor that their mother would erupt like Mount Vesuvius as a result. Equally they knew their father would be totally supportive, as they were. So when their mother had rung them early on Saturday morning looking for a sympathetic ear, she was told to grow up. Auntie Helga had indeed run up a dry gully, which left her speechless with rage, crying and screaming all at once as we walked in the kitchen door.

She spotted Emma and Megan and tried to get them to leave because this news was too terrible for such young ears, but Mum stepped in and told her very firmly they were staying because this was a natural and normal issue and Emma and Megan were perfectly okay with it.

"Aren't they, Dean?" Mum asked.

"Yes," I replied with a smile on my face, "they were just so cool when we told them about me."

Aunt Helga's face suddenly wrinkled up like a bull mastiff in season as she tried to absorb this new information. "You, Dean," she barked, "what about you?"

"Auntie Helga." I smiled nervously but took my time because I had the element of surprise. "I'm sure we would find some genetic links in previous generations of our family if we looked hard enough, but these days no one really bothers about stuff like this. Toby isn't the only gay person in our family, because I'm gay too."

"You've corrupted your cousin," she shrieked at poor Toby, who was doing a good job of trying to fade into the wallpaper and disappear from sight.

In all the years I'd spent around Uncle Ted, the only time I'd heard him raise his voice was when he was trying to catch Jigger, so it was quite shocking to hear him roar at his wife the way he did.

"Helga," he shouted, "don't be bloody stupid and irrational! If you insist on treating your own child like this, then you're not a fit and proper person to be around him. Our son is a wonderful young man, and you're being hysterical and ignorant. Now unless you can calm down and apologize to your son and nephew, I suggest you go to the bedroom and retire because you have nothing to offer this conversation at the moment."

We all felt terrible as Auntie Helga burst into tears and ran from the room. Uncle Ted apologized to Toby and me.

MUM AND Dad looked at each other. Whenever there were family problems, food seemed to be the answer, so Dad fired up Prentice Central's barbeque, which in turn drew Aunt Helga out of seclusion and reinstated the status quo because her role in life was to feed everyone. As if by magic, Gail, Brian, and their families arrived, and the whole silly affair dragged through lunchtime and well into the afternoon.

Rather than ostracize her, we all felt sorry we'd had what amounted to a family storm in a teacup. Aunt Helga acknowledged that the Netherlands, the place of her birth, now led the world in areas of marriage equality, and same-sex-attracted people had exactly the same rights and privileges as everyone else. But to have a gay child was such a shock to her, she said, and it was the last thing she expected. Now she'd had time to think about it, she could see some positives. It was quite obvious that Toby would be a captain of industry, a financier no less, and that I would be a famous veterinary surgeon, because gay people worked harder than anyone else. On and on she went, and if Toby and I looked a little bewildered, it was no wonder.

Aunt Helga was, after a few hours of intense family scrutiny, a convert—as blinkered and one-eyed as if she had seen Jesus at the farm gate.

She could easily have gone from door-to-door in town and instead of selling the *Watchtower*, she could have sold gay porn magazines.

Later in the day, I got to spend some time with Toby. Without hesitation, I told him about Danny and my reservations about the relationship, particularly the reasons why it could so easily go off the rails.

He agreed, which shocked me, but also brought me down to earth again.

"It's all right, cuz. People in love are never rational. We always want to believe the best, even if our partners are cunts. We make allowances for them, and we give them latitude, even when we know they're wrong and particularly if they treat us like shit. One of these days your knight in shining armor will come along, and you'll know all about it, I promise."

Suddenly, the penny dropped. "So, are you speaking from experience, cuz?"

Toby nodded, a faraway look on his face. "His name's Robert, Robert McNamara, but everyone, including me, calls him Macca. He's about five years older than me, had lived as a straight man until I got him between the sheets, and in a very short time he's become the rest of my life. By the time you come to live with us, we'll be in our house. We signed the papers yesterday."

I looked at Toby, and I couldn't hold back the damp eyes. "You must love him, Tobes."

Toby just nodded, and I thought a day that had started with such drama now couldn't get much better.

CHAPTER 4
THE SHIT HITS THE FAN

ONE MORNING about the middle of the following week, I couldn't find Danny.

We'd always meet on our bikes at his farm gate and ride to school together. Bruce wasn't happy either, and, as a creature of habit, he was clearly put out that his other favorite person was missing.

Because I was running a little late, I thought maybe Danny had gone on ahead, and Bruce and I sprinted to school.

Still no sign of him, so I sent him a text, but by the time class was about to begin there was no reply to my text and no sign of Danny.

I started to worry and sent a further text. And still no sign of him.

Finally at lunchtime I caught up with him in the school canteen, and even though our eyes met for a moment down the line, he looked like he actually wanted to avoid me. Taking his food, he strode across the room to Phillip Harrison's table, sitting there with his horrible cronies, who looked back at me and laughed.

Suddenly I wasn't hungry.

I ate sparingly and left, heading over to Bruce, whom I let off the chain, and we walked together down the path to the little creek at the rear of the school grounds. There were a few kids there, mainly the smokers, who waved cheerily at me and continued puffing away.

Bruce cocked his leg and had a nice drink from the stream as I sat on the bank and tried to work out what was going on.

What was different to last week, I wondered. What had changed?

Then it hit me like a tonne of bricks.

Toby and his news, outing himself to the family group.

But that was sort of family business, so Toby could eventually bring his boyfriend home to meet Uncle Ted and Aunt Helga. I wondered why would anyone worry about someone who had already left school years ago and was already in the workforce?

I dragged myself back to class, but my heart wasn't in it, so I feigned a headache, and Bruce and I left early.

Fuck it, two can play at the no-speaking game. I'll go home, do my homework, and see if he shows later.

I HAD no appetite at dinner, and Mum and Dad knew something was wrong. Nothing had prepared me for this. I'd always been confident and outgoing at school, and while we kept to ourselves, Danny and I were still popular in a nice, uncomplicated way.

But this was different, because as well as Danny's change in attitude, I'd noticed a few nasty stares from kids I normally got on well with.

Mum didn't think people could be so shallow, and she was upset that Danny had treated me so rudely, but Dad was a realist, and he agreed it had to be something to do with Toby's revelations at the weekend.

"I've been expecting something like this," he said sadly. "That's why I was so insistent that Linh trained you to defend yourself. This could get nastier before it gets better, Dean. I'm sorry, but it looks like you and Danny as a relationship are in trouble, and that's terrible because it's no fault of yours."

Just then there was a scrape at the backdoor and I flew over, throwing it open.

He stood there, guiltily hanging his head, looking from Mum to Dad and back to me again. He had his laptop bag with him, homework ready as if nothing had happened, but his demeanor and his body language said the opposite.

Dad wisely didn't get involved as I motioned to Danny to follow me into my bedroom.

"So what's this shit about, then?" I asked him curtly.

"Dunno what ya mean," he replied defensively.

"Well, let's put it this way, Daniel," I said, using his full name to telegraph my very pissed-off state of mind. "Why did you go off to school by yourself, then proceed to ignore me for the remainder of the day, choosing to mix with the town trash instead?"

"Because they're not gay!" he shouted.

"Daniel Morgan, if you ever raise your voice to me in that way and attempt to insult my intelligence with such bullshit, I'll drag your arse over to your old man, tell him what you just said to me, and let him deal with you."

"Oh no, don't, Dean, please, don't tell Mum and Dad about any of this."

"About what?"

"Your Auntie Helga was at a CWA meeting on Tuesday, and someone started criticizing gay people, and she cracked it big time. She told everyone about Toby. How he had a big job at the bank, and that he was a gay man, and how everyone should make gay people feel more welcome down here. Then she went right off and screamed at the woman who was carrying on and told her to try saying something nice about young people instead of just hangin' shit on 'em all the time. She musta really stirred 'em up, because it's all around the place now."

I had to giggle at Auntie Helga. There was no way she'd allow any criticism of her kids, and Toby's news must have made a juicy morsel on an otherwise dull day bereft of any "scandal."

"So even though she never mentioned me, I'm guilty by association," I snarled back. "Just because my name's Prentice as well."

Danny nodded miserably, looking like he didn't want to be around me, which was probably understandable. What made me mad, of course, wasn't poor Aunt Helga's opinion on the matter, because she had changed into a pro gay rights activist overnight, and I knew she would fight to the death for Toby and me. No, what appalled me was the level of ignorance and stupidity involved in our peer group at school and their parents.

"So you suddenly wanted to ditch our lifelong friendship, and dare I say our relationship, because your new mates don't like gay people, is that it?"

"I'm not gay!" Danny shouted, out of control.

"Well, you'll pardon me for doubting your opinion when I distinctly remember being chock-a-block up you on Sunday night, with you screaming out 'fuck me, fuck me' at the top of your lungs," I snapped.

"I'm not gay," Danny cried. "I read on the Internet that straight guys sometimes like to fool about with gay guys, and that's like me."

"Oh," I replied, somewhat dangerously, "and where's your straight credentials? When was the last time you stuck your dick up a pussy, may I ask? You're kidding yourself, Danny, but that doesn't matter. What does matter is that whatever your sexuality might be, you still don't want to be seen with me because some of your new mates think I'm gay. It's that simple, isn't it? You'd rather hang around with those fucking cretins you were with today because they're supposed to be straight?"

Danny hung his head and literally sobbed, and I drove my point home.

"My dad and mum have known I'm gay for some time now, and they also know we've had a relationship of sorts. Frankly I think you underestimate your parents and certainly one of your brothers."

Danny's mouth dropped open in alarm. "Which one?" he croaked.

"Simon, of course. He and Julie love us, Danny. They think we've got great potential as a couple."

"Don't you breathe a fuckin' word about me bein' gay to anyone," Danny threatened. "Particularly not to my family, right." He poked me in the chest with his finger.

I stood up and steadily met his gaze. "I think you've forgotten your manners again, Daniel. Only one day of mixing with the town trash, and you're already starting to sound as ignorant as they are. Oh, and before you go, there's something you should know about one of your new friends."

He looked at me like a rabbit caught in the headlights. "Those people who openly criticize gay people are usually insecure about their own sexuality, and one of your new cronies came on to me so strongly a few weeks ago it was embarrassing. So if you receive some unwelcome attention from one of them, I'm sure you'll know how to handle it, you being a straight guy these days."

Danny visibly wilted at my bitchy tirade, but hell, why fuck about when there's a few things on your mind?

"What those guys don't understand," I continued, "is that homophobic remarks and behavior aren't tolerated at school anymore, and I'd like nothing more than to have my parents sue the pants off anyone who opens their mouth. And that includes you. So why don't you fuck off, you fucking loser?"

Danny's tears flowed again as he ran through the house and almost flew out the back door.

IT NEVER got much easier. The following weeks went by in a blur as I determinedly worked toward my grades in preparation for Veterinary

Science School. I'd even taken an extra subject online so there could be no argument that I'd fulfilled all the college prerequisites and could move away from this fucking hellhole.

There was almost no sign of Danny. I saw him infrequently at school. We had effectively vanished from each other's lives, and I felt a vacuum where he once was. To say I missed him was an understatement, but I had the added emotional burden of a love affair gone wrong. Not a case where he'd taken off with someone else, which would probably have been easier to put behind me and move on, but a situation where, even in this modern society, he was lying to himself, and because of that I felt only sorrow for Danny and for myself.

He'd hurt me badly, I'd reacted harshly, and we were both paying the price.

The one bright spot was Simon, Danny's brother. He and Julie never gave up on me, they often took me on outings with them, and their kindness was amazing. One Sunday they brought Danny with them. He stomped along behind, obviously not pleased. Mum saw him first and made a huge fuss of him. Then he saw me, and we got emotional.

That night we cuddled together in my bed, and he left to go home around 2:00 a.m. We made our peace with each other, but he made no secret of the fact that he was still determined to eventually live a straight lifestyle.

Then he dropped the bombshell that he now had a girlfriend, and when he told me who it was, it was hard to be jealous.

He was dating Suzanne Crosby, who was a very healthy girl, raised on good farm produce to keep her strength up. She had managed to work her way through an Aussie Rules team, the cricket club, and the anglers' association, the latter consisting mainly of married men.

It was common knowledge she'd had at least two abortions and been instrumental in the demise of several marriages, all accomplished under the age of nineteen. Of course she welcomed Danny as her boyfriend. She had a penchant for well-developed schoolboys anyway, but I knew poor Danny would be the laughingstock of the town. Suzanne needed a nice boy who wasn't attached to anyone else so she could display him as a trophy, and in that respect, she and Danny were on the same wavelength.

But there was no way I was playing second fiddle to anyone else, least of all Suzanne Crosby. I took care not to criticize either of them. This was a path down which Danny would have to travel without my assistance in any way.

"Sorry," I said to him softly when he arrived a few nights later. "You can't have it both ways. If you're serious about eventually settling down with a girl and having a family, then I can't stand in your way."

He tried to pretend he didn't understand me, but he knew. He knew I was too proud to be an object of sexual gratification while he had the town bike for window dressing.

But we agreed to always stay friends. Both of us knew at this stage of our lives that friendship was probably more important than anything else.

WHILE DANNY'S hang-ups about gay sex continued to haunt him, I now felt less constrained because our relationship was over. Even though I hadn't come out at school, I increasingly stuck up for myself as the name-calling and homophobic comments continued, both in the school ground and on Facebook and Twitter, where the insults flew through cyberspace totally unchecked but unfortunately believable in the absence of any defense.

I was constantly called "PP" for "Poofy Prentice," which was really stupid simply because my cousin had been outed by his mother!

I remember thinking to myself that maybe it could be worse. How would I feel if I'd been a straight boy faced with this unrelenting bullshit? At least gay guys have an expectation they'll probably have to travel a rough road before they reach the highway, but for straight guys this would be the ultimate insult—because gay guys aren't as good as straight guys, are they?

I was also hated because, with the homophobic rubbish being thrown at me, I still managed to achieve A levels in every single subject, which I needed if I was going to leapfrog into the Veterinary Science School. Which meant, in their eyes, that a gay guy was smarter than they were, and that obviously hurt them heaps.

My old nemesis Phillip Harrison was still leader of the trolls, some of them farmers' sons and all who should have known better.

One was Oliver Brown, who had come on to me some months prior and whose advances I had rejected. Oliver was really pissed off because I now had something on him, and he couldn't afford for that to be public knowledge, so he, Harrison, and four other arseholes began a campaign of sorts, trying to force me to leave. But if brains were dynamite, then it wouldn't have even parted their hair.

So rather than be physically confrontational, Dad and I put our heads together and got the local branch of a legal firm experienced in personal libel and slander to issue a warning to their parents. The small fee was worth every cent.

We sent a copy to the headmaster, for good measure.

THEY CAME at me from around the corner of the lockers, surprising me, dragging me outside, down toward the creek. It was a winter morning, and some frost remained on the ground, which made standing difficult.

They made their first mistake when they let me go so they could bash me and verbally hammer home the message their fathers had instructed them to deliver. That they were heartily sick of the young bloke who was making their kids look stupid and who was just one of the Poofy Prentices anyway.

I was now exactly where I needed to be as I pressed the button on my mobile, our prearranged signal. Somewhere in the school administration building, the headmaster was answering the phone to my father, who was suggesting he'd better make sure I was safe, as the first one ran at me. My training kicked in, and he went down, screaming in pain as he tore his knee open on the still frozen ground. They took it in turns to throw punches, which was a bit silly because I simply continued to take them out one at a time.

Danny arrived as big fat Phillip Harrison started to run in the opposite direction. Danny intercepted him, kicking him in the nuts as he fell to the ground screaming. Several teachers appeared over the horizon. Only Oliver Brown remained, his face white.

"So what's it to be, Oliver," I whispered, "a smack under the ear or a head job?" His mouth fell open as I made eye contact. "You could have had yourself a good time, Ollie," I purred, "if you'd played your cards right, because I really am an excellent cocksucker. But you and quite a few others want to hide behind your girlfriends' skirts while I've been really enjoying myself. I might even mention to Daddy that if you play your cards right, I could be his new daughter-in-law. He'd be really impressed with that, wouldn't he?"

The look on Danny's face was priceless—total jealousy mixed with anger and then guilt, a heady combination.

CHAPTER 5
ESCAPE

I REALIZED I was an unsophisticated eighteen-year-old from the bush, but what amazed me was how easily I adapted to my new home and way of life, as did Bruce, who seemed to thrive on all the attention.

Thanks to Dad and Mum and the Internet I knew my way around many of life's questions, and through Danny I'd experienced the highs and lows of a relationship, so I wasn't at all naïve for my age.

Which was certainly a great way to be, because Toby and Macca's home environment was anything but traditional.

I was introduced to Macca, and I thought about how hot he was and told my lovely cousin we had similar tastes in men, causing the three of us to laugh our heads off. Realizing what I'd implied, I tried to apologize, but they just laughed even more, welcoming me as a fellow traveler into their family.

"At least I'll know where to find him if he strays," Toby said, grinning. "I'll look in your room first."

Macca was a bit of a bear in appearance—a ruddy weather-beaten face, a broad hairy chest, thick legs clad in work pants and shod with Blundstone work boots. He had tight curly hair—almost African in appearance—nut brown in color and mostly hidden under one of his collection of baseball caps.

But Macca's crowning glory was his beautiful smile. It welcomed you into his world and reassured you that because you were family, he would do anything it took to make sure you felt loved and safe.

MACCA WAS self-employed. He had a concrete-cutting business, and as I drove into their driveway, he was in the process of taking delivery of his second work van—business was evidently booming.

Their house was a big old cream-colored Californian bungalow on the eastern side of the city on a huge block of land, with a little sleepout in the back yard. It was Friday afternoon, and Toby was still finishing up his working day at the bank, so Macca introduced me to the other members of their family group—Paul and Dougie, two young blokes who occupied the bungalow with their twelve-month-old baby, Jenny.

Paul was quite tall, well built, with brown hair, and looked like a college jock, while his mate Dougie was smaller, with fair hair and complexion and the most amazing combination of tattoos and piercings I'd ever seen. There was hardly a square centimeter of his body visible that wasn't covered in ink or didn't have some metal hanging out of it.

Dougie had Jenny in a little stroller, and as I looked down at the chubby little creature, she returned my gaze with a beatific smile, obviously directed at me.

"Oooh," Dougie said, "she only smiles at the good-looking blokes!"

Paul laughed. "Yeah, but she's got good taste, darls, because she always grins at you first."

How nice that they can openly flirt with each other, I thought, watching the language of intimacy between them.

So here I am, ready to begin university, and I've gone from a rural community knowing just one other gay guy to a household with two same-sex couples and a kid. How amazing was that!

And I realized it didn't stop there. This regional city was clearly more advanced socially than either the tiny rural center of my birth or even Melbourne.

Toby and Macca were part of a group of like-minded couples, most of whom I'd already met—Craig, a builder, and Teddy, an architect. And Steve, a Senior Constable, was with his partner Aaron, an IT specialist.

In the same period, at Henry University, where I was about to spend the next five years of my life, the headquarters of the International Center for Human Partnerships—ICHP—had been founded by two Americans, Alain Le Maitre and Kenneth Osborne, close friends of Craig and Teddy, and was quickly becoming an international beacon for same-sex people.

RIGHT NEXT to Toby and Macca's room was my new bedroom, with a view out into the backyard and the sleepout. Toby had found a nice secondhand desk from an auction, and Macca, ever the handyman, had repolished it so it looked brand new up against the wall with the Internet connection right beside it.

Christ, I'm one lucky dude to have the most perfect home environment for the foreseeable future. Other kids had to put up with dorm life or share shitty rented premises, and here I was, invited by Toby and Macca to live with them in these beautiful surroundings before I even had a chance to ask them.

As had been my custom at home with an unwell mother and a father who worked long hours, I began preparing the evening meal, knowing Bruce would enjoy any leftovers the next day and that Dougie had already organized Jenny's meal.

I was working away at the sink, peeling veggies, when I felt a pair of hairy arms slip around me, then a sloppy kiss on my right ear. "Tobes said you'd just fit in so well, and he's right." Macca said, "There's no work roster here. If we're in a good place without any deadlines, then we sorta take it in turns to do the evening meal. We're all passable, but Tobes said you're an ace cook."

"Oh, thanks very much," I said. "Now the fuckin' pressure's on."

Paul, Dougie, and Macca were all pissing themselves when Toby walked in the door, head down, obviously on a mission.

"Relax, darling," Macca said, "we've got a cordon bleu chef, and ya got th' night off."

IT WAS after dinner that first evening that I asked about Paul and Dougie's story. I was intrigued and quietly asked Toby how they came to be there so I wouldn't embarrass them by asking them direct.

Toby shook his head and smiled, leading me into the big lounge room where Macca softly snored in an armchair. Jenny was also fast asleep in her carry basket in the corner, and Paul and Dougie had cuddled up together on the big old sofa.

"Guys," Toby said, "Dean wants to know all about you two and how you came to be part of this family. What do you reckon?"

Paul's face registered pleasure, I noticed, and probably pride as well. He smiled at me and patted the sofa next to him.

Toby grinned at me and left the room.

"Well, it all started with me, I suppose." Paul smiled. "I was living with my mother in a commission house in the western side of town. Never really knew my father, so for years it was just Mum and me plus whatever boyfriend she brought home—and there were plenty of them. She was always high on something, so that's why I learned to cook," he said sadly. "We never had any spare cash even for McDonald's or KFC, so I managed to find some meat and veggies, usually the chuck-outs from Safeway. They were really good to me there, and I sorta kept us fed. But she kept fallin' behind with the rent, and we had social workers and commission people there all the time. I learnt how to do the washing and ironing," he said proudly. "And I even started to do okay at school, but when I was about sixteen she just pissed off with the latest boyfriend and went to Queensland, and I've never seen her since. Wouldn't know if she was dead or alive.

"So that's when I lost it," he said with a sob in his voice.

I felt terrible that I'd asked him to rehash part of his life that obviously held painful memories.

"No," he said as if sensing my discomfort. "It's over now. I got in with a really, really bad mob. They made their living dealing, and I had to be a courier around the place on my bike. I mean, what could be more innocent, a kid on a bike? Even then I realized I was gay, but I was smart enough not to tell anyone because I would have been in real trouble, simple. So there were some chicks who used to hang around with the guys, just moles they were, and one of them took a fancy to me.

"I managed to get it up long enough to bang her, and that's how I got Jenny." He smiled. "After she was born, her old man arranged for a DNA test, and there was no doubt I was the father. That was an eventful week." He sighed. "Jenny's mother pissed off with some bloke, and I was handed my kid to look after. Then the bailiffs arrived and took all Mum's stuff, and the commission threw me out of our house."

"You're getting ahead of yourself again." Dougie said. "I was in the same gang," he said. "And we realized we were really hot for each other, but they would have fucked us over properly if they found out. So we'd sneak away to a squat I knew and spend the night there, and it didn't take long for us to grasp we had somethin' special, like we loved each other."

A tear began sliding down Paul's face, and I held his hand. He knew I understood, and he continued. "Dougie was amazing. He somehow got all this formula to keep Jenny fed. He got food for us and a little gas stove to cook it on, and we fled to the squat to hide. We only had the clothes we stood up in, so I was on laundry duty every day.

"We were at the squat for about a week when the coppers found us one night."

"Not Steve?" I guessed.

"Yep. Senior Constable Steven Norris, our guardian angel. They made up a bed for us at the station, and the next morning they brought us over here because Steve said Macca and Toby were part of this volunteer group. We walked in, and they had breakfast ready." Dougie grinned.

"We were nearly sick, we ate so much," Paul said quietly.

Just then Toby came back into the room. "What they didn't tell you, Dean, was that they wouldn't touch a drop of anything until they'd bathed Jenny, dressed her in some clean clothes, and after feeding her, put her down for a sleep. Macca and I watched with our mouths open. After that experience we reckoned we just had to make them part of our family. Anyone as unselfish and caring toward a little child and each other meant that the cycle of self-abuse had been broken with these two. Neither of them do drugs—don't even drink alcohol, can you believe that? All they needed was a chance, and we've given them that. Paul is at night school three nights a week and helps Macca during the day, while Dougie works for the wholesale florist down the road. Mrs. Browning next door looks after Jenny when none of us are here, so if you don't mind, you'll also be required to do some multitasking as time goes on. Okay with you?"

I nodded at Toby and the boys. I loved babies, and having a chance to look after Jenny was a no-brainer for me. There was no doubt she recognized a queen when she saw one, so we already had a great relationship.

CHAPTER 6
A NEW LIFE

DESPITE DAD and Mum lovingly describing me as a child prodigy, I always understood university would be no pushover but a real stretch academically from my high school and college years. And it bloody was.

Subjects such as Veterinary Anatomy, Biochemistry, Physiology, Animal Systems, and Veterinary Professional Life were just as dry as they probably sounded to a layman, and even though I had lots of practical, hands-on experience in Tim Rodgers's practice, nothing prepared me for the reality of this mountain of information that my poor brain had to absorb.

And if that wasn't enough, the whole experience was all the more stressful because I didn't know a single soul in this new place.

But then orientation week kicked in, and the puzzle began to resolve itself.

But what really helped was meeting Sarah and Will.

They were locals, were in the same stream as me in the Veterinary Science School, and we became great mates immediately. Sarah was a bubbly, gregarious, in-your-face redhead, while Will was a touch geeky, quieter and more introspective, tall, slim, and dark. But I loved them because they weren't up themselves—they were here to learn, like me, and didn't waste time with "look at me" behavior. And they both had a wonderful dry sense of humor. We did the guided tour together—library resources, lecture theaters, bistro and café, dining hall—and at every turn "the facilities" were pointed out.

"Christ," I murmured to Sarah, "they really want us to know where to shit, don't they?"

"Maybe if the lectures don't move your bowels, then the food will," she bellowed, and our guide, a postgraduate volunteer, looked a touch askance.

Will nodded. "And as long as they've got some nice glory holes for our mate here"—he pointed at me—"then hopefully they'll serve a dual purpose."

I felt the heat rise to my cheeks as they looked at me, grinning. Three days into this place and my cover was blown, our guide finally laughing at our antics.

"Well, there are a few, so I've been told," he said. "But you'll have to establish their location for yourself."

His brusque manner returned as we staggered along behind him, trying to keep our mirth in check.

We eventually found ourselves back at the café, and while I wasn't upset because my lifestyle was now public knowledge, I was still curious.

"Surely I'm not that obvious," I said to Will and Sarah.

"No, only to the trained eye," Will laughed. "We've both got same-sex siblings, so we grew up with queens all around us. Sarah has the most beautiful tits, which you totally ignored, but your eyes kept wandering to my crotch. You like what you see?"

"Yes I do, as a matter of fact," I said calmly, calling his bluff. "You want to give me a demonstration?"

"Maybe later when Sarah isn't looking."

"You can borrow him any time you like, Dean," said Sarah. "I'm totally tired of it."

I realized I now had the upper hand as Will began squirming in his seat, looking a little under pressure.

"Premature ejaculator?" I inquired of Sarah, deliberately ignoring him.

"Among other strange nocturnal habits," she replied with a straight face.

"What a pair of fuckin' bitches you both are," he laughed.

"Takes one to know one, dear," I said to my newest straight mates, and everything in my world was just a little happier.

OUR DAY just got better from there on. The final destination was a presentation and drinks at the ICHP, an annex of the university. I smiled inwardly. This mob must be pretty smart. University students by definition are always impoverished, so in order to maintain an enthusiastic focus on their material, they were holding a mini cocktail party afterward. Free booze and finger food. No wonder the place was packed to the rafters!

The presentation talked about the ICHP as a unique institution, its work in third-world countries and others with traditional values. It was evidently regarded with respect worldwide, encouraging governments to treat same-sex-attracted people as a legitimate part of societal structure through proper legislative process.

The ICHP also ran another business in parallel with its humanitarian pursuits—surrogacy. It arranged, controlled, and managed surrogacy services for same-sex and hetero parents-to-be from sources all over the world and at home in Australia—a highly profitable and complex business.

I'd heard about this place, and after the presentation by its founders, questions were invited. I had to ask about the name.

"Why not call yourselves Gay International?" I laughed.

"That's actually a very good question," Kenneth Osborne said, a strapping big African-American, probably in his late thirties. "The charter of this organization is to fight homophobia and prejudice. If we showed bias by not including hetero people, then we could be accused of prejudice ourselves. The fact is, our straight mates are the ones driving marriage equality here in Australia, and of course we should never forget that we're all human beings anyway."

Which is a nice way of saying that in this society of profoundly changed attitudes, kids were exploring their sexuality like never before. I nodded my thanks to him, while being mesmerized by his presence. I'd never really noticed older guys before, but this guy was just so sexy he could have told me anything, and I would have believed it.

My new friends picked up on my body language straightaway, and I blushed deep beetroot as they led me toward the food and drinks, still laughing their crazy heads off. The bastards could read me like a book already, and if we all stayed on track with our studies, I had five years ahead of me being teased mercilessly—except I had a great memory, and they'd better not let their guard down around me because retribution could be a real bitch.

THERE WAS a mini guided tour around the ICHP, and I had to pinch myself.

Here was this vibrant, effective, public organization devoted to supporting same-sex-attracted people around the world.

Yet just over one hour's drive away, where I was born and lived for the first eighteen years of my life, the law may have changed, but attitudes remained just the same—similar attitudes to those Irish immigrants who'd settled the district nearly two hundred years ago.

If anything, because attention had been drawn to the issue, the social stigma was even worse now than physical violence. A person even perceived to be same-sex attracted was simply ignored. Membership applications for local clubs were misplaced, lifelong friendships disappeared overnight, and the sounds of silence were deafening.

That was the atmosphere I'd left behind and the atmosphere Danny was part of more than ever—living with his girlfriend in town, still downplaying his links to the Poofy Prentices, and trying desperately to reinforce his butch image as a diesel mechanic in any way possible. I knew it would never last. With resources like the Internet and understanding Danny as I did, I knew he was headed for trouble unless he relented and began living a life that was more natural and fulfilling.

"IT'S MUCH more sophisticated here," Toby said after dinner that evening. "This place has a very embracing attitude, thanks to the university and the work we all did after Craig and Teddy became a couple. Nowadays the city council has outreach programs, and the police are totally on side. But this place is still a town in transition."

Macca agreed with him.

"What do you mean, guys?" I asked, full of curiosity.

"Well, mate," Macca explained, "in simple terms, blokes just got married. Didn't matter if you batted for the other team, you just managed to get it up somehow, then hey presto, you've got a couple of kids and you're flying. I mean, you've proven your manhood, and you just give the little woman a fuck once a month and it's all cool. Fact is, of course"—Macca smiled gently—"the poor girl is so fucking tired raising kids and usually working full-time as well, she probably doesn't want much sex anyway. Then about five years ago, the shit really hit the fan for these guys.

"Suddenly being gay wasn't the worst thing that could happen to a young bloke. In fact, it became cool to be out and proud. Public opinion changed with the speed of light. Can you imagine how some of these guys felt? All that play-acting, living a double life, and it had all been for nothing! Marriages broke apart without warning. Blokes like Aaron, Craig, and even me realized there was an alternative. And just look at us all now." He grinned, pinching Toby's cheek affectionately.

"But obviously there are a lot of successful hetero marriages," Toby said. "Or at least marriages where guys were happy to stay in the closet, and consequently this place has more than its fair share of married guys who are still having two bob each way," Toby said with a grin, using a famous, old-fashioned Australian idiom, typical of we "bushies."

MY PHONE beeped, and I knew it was Danny. We played games like this all the time. He'd pretend he was pissed off with me and not ring or text for a few days.

I knew he hated gay names, so I'd always stir him along.

hello princess, I texted back, *how's the smell of diesel, still turning u on?*

There was no answering text. Instead the phone rang, and I walked outside to take his call. He admitted he was lonely. Even though he was living in town with Suzanne, his dispirited tone of voice gave him away instantly.

I refused to give him any comfort by admitting I was also lonely. He'd walked away from our relationship, and now that I was living over an hour away, I realized he was jealous. Danny wasn't stupid. He knew I'd find myself a sex life of sorts away from the prying eyes at home, and there was always the possibility of a new boyfriend or partner, which meant he'd lose me for good.

CHAPTER 7
INNOCENCE LOST

IT'S NOT fair when everyone around you is getting a bit and you're a horny nineteen-year-old with a libido that just won't quit. I'd been in a close relationship with my right hand for some months, ever since Danny and I had ceased to be an item, and in my new home I was constantly reminded that the two couples with whom I shared were busy in the bedroom. Added to that, their friends who floated in and out were as hot as hell—so much so I'd have to excuse myself at times and "retire" to my room to beat off.

Arriving at university, I really didn't set out to hunt for sex partners, because my studies came first and I wasn't about to be sidetracked from the academic goals I'd set myself. I certainly wasn't a child from a wealthy family who just wanted to party the time away on Daddy's money, yet I wasn't Miss Goody Two-Shoes either. I loved a party but not the scene that went with it—the drugs, the hangovers, and the waste of time when I could be doing things that really turned me on, like making real animals feel better, not the human variety.

I also realized I was still just a little hung up on Danny, and it was hard for me to separate sex and my emotions. I obviously needed time to get my mind right.

But nature and opportunity overtook me. I was having a leak after lunch one day, when I became aware of a presence beside me at the urinal.

Normally it was Will who shadowed me everywhere, but I hadn't seen this bloke before. He was average-looking, not really wank-off material for me, but he had one asset that galvanized my attention. His cock was so long it nearly touched the porcelain in front of him, and he smirked at me as I enjoyed watching him bring it up to its full potential.

"Not here," he whispered. "The bog near the ICHP, after five. See you there." With that, he stuffed his monster back in his pants and disappeared out the door as Will ran in. Quickly, I finished my business as

Will grinned at me with a knowing smile but thankfully didn't say anything. All afternoon I had difficulty concentrating, and Will picked up on my mindset. "You meeting someone?" he asked evilly, raising his eyebrows, correctly analyzing my situation.

"Perhaps. And what's it got to do with you, bitch?"

For once, Will apologized, realizing he'd overstepped the mark. But I knew he wanted to take our friendship a step further, and he was displaying all the signs of a jealous lover without actually being one.

What a bloody dilemma. Months with nothing, and suddenly there are two blokes after me, possibly more!

"Look," I said to Will privately after the lecture had finished, "you and Sarah have been really kind to me. I simply can't do anything to upset that friendship."

"You won't be doing that, because she and I aren't really a couple, haven't been for a while. We've never lived together, and only very occasionally do I stay over. The last time was orientation day. So where are you meeting your friend?"

"I'm not," I said. "I'm going home with you instead."

He looked at me askance. I'd called his bluff, and he could back out or get on with it, and he smilingly chose the latter.

"That'll teach me to watch my big mouth, won't it?" he whispered. He was trying to cover up his excitement, I thought, just as I was.

We literally ran in the door of his little unit. He hurled his briefcase at the old sofa in the corner and dragged me into the bedroom, where he looked a bit bewildered. His bottom lip quivered. He suddenly looked like a lost little boy, and the experienced man-of-the-world persona disappeared. I realized he was as inexperienced as I was, perhaps even more so.

"Don't worry," I said, picking up on his mood, "I'm pretty inexperienced too, you know. We'll have to teach each other the ropes."

We sat on the end of the bed and grinned at each other. The desire hadn't diminished and we were raring to go. I leaned in and kissed him, and he suddenly relaxed, returning the favor with what seemed like a very long and athletic tongue.

I'd been such a slut through all of this I hadn't even asked where Sarah was. She wasn't at lectures, and I'd taken copious notes for her information, but none of that seemed to matter as Will and I tongue wrestled on the bed, finally almost tearing each other's clothes off to unwrap our presents to each other.

He was long and quite thin. I was shorter and thicker, much thicker in fact, and he was enjoying every centimeter.

He insisted he wanted to be fucked, pleading with me, despite my warnings that it usually took some practice to enjoy it fully.

So, just as I'd educated Danny in the shearing shed, I supervised his cleaning routine, then opened him up using an old dildo that somehow appeared like magic. Then I told him to sit on me, and he did, at his own pace, finally enjoying himself as he relaxed and got into it, his dick along my tummy, his eyes boring into me, looking for approval.

He rolled onto his back, and I stayed with him, pushing up into him as he yelled with pleasure. Only a few minutes later, I felt the impending orgasm building. I came with a huge rush, Will squealing like a big girl as he joined me.

I sort of knew what was coming next. I may have been a country hick on my second sex partner, but I could have written the script, because the Internet was full of confused straight boys, and I'd already worked Will out.

The look on his face was priceless—something approaching outrage, because he'd so obviously enjoyed what he'd done with me more than with Sarah and the other females who had been silly enough to allow him to play hide the sausage. And with me, he felt guilty because he'd enjoyed what he thought he would hate. More than enjoyed it, he bloody loved it.

Here it comes, the end of a lovely friendship, partly because I can't keep my dick in my pants. I knew he had to accept half the blame, his hormonal drive very much in evidence since the first day we met. But I was surprised at his honesty.

"That's my first time with a guy," he admitted. "Guys like my brother and you are lucky, because at least you know where you are, what turns you on, but I still don't. I thought having sex with a guy would finally get my mind focused in one direction or the other, but it's just made me more confused because you're just so amazing."

I smiled at him but didn't respond. He obviously wanted to talk it out.

"I don't think I'm a bi guy," he said. "The idea of jumping from a chick's bed one moment and into a guy's pants the next doesn't do a thing for me."

"So why did you flirt with me so outrageously?" I asked.

"Because you're different." He smiled. "You're smart, you're hot, and you're just a lovely person, and I couldn't help myself, sorry."

At the mention of "you're just a lovely person," my defense mechanisms were suddenly on red alert. It was clear Will had a crush on me at the very least, or was in love with me in the worst-case scenario.

"I don't love you, Will," I said, sadly but truthfully. "I wish I could say I do, but I think my emotional self is still tied up elsewhere, otherwise we'd set this place alight. But the sex was lovely. You have absolutely nothing to be ashamed of in that department."

I remembered meeting two of Macca and Toby's younger friends; they reminded me so much of Will, and I told him so. "Those chaps identified as straight, Will, but they also found guys turned them on, and they explored a little more. Then they found each other, and according to Toby, it was like they lit up the sky because they fell in love with each other. They've been a couple for around two years now and are devoted to each other. And that, Will, is probably what will happen to you, unless you fall in love with a nice girl beforehand."

Shit. I'm starting to sound like my mum and dad, but I can see where Will is at, and because he's so honest I reckon he'll be okay.

We cuddled up on the bed, and Will looked at me with new respect, except he was as hard as a rock again.

"Seems a pity to waste that," I said and threw myself at it, engulfing him in one movement.

At last Will's sense of humor returned, and he roared with laughter as we got it on again, fucking like bunnies. I told Will he'd be sore tomorrow, and he said, "Not to worry, it'll be a pleasant reminder."

I TOLD Toby, and he giggled his way through it and made me retell it all over again. He suggested, with a smile, that Macca was still a little naïve about these things and could perhaps be a touch judgmental, without ever intending to be so. But I took his point, and we kept the luscious details between us. It was important because I took the running of our household quite seriously, and while I hadn't reneged on any of my duties, my routine had changed and would change again in the future as I spread my wings.

But by the time I arrived at uni the next day, I was a nervous wreck.

I accepted that my hormones—and Will's—had overtaken us, but there was still the matter of Sarah. I worried that, despite Will's assertions, they may still have been a couple, and I might have wrecked it all. Worse still, it could mean that the two people whose friendship I valued most at uni might never be my friends again. I dragged myself over to the workbench, and her eyes caught mine, and she smiled her beautiful smile at me. *Christ, no wonder Will's attracted to her—she is just so gorgeous inside and out, and if my orientation were different, I'd be at the front of the queue trying to bed her.*

Sarah was great. She smiled her knowing smile at me, and I understood she knew that Will and I had become more than friends.

So I confessed and was unsurprised that she was still supportive of Will. When I told her that it was just physical and how I'd practically counseled him, she was really happy and said so.

"I knew he was a troubled puppy," she said. "You've probably saved him from a really difficult period in his life by giving him the outlet he needed."

"Well, don't worry," I said. "He's still getting treatment—he's a good student."

She squealed with delight. Her two favorite men were really looking after each other, and she thoroughly approved.

WHILE I was close to Will, I continued to be truthful about my feelings, and he understood. Well, I hoped so anyway, because, being selfish, I wanted more of that action but with no strings attached.

Bugger it. I want more action period, with or without Will. That little sojourn with him had awaked my libido from a long sleep, and now I was raring to go.

I finished class for the day. Will went off with a cheery wave, as did Sarah—and in separate vehicles, which made me feel even better.

It was time to check out the "facility" near the ICHP that was supposedly a hotbed of vice and a den of iniquity. I'd heard about the "beats" from the Internet, realizing there was at least one in my hometown, and my cousin knew them all here in the big town. A place for quick anonymous sex—dangerous because the likelihood of being caught was real, and if a copper apprehended you in the act, then anything could happen, including charges being filed and the public humiliation of a court case that could follow. That had always been the case; the law hadn't changed to allow any two people of whatever gender to have sex in public.

This one was perhaps different in the eyes of the law. It was actually within the grounds of the university—just—and yet the car park that abutted it was open to the public. But it was still a public place, so I knew I must be careful.

I kidded myself I'd just go for a look, but the moment I walked in the door, I realized how addictive this could be.

The guy I'd met in the dining-room toilet was standing at the trough, a big smile on his face as another, older bloke, probably in his early thirties, was going down on him. Another guy, around the same age, looked on.

They stopped for a moment, not out of fear, I suspected, but just to look me over as I almost ran into the nearest cubicle and quickly closed the door.

To my amazement, before my bottom had even hit the seat, two obviously well-endowed guys decided to make me feel welcome by extending the hand of friendship through the glory holes on either side.

Oh Jesus, Christmas has arrived early. What do I do now?

So I did my community service/social networking and blew both of them, before flying out the door, mindful of the fact that I had just knowingly broken the law, albeit in an attempt to help my fellow men, and of course getting my jollies at the same time. Inside, Sodom and Gomorrah reigned supreme with no thought of modesty or caution, which really worried me. Outside, the car park was nearly full, blatantly advertising the fact that this cottage had plenty of delights inside. Toby had told me what to look for, and I did as I walked away and back into the university grounds to my car.

At the very least, 50 percent of the vehicles were fitted with child seats, and I recalled seeing fingers with white circles around ring fingers and hands with gold and silver bands whose owners simply didn't bother to remove them. Why should they? Just having a bit of fun with the boys on the way home.

CHAPTER 8
THE GRINDSTONE

THERE WERE never enough hours in the day to get it all done, but after successfully negotiating year one, the course material had started to make sense, and even though I came home many nights stinking of formaldehyde, I was actually enjoying the experience. Yes, we'd started doing surgical procedures on animal cadavers, and I enjoyed it!

Sarah and I usually worked together, while poor Will was constantly sick.

We tormented him mercilessly, said he had morning sickness, and dutifully asked if he could feel the infant kicking yet.

But he wasn't the only student so affected. At least three others were similarly affected by the smell and knew they'd better get over it—quickly, because bad smells and veterinary work obviously went hand in hand. Weak tummies had the potential to circumvent promising veterinary careers.

I became a hero to those four students because I remembered Aunt Helga had a similar problem when she married Uncle Ted and came to live on the farm. Aunt Helga's family had brought with them a calming herbal remedy for the digestive system, and it worked like a dream.

Shortly after that Will disappeared from my life, and from Sarah's as well, because his dream of becoming a veterinarian in a lovely white coat and an immaculate surgery had not allowed for the reality of blood, guts, and the smell of shit and piss everywhere. And he realized the long, tedious hours of a practicing vet and the fieldwork in all weather, often in the middle of the night, was a fact of life. So he dropped out, much to our disappointment, because in deciding he'd pursue a career as a science teacher he had to transfer to another university in Melbourne. So we farewelled him collectively, and I gave him the mother of all roots to remember me by. We were smart enough to know our arrangement simply couldn't last: attractive girls and boys would seek Will out, and he would certainly be popular, in bed and out of it.

AROUND THAT time I was lucky enough to get part-time weekend work with Brett Walker, a local vet and equine specialist. Brett had a practice based on showjumping, dressage, and eventing and had a well-deserved reputation as an equine surgeon. It was very much a niche market, with queens on horseback throwing hissy fits at a moment's notice, and spoiled brats driven by their status-seeking parents who wanted their kids, particularly the girls, to participate in something with other "nice" families.

It was a busy place, never a dull moment. Brett was always full-on in the operating theater, so I was on a crash course to learn all about horses on my weekends and "spare" time after lectures, whether I'd planned it or not. I began to appreciate the many centuries of human and equine interaction because the horses remembered me, and they remembered Bruce, who was always with me. Brett reckoned I was the only student who turned up with a dog for the initial interview, and, thank heavens, he was impressed with me, and he really loved Bruce.

Bruce was extraordinary. Brett watched with horror one day as Bruce got into the loose box with Top Flight, a racehorse famous for his bad behavior.

"Jesus, Dean," Brett said to me. "Get your bloody dog out of there, or that bastard will kill him."

Everything seemed to move in slow motion, but the thought of Bruce being in danger put wings on my feet.

As I ran over to the half door, I looked over and froze in place. Turning to Brett, I put my finger to my lips to be quiet and beckoned him over.

The aggressive, skittish stallion had a silly look on his face as Bruce, standing up with his feet against the door, licked Top Flight's muzzle.

I took a risk and said quietly to Brett, "There you are. No one knew he needed some male bonding. I suppose the owners have been trying to breed from him."

Brett giggled. "Yeah, they gave up trying to get him to top a mare and used artificial insemination. Well, they all do now anyway. What are you tryin' to tell me, Deano, you reckon old Top Flight's gay?"

"Yeah," I said before I even thought about it, "like me, and I think my bloody dog is too."

Brett roared with laughter, and a friendship began out of mutual respect and honesty.

Brett's wife Heather was in the house next door raising two little kids. He was just so lovely and human. So masculine, yet so gentle. No wonder the horsey people loved him.

"You're always welcome here, Dean," he said to me afterward. "As long as I'm a vet in this place you'll have a job with me. Good people are hard to find in this business. Good people who are good vets are even harder. When you finish uni, I want you here," he said. "With Bruce!"

CHAPTER 9
HOMECOMING

THE EASTER holidays were nearing, and I packed my things for the break.

Bruce seemed to know we were heading home. Like most dogs, he was a creature of habit, but he was still eerie in the way he could accurately pick the signs of any departure from the normal routine—a toilet bag packed, perhaps my little suitcase on a chair instead of in the wardrobe.

On the Thursday night just before we were to leave, he went out the back to Paul, Dougie, and Jenny, scratching on the door until they let him inside.

I marveled at how my dog could teach me some manners. I'd been so wrapped up in my own affairs I'd completely forgotten to say good-bye to these beautiful people who had become part of my family for the last sixteen months of my life and who cared for me as much as I cared for them.

Bruce held up his paw to shake hands and gave Jenny's hand a lick before running to the main house to find Toby and Macca.

I hugged the guys. They were so affectionate and caring, telling me to drive carefully. I picked up Jenny, and she gurgled with joy. I'd never focused so much on a child before—she was a great learning curve for me, and I realized as a result that I wanted babies of my own one day.

Then Toby and Macca came out to farewell me, with an enthusiastic Bruce following. Game, set, and match. My "other" family at least loved my dog as well as me. How bloody lucky I felt!

I HADN'T been home for nearly three months. Dad and Mum understood, Dad offering to support me with extra funds if I needed the cash, but I realized my work with Brett Walker was valuable experience as well as income, and I declined with thanks. It was great to see them all. My sisters were growing up and wanted to know if I had any romantic involvement with anyone. I was able to assure them that I certainly didn't and just as certainly didn't want to start a relationship.

Mum and Dad just laughed at them. Emma and Megan were supposed to be a real problem because of postpubescent hormonal urges, but they were totally taken over with romance and the idea of a Prince Charming riding over the hill on his beautiful white steed, sweeping them into his arms, and living happily ever after. The only point of argument would be who got to him first! But they were just perfect in my eyes. Thanks to our parents' guidance, their lovely natures hadn't altered even through the homophobia of my final year at high school. It was nearly 9:00 p.m. when Bruce and I walked in the door. There was pandemonium and even tears from Mum—her chickens were all together again, at least for a few days. Bruce ran over to Dad, hurtling into his arms like a child, head on Dad's shoulder, licking his ear and making little squealing noises and adding to the mayhem.

"I think you're glad to be home," Dad laughed.

I told them how Bruce had charmed old Top Flight, the nasty stallion, and no one was surprised.

There was more to celebrate than usual. After removing Mum's medication in preparation for a new regimen, they'd watched her condition improve almost overnight, her original diagnosis now in question. The dizzy spells were still apparent, but she was walking again and was exercising and strengthening muscles she'd only partially used since she first became ill. Neither she nor Dad wanted to discuss it because they simply didn't have enough information, and, I suspected, didn't want to disappoint us if it didn't work out.

But for the time being, the household sang along with quiet optimism, and it looked like the best Easter for a long, long time.

BRUCE WENT outside to his old kennel. Dad and the girls had thoughtfully washed his blanket, and the noises he made organizing his nest for the night were hilarious. I said good night to everyone and showered before bed. I opened the window about halfway. The bedroom was airless, but it was a cool April night outside, and I rolled into my bed, breathing in the fresh air, slipping off to sleep almost instantly. I was a deep sleeper but always a dreamer in the literal sense. Mum and I were similar. We could sit around the breakfast table and describe our dreams in great detail, much to everyone's disgust and total lack of interest.

Tonight I dreamt I was walking through a grass paddock with Bruce, rounding up a mob of something or other, but I discovered he'd rounded up a mob of blokes, and naked ones at that! I wasn't close enough to study any of their faces or other interesting bits, but Bruce was bringing them all closer to me, about twenty of them.

"I'd better not tell them about this dream at breakfast," I chuckled to myself, away in the Land of Nod. There was this noise like distant thunder. *Christ, these blokes are going to get wet. There's a thunderstorm brewing*, I thought, in my utter stupidity.

The noise got louder, and I awoke and sat up in bed, realizing the "thunder" was coming from my window. It was just like the staccato noise on the glass that heavy rain made. Then, as the noise went up another octave, I leapt out of bed, throwing the window wide open.

It can't be.

And of course it was, and I stood groggily to one side as something like an overnight bag came hurtling into the room, landing up against the door. Then there was a foot wearing a very large boot, followed by another, and then the remainder of Daniel Morgan wearing a huge grin fell into the room, with Bruce making a huge fuss outside. If it had been anyone else, they wouldn't have made it over the fence, let alone into the house. But Bruce knew who it was and was behaving like a lovesick child. Danny leaned out the window and grabbed him by the collar, dragging him inside as I watched on. Bruce just looked at me as if to say "He says I can come inside, bitch, try to piss me off now."

I pointed to the far corner of the room, finding a blanket for him as Bruce decided discretion was the better part of valor and quietly made his way there. But he looked at Danny as he slunk past, wagging his tail, and we laughed at him.

"You coming for the weekend," I said drily, pointing to his bag.

"Yeah, if you'll have me."

"Daniel," I said wistfully. "You know the rules."

"Yeah, and I agree with 'em, one person at a time. That's why I'm here, hoping we might be able to sort a few things out."

I must have looked at bit puzzled because he grinned at me again, that beautiful bloody smile that always sent my insides into turmoil and my heart racing.

"I broke up with Suzanne," he said, "over two weeks ago. Been living back home with Mum and Dad since then."

He hung his head, looking embarrassed, then looked me straight in the eye, welcome behavior I hadn't seen for some years.

"I fucked up, Deano," he whispered. "You were always more mature than me, and I just wasn't ready to be part of a gay couple. I still can't hack it down here. They're bloody cruel with their gossip, and I wouldn't do it to Dad and Mum. But you always said I needed to get away from here regardless of whether you and I were an item. I've got a good chance of a new job up there with the Ford dealer. They need diesel engine expertise now that even small cars are goin' diesel."

"What about Staines Farm Machinery?"

"Well, things are a bit quiet in the bush at the moment, so they're quite happy to let me go and transfer my apprenticeship. But I have to get the new job first. I've got an interview next Friday."

He looked at me rather like a naughty kid, that smile playing around the edge of the very full, almost puffy lips I loved so much. Then he was serious, and he looked me in the eye again.

"Sayin' I'm sorry, Dean, for all the shit I put ya through would mean I'd still be sitting here in ten years' time, and that wouldn't achieve much, would it? I mean, thanks to Simon and Julie we made up again, but I'd forgotten about our friendship and the loyalty part because I was so frightened about what would happen to us if we got caught."

He looked beseechingly at me, grabbing hold of my hands. It was confession time.

"It was all right at first," he said. "Suzanne was good company, and we seemed to get on well together. I just told her that I had erectile dysfunction from time to time, that it was a family thing, but the doctor told me it'd still happen now and then, and that seemed to keep her happy. But the fact was I couldn't get it up with her most of the time.

"Because I'm gay."

He looked at me, not upset now but with eyes twinkling, and I realized he'd finally made the leap of faith that allowed him to be a fully functioning part of the human race by being totally honest with himself.

"She wanted to fuck around again," Danny continued, "and said we should open up the relationship, like with the odd threesome every now and then. But word travels quickly in this bastard of a place, and before I knew it, she had gang bangs happening everywhere—at home, down by the lake, at one of the guys' houses. I never went near her after that. She reckoned I was sulking, but I just didn't want to catch anything because none of those guys wore a condom. Those blokes were the most two-faced arseholes I've ever met," he said to me, eyes blazing. "Most of 'em had wives or girlfriends, but there's a code of silence down here. No one talks about it, and it's just like it never happened. I was around her most of the time"—he grinned—"because I liked lookin' at the blokes. One of 'em took me outside one night, and we did everything except anal. Then his mate did the same thing another night—Dale Fairweather and Jimmy Coxon."

I nodded. I knew the guys, but their behavior didn't surprise me as much as it had stunned Danny.

"Two days later I was outside the supermarket where Suzanne works when Jimmy came past with his missus and kids and Dale with his girlfriend. Both of 'em pretended they didn't even see me. Christ, why would I dob 'em in? I had as much to lose as they did. Those two blokes are as gay as; the most dishonest pricks I've ever known, mainly because they're using women, like I did for a while. I'm ashamed of meself," Danny said, almost in tears.

"I used Suzanne because I thought I might have been straight or perhaps even bisexual, but I had the guts to set her free without her knowing why. But at least I did it. Bloody Dale and Jimmy were laughing about the guys they'd had sex with. They even go to Melbourne to do the saunas once a month."

Danny paused for breath, and I could see it was getting to him, but there was more to come.

"Dean," he said, "I love you."

MY SLEEP-STARVED brain was having difficulty, at 11:30 p.m., trying to focus on the mountain of information my ex-lover and friend had imparted in the last hour or so.

He sat cross-legged on the end of the bed, with the famous four-letter word fresh on his lips, and it was all I could do not to throw myself at him, promising endless love.

But I'd been burnt before, and I was cautious—bloody cautious.

I looked at him and asked the only question I could, given his lovely lack of sophistication. It was clear Danny had come a long way, but I wondered if he understood completely what I'd laid on the line around two years ago. I knew what I wanted back then, and it hadn't changed. None of the blokes I'd been to bed with could even come close to what I'd had with him. I knew I'd been emotionally faithful to him since we parted—in fact, the emotional bond between us had prevented me from getting permanently involved with anyone else.

"Danny," I said, "what do you mean when you say you love me?"

He looked at me with that smile again, and his reply shocked me. It certainly wasn't what I expected.

"What I mean is that I want to spend the rest of my life with you. I want us to be a couple, just you and me, monogamous. In a few years the law will change. We'll be able to get married, and if we're still going strong, that's what I want to do. Mind you, I'd have to be asked first," the cheeky bastard said and grinned at me a bit uncertainly.

But it was still a grin.

"And I remember you wanted kids, and so do I, and because we'll never grow up, the kids should be right at home! If you want to think about it, I'll understand," he said seriously. "I've heaped a lot of shit onya tonight."

I simply sat there with my mouth open, and I felt I'd never close it again.

My mind was whirling. Despite being a closeted country boy, Danny had done a complete 360-degree turn in his mindset and attitude. I must have looked confused as the beautiful big bastard slipped his hand around behind me to massage my neck muscles.

"Simon helped me, and Julie," he whispered, "and I talked to some pretty smart people online. I worked most of this out while I was still living with Suzanne, so I had to be discreet. I gave her six months' rent when I left and tried to leave on good terms because she's such a fuckin' bitch, and Simon reckons she's a real loose cannon."

Suddenly I wasn't tired anymore. I was as hard as a flagpole and raring to go. Speech evaded me. I found all I could do was to mumble at him as I quickly rid myself of my trusty boxers.

"I take it your answer's yes?" he said, quite seriously.

"Of course it is, you fool. Now get your lips around this," I said, finding my voice and thrusting all I had in his face.

He kissed the end of it and gently stroked me, sending waves of pleasure through me.

"Darling Deano," he said, and I nearly swooned at the newly found intimacy. "I'm fine to be out around your family but not yet around my family or anyone else in this cunt of a place."

I can live with that. Nothing is ever perfect in this life, and perhaps I should be a little more understanding and less judgmental, considering his amazing change of attitude and level of maturity.

"Yeah, no worries, I do understand. Now get your gear off."

In the corner, Bruce made a gagging sound. Whether it was intentional or not, I don't know, but it sounded so funny we held on to each other and laughed at him until the tears ran down our faces.

THE NEXT morning, clad only in my old ratty dressing gown, I put Bruce outside to pee, finding Mum already up and with breakfast started.

"Ah, we've got a visitor for breakfast," I said, blushing a little.

"I know, dear," she said. "Have a nice night, did we? I expect you'll need to build your strength up."

I flushed even deeper and suddenly realized this was no surprise to my mother. "Have you two been talking?" I said, knowing that she and Danny had always been close.

"Of course, darling," she said, taking my hand. "He wanted to leave no stone unturned because he realized he had a fight on his hands to get you back as a proper boyfriend this time. The girls don't have any idea yet, but I doubt if you'll be able to get them out of bed this early on a holiday morning."

"Leave it to me," I said. "Start their brekkie as well, they'll be here."

"HEY," I said, not angry with him, just amazed at the trouble he'd gone to. "Why don't you get your reasonably attractive arse out of bed and into the kitchen? Your partner in crime is cooking breakfast. 'Just so we can keep our strength up' were her words, I believe."

He giggled, and I kissed him and pointed the way to the shower.

"When you're finished in there, would you please wake my sisters up? Mum reckons they'll be there until midday, but I think you can do better than that."

He knocked on their door, and they struggled awake, moaning and complaining until they saw who it was. Then there were screams and laughter as he tickled them and teased them. There was no way they were staying in bed under those circumstances. Even Dad, who had been enjoying a rare sleep-in, joined us all for a beautiful breakfast.

Good Friday breakfast with lots of home-cured bacon, eggs, and not a sign of fish.

We sat there as a peaceful family group. The girls had always adored Danny and crawled all over him—with my permission, of course. They might have been my little sisters, but they understood I had my boyfriend back, and while they would never mention it outside our front door, their affection for us, as a couple, was beautiful.

Mum had always been besotted with him. He could do no wrong in her eyes, and unbeknown to me she had always kept in touch with him. When he finally woke up to himself, Mum was one of the first people he turned to. My beautiful Mum—she had counseled him, helped him with homespun advice, and then bloody conspired with him! There was a bond there between them. He may have had a different surname, but so far as she was concerned, he was really a Prentice, not a Morgan.

Dad looked just mildly troubled, but I was so over the moon I really didn't notice. He kept a small office at home, and after the breakfast dishes were done, he asked Danny and me to join him in there.

"Congratulations," he said, quite formally, and suddenly my guts froze for some reason because my dad looked quite stern.

"Margaret and I are very pleased for you," Dad said. "We always hoped you two would get your act together and get on with it, and now you have. There's very little more we can do now except be your backup and support. That's what families do for each other, particularly if you need money or help in any way. Now, Daniel, tell me about this new job you're going after."

Danny gave Dad chapter and verse about the new position and stressed he still had to be interviewed. But he wasn't finished yet.

"Mr. Prentice," Danny said, "there's a few things that I think have been on your mind, and you're too much of a gentleman to say them, so I'll say 'em for you.

"Excuse me for using bad language, but two years ago I fucked up completely and let the only person I've ever loved slip through my fingers. The only excuse I had at the time was that I was totally inexperienced and a bit naïve about life, despite you and Mrs. Prentice making things really easy and open for us as gay boys.

"But through some really bad experiences I've grown up, and because I know you all love Dean so much, I want to assure you that what happened two years ago when I hurt him so badly will never happen again, Mr. Prentice. Ever."

Dad, like me, looked at the new, very articulate Danny with disbelieving eyes, and this was the first time I'd noticed my father unable to speak because he was choked up. He cuddled us both, suggesting he, Mum, and the girls might go for a two-hour drive down the coast, mentioning that we'd probably find something to occupy ourselves with.

They were hardly out the door when I pounced on Danny, but he was ready for me and beat me into the bedroom, stripping off his gear and wearing nothing more than a big, beautiful smile.

He'd grown bigger, like a bear. But a young bear, with a truly dark, hairy barrel chest and a broad treasure trail leading down to his amazing dick—everything in proportion. It was familiar, like being back home again. Our home, with me inside him and Danny purring away in pure pleasure.

After finally exhausting ourselves, we sat around the kitchen table again as I began cooking a late lunch for us. I looked on in amazement as he shepherded me back to my seat and took over.

"I did learn something, like how to use the kitchen or starve," he said with a grin, producing a magnificent quick meal for us.

"So if everything goes okay for you with this interview," I said, "you'll need somewhere to lay your head, as we discussed. Do you want to move in with me, or do you think we should get a place of our own?"

"Nah," he said, full of authority because he'd obviously thought about it. "I'd love to move in with you guys. Toby and I've always got on well, and it would be a lot cheaper to start off with."

"Okay," I said, "I'll ask Toby and Macca."

"No."

I looked at him, a little puzzled.

"I should do the asking, darling, I'm the one who has to take some responsibility for a change. Do you mind?"

All I could do was to shake my head and nod in the right places. It had been one surprise after another this Easter.

I'd arrived home single and was going back to uni very much committed to my boyfriend, who had gone from zero to hero in my eyes and in the eyes of my family.

He'd matured beautifully in our time apart, completely blowing away any reservations I'd ever had.

Not only had he told me he loved me, but he'd planned this reunion. And the best of all? He called me darling, and I would have walked over red-hot bloody coals to keep him as a result.

CHAPTER 10
A VERY ORDINARY TIME

DANNY FLEW into the position at James Kitchener Ford. They had begun a little sideline in rebuilding injector pumps and injectors and needed someone knowledgeable to do the grunt work, and he was a bargain on apprentice wages. Regardless of the low salary, Danny loved the work. The compensation was lots of overtime, and he settled in well.

At home, he was an immediate hit. Paul and Dougie loved him, and Jenny had yet another man doting over her.

It wasn't all plain sailing. Danny began to understand, finally, how difficult a task I had and how hard I needed to work and apply myself to my goal of becoming a veterinary surgeon. Quite often I was still at uni when he arrived home, and sometimes when he worked late I was home before him. And when I worked with Brett Walker on weekends, he was often at a loose end. Toby sensed we were having "teething troubles," as he put it, and to my eternal gratitude he kept Danny busy at home, particularly in the garden, which Danny seemed to find some comfort in. Then Macca stepped in and put him on one of his vans at weekends, and Danny put some serious money in the bank.

I began to realize that being madly in love with someone wasn't just playing happy families. He was always delighted to see me, perhaps even too much, but particularly after some lovemaking sessions, he seemed rather sad and withdrawn. I asked him what was wrong, and he defended himself, as most blokes do, and claimed he was just a bit tired. In fact, we both had issues there, but we always resolved them. I forced him to tell me what was on his mind at times, and I made him promise never to go to bed angry.

He giggled and agreed, saying it was bloody impossible to have a root with someone if you were pissed at them.

We always walked Bruce before bed. The others understood it was our time and gave us our privacy. We strolled around the general cemetery, which was just two streets away. Danny said I was fucked in the head for going anywhere near such a place, but after a while he relaxed and began to enjoy our nightly ritual, and we actually walked inside. His sense of humor started to creep back. While there were times where he seemed out of it and moody, there were others where we laughed until our sides ached—like tonight, as we walked, hand in hand down an avenue of graves.

"Why does bloody Bruce cock his leg on that grave all the time?" he asked.

It was a silly question to ask a veterinary science student. "Because it's Mr. Bone," I said, trying to keep a straight face.

"Mr. Bone."

"Yes, give the dog a bone."

"You're a fuckin' idiot," he squealed, almost pissing himself with mirth. "I asked for that, didn't I?" He laughed again as we ran home, the humor working like an aphrodisiac.

IT HAD been three months since Danny and I had resurrected our relationship, and the early misgivings I'd had were long gone. Only occasionally was there tension, and we soon resolved that with a good rambunctious fucking and promptly forgot about any arguments.

It was a Saturday night in late July. I'd worked late, and he'd actually cooked me dinner, which was beautiful, both the meal and the thought behind it, because the others had eaten and were relaxing in the lounge.

Paul and Dougie were happy to stay home. Jenny was growing in leaps and bounds and was full of energy. Raising her properly was important to them, and they were good at it.

Apart from the odd date we sent them on with each other, they spent all their free time with their child because they wanted to.

Toby and Macca were similar. They had a ready-made family circle and wanted to keep it the way it had begun, with love and respect. The winter weather was a sheer bitch—much nicer to be around a warm fire, particularly if the company was good, and it was. We were just so compatible with each other.

Both of us had work the next day, so we excused ourselves, walked Bruce, showered, and went to bed like an old married couple, followed not too much later by the other two married couples in the house.

Danny and I made love gently and sweetly, my beautiful bloke almost purring with pleasure. We cleaned ourselves up, and he slipped behind me, spooning me, our usual sleeping position.

I woke up with a start, a high-pitched noise still stinging my consciousness.

The bed was empty beside me. *He must be in the toilet.*

But his side was cold, and I realized he'd been gone for some time. So instead of slipping back to sleep as I normally would, I struggled out of bed to find him. Perhaps he couldn't sleep, but that was unusual. Danny wasn't as deep a sleeper as me, but he usually slept well enough. I'd never known him to be out of bed very long, particularly on a cold winter's night.

My feet hit the floor and I realized the high-pitched sound had come from my phone. Who in Christ's name would be sending me a text at 3:15 a.m.?

I picked it up and it had come from—Danny.

Why would he send me a text? Why would he get out of a lovely warm bed next to his boyfriend and send me a text?

I scrolled down to the body of the message, and all it said was "I love you."

I tried texting back, but there was no answer.

Suddenly my blood ran cold. I knew something was wrong, and I ran out the bedroom door, nearly knocking Dougie over.

"I saw him go," Dougie whispered. "He backed the ute down the driveway without any lights, and I wondered if you guys had a fight, but everything was fine earlier, so I thought I'd better not interfere, ya know. But Bruce wasn't happy, and I thought I'd better come in and see if everything's all right."

Just then, Bruce started a dreadful, mournful howling, and I felt palpitations in my chest as hell on earth appeared to be asserting itself. There was no doubt in my mind that something dreadful had happened to Danny. I'd seen enough animal reactions to know that Bruce had sensed it, and my first reaction was to comfort him. I opened the back door, and he tore inside, leaping into my arms, shaking, crying, and whimpering in terror.

All the noise had woken Toby and Macca, and they struggled into the kitchen, eyes wide open, struggling to understand the drama. As logically as I could, I explained to Macca the train of events as we knew them—that Danny had left our bed, dressed, and driven away, probably around 2:30 a.m.

He'd sent me a message around forty-five minutes ago. I'd sent one back, but there'd been no response, nothing.

Paul staggered in, taking in the scene with disbelief. The house had gone from a pleasant suburban family nest on Saturday night to a hellhole in the early hours of Sunday morning. One of our number was missing, and unanswered questions hung in the air, making a logical next step impossible.

My whole body felt cold, and I supposed—quite correctly as it turned out later—that I was in a state of shock. Even my brain seemed to freeze.

Macca took charge, as he normally did in any crisis, and I felt just a little better as a result. Let's face it—in my short life I'd never had to face any real crisis apart from the bullies at school, so I had no template to follow, nothing like this had happened to me.

"Where would he go, Dean, where?" Macca asked.

"What?" I said stupidly.

"Think, sweetheart," he said, "where would Danny head to?"

"There's only one place," I said with certainty. "Home, to his parents, to the farm."

"Nowhere else?"

"No, it's been months since he's even talked to his ex-girlfriend, and there's nobody else he's really close to except Simon and Julie."

Deciding not to worry his mum and dad at that moment, we instead rang an astonished Simon, who was instantly awake and promised to ring around, including the local police.

Finally Macca rang Steve Norris, apologized for the timing of the call, and explained one of the "family" was in trouble.

"Leave it to me," Steve said, understanding that we wouldn't ring him unnecessarily, and asked to speak to me.

I told Steve all I knew. No, he'd never done this sort of thing before; no, he hadn't been moody lately—in fact, he seemed to have settled down quite well, seemingly adapting to his new life in the big town. Steve agreed and said how well liked Danny had become with all Toby and Macca's friends.

"Anyone who wins your heart has to be special," Steve growled, obviously trying to settle me down with a bit of flattery, and mostly succeeding.

CHAPTER 11
THE END OF AN ERA

THE POLICE van was only five kilometers from Cameron's Corner when the report came in.

They called for an ambulance with a paramedic immediately, switching the lights on but no siren, as there was nobody to warn at 3:45 a.m. anyway.

The rookie constable jumped from the van, eager to help, but it was obviously too late— nothing could have survived the force of that crash.

The ute was driven up the big white gum with an air bag waving lazily through the crumpled and slightly open driver's door. The rookie pulled the door open wider, and some specks of Daniel Morgan's brains fell onto his nice regulation black work shoes. He turned quickly, vomiting on the broken twigs and leaves that covered the forest floor.

I SUPPOSE the old saying "no news is good news" is applicable. As much as you know something awful has happened, as long as nobody confirms it, life just bowls along, albeit slowly.

It was nearly 10:00 a.m. when Steve Norris drove into the driveway and parked next to one of Macca's vans—the very one Danny should have been driving that morning.

My heart sank as Toby opened the door and Steve walked straight over to me, his strong arms folding around me.

"Dean, I'm so sorry," he said, "but it's all over for Danny. Terrible car smash at Cameron's Corner."

I nodded dumbly. For years Danny and I rode around Cameron's Corner every day on the way to and from school, with Bruce beside us.

Toby, Macca, Paul, and Dougie looked stricken. Jenny, the innocent little thing without the cares and woes of adults, cooed quietly to herself in her high chair.

Toby helped me to a kitchen stool, and I sat there, stone-faced and dry-eyed.

After all we had been through, having agreed to rekindle our relationship properly and sleep in the same bed every night, Daniel was no more.

I felt numb, as if I was under anesthetic, and sometime soon I'd wake up, and everything would be okay.

But now I knew it certainly wasn't, and I had to handle the facts as best I could.

"Dean, there's more." Steve was speaking again.

"There are some facts you should know about this tragedy because you deserve to. However, as you are theoretically not next of kin, this is private information, and I know you understand I could be fired if anyone found I'd passed this on. Are you with me?"

I nodded and thanked him. Despite my state of grief, I could still appreciate the personal loyalty and integrity of Steve Norris. Paul, Dougie, and Jenny were part of our little family group because of him, and so trust was implicit among us all.

"Steve, we all need to hear this," I said, and the guys gathered around me, Jenny still gurgling away happily in her chair, chewing on some toast.

"Dean," he said, "Mrs. Cameron suffers from insomnia and was sitting in her lounge room only a hundred meters away, and she heard the engine note increasing before the impact, and then she phoned 000. Mike Stringer, who was on duty last night, is a great mate of mine, and he said there was no question, given the logistics, that this was deliberate. I'm very, very sorry."

My head spun like a top. I felt disoriented trying to take in the information, which was becoming more and more ghastly. Danny was gone forever. In time I supposed I would have to handle that, but suicide? My mind swung crazily from guilt to anger, backward and forward as I tried to rationalize the awful train of events.

"Mike Stringer is one of us, Dean," Steve said gently. "His boyfriend was the other officer on duty with him. He's only a kid, a rookie, and he's terribly upset. It was his first motor vehicle fatal," he explained. "But he had the presence of mind to retrieve Danny's mobile, which will be handed to the coroner for evidence. I know I'm asking too much for you to look at them yourself, so let me read them in succession. The first was from a Suzanne, I presume his ex-girlfriend, at just after 2:00 a.m. today.

Suzanne: I'm pregnant need money ur fag boyfriend has plenty I want two grand by 2 morrow.

Danny: the kid's not mine and u know it y pick on me?

Suzanne: no money & I tell ur stuck up family that ur a poofter livin with ur mate up there

Danny: ur a bitch get the real father 2 pay or don't u know who it is

Suzanne: u left me on my own now u can pay poofter cunt ur name will be mud after I finish with u

"I think you get the drift," Steve said. "There's more, but you don't need to hear it unless you really want to. Don't worry, she's in custody right now, and she'll face some serious charges, not the least of which will be blackmail."

The train of events was now clear to me, and that lessened the pain just a little. Now, with the facts at my disposal, as wretched as they may be, I could focus on the events and the people who had directly or indirectly caused my other half to take his own life. And it was all just so ugly.

But I remembered my manners and the course of action involving personal risk that Steve Norris had undertaken on my behalf. "Steve," I said, "I'll never forget your kindness and consideration. I appreciate everything you've done."

Suddenly everything went black, and the floor rose up to meet me.

When I came to, Toby had stripped me and was putting me back to bed. Their GP, Darren Clarke, was giving me a needle of some sort, explaining I was in shock and this would help the symptoms and allow me to sleep.

I felt a prick in the arm and slipped off, with Bruce lying next to me and refusing to allow anyone else in the bedroom.

BRUCE AND I arrived home two days later with Toby and Macca for company, refusing to let me out of their sight until I was safely in my parents' door. I was in control, or I thought I was, until I saw my parents, and the dam burst. Mum and Dad had adored Danny. Yes, there had been some difficult times, but everyone, including me, had thought those dark days were behind us.

So we allowed ourselves to feel bereaved and sad for a while. The girls were at school, so after we had a good howl around the kitchen table, it was me who reminded the three of us that there was nothing we could do to bring him back, and Danny would probably hate the fuss we were making.

Then my phone went off. I was still gun-shy at the sound, but when I looked, it was Simon. He and Julie were as devastated as I was, but if ever one believed in the power of partnership, it was Simon and Julie. They were looking after the funeral arrangements because Danny's parents were so devastated they felt incapable of making any decision at all. So Simon, with Julie's help, had stepped in and taken over, and that included the farm for the time being, Dad informed me. Simon asked if I'd be free in an hour or so because the celebrant was due to interview them, and his parents had specifically asked me to be there.

The request didn't surprise me. Apart from anything else, I was Danny's oldest friend from when we were not much more than babies—until now.

I agreed to go over but asked if I could bring Dad with me, to which Simon warmly agreed. He and Dad were favorite people to each other, and Simon knew Dad's common sense would be an asset to the process.

We walked through the bush on the same path Danny had used for all those years. I knew my sentimentality was showing, and so did Dad, so he took my hand as if I were a little kid, and I squeezed his big hand back, and I knew I simply had to hold it all together for his sake.

OBVIOUSLY NO parent is ever prepared to bury their own child, particularly when that child was in the absolute prime of his life.

Mrs. Morgan looked tired and worn out—rather like I felt. Mr. Morgan looked dreadful. He was clean-shaven and composed, but clearly he'd taken the news totally to heart and looked twenty years older. I knew the grapevine would have been in overdrive. The lounge room down the end of the hall was full of neighbors and friends who, in time-honored country tradition, called in to "pay their respects." Many brought food, desperately seeking to do something practical that would perhaps ease the agony a little. But most just sat there, drinking interminable cups of tea, trying to remember something nice about the deceased, genuinely trying to be there for the bereaved family.

Regardless of custom and at the risk of offending the gathering hordes, a clearly frustrated Simon asked me what he should do. He needed some peace and quiet while the celebrant was visiting, because the risk of overheard and misinterpreted information was not something the family needed at this point.

When I suggested Mum and Aunt Helga, his face lit up. Simon understood the Prentice family had displayed their good breeding and discretion thus far, but I knew the combination of Mum and Aunt Helga would soon bring about some peace and quiet.

Within minutes, they were there. I could hear Mum's reasoned tones, thanking everyone for showing concern but asking if the family could have some privacy while they made the funeral and ceremonial arrangements. I heard some muffled remarks, and then I heard Aunt Helga bark, and I pictured some poor soul backing out the door with terror in their heart. Dad grinned at me. At least we'd started this process the right way, with humor.

Mr. and Mrs. Morgan both embraced me, with Simon and Dad looking on, and the sense of guilt that had been with me since this happened suddenly overwhelmed me.

"I'm so sorry," I said. "I had no idea. He seemed so happy, particularly since we moved in together."

Before his parents could say anything more, Simon cut in.

"It's all right, Dean, relax." He smiled. "Mum and Dad have always known how close you two were, including the nature of your decision to move in together."

My face must have fallen to my boots. Danny had ended his life when the very people he most feared hurting had known all along. My darling bloke had just wasted his life—an utter, complete, and senseless fucking waste.

DAVID CANNING, the celebrant, arrived a few minutes later. Balding, bespectacled, and with a close-cropped white beard, he was everyone's grandfather. He'd been recommended by Macca and Toby at Simon's request, and after being introduced, he made us all relax as best he could. At times he held both Mr. and Mrs. Morgan's hands, an action so strange in this bastion of concealed feelings. But it was reassuring because the conversation was getting down to the facts, and this bloke, while seemingly understanding our grief, was showing us a way to deal with it.

It helped that he was a gay man in a very long-term partnership and that he'd also been raised in a rural area even more conservative than this one. He seemed strangely familiar with the awful train of events that had led to us sitting around the dining table in the Morgan family home.

An hour passed. We found ourselves blurting out all sorts of information. In particular he covered the years of our partnership with empathy and understanding, and somehow I felt totally free and without embarrassment speaking of our love affair, such was his skill in extracting the information.

Mr. Morgan again surprised me by rubbing the back of my hand.

"Daniel had grown up, and while for Beatrice and me he'd left the nest, a child never leaves your heart. But the point I really wish to make"—he looked at the celebrant—"is that we should be directing our sympathy in the first place not toward ourselves, but to Dean as his partner."

"I agree completely," said David, "and thank you for making the point. It's so refreshing."

We broke for a while. Mum and Aunt Helga put on a light meal, and we sat around and just talked like a normal family. Old David asked if he could go for a little walk to clear his head, and Dad offered to show him around.

According to Dad, his eyes sparkled at all the farm gear. His family had been farmers in Tasmania for generations until his lifestyle drove him to Melbourne and eventually to the same town we lived in.

He and his partner Peter had been flower growers and bred stud sheep and Kelpies at a little property in the area. He saw Bruce and asked if he was my dog, and Dad nodded. "Animals grieve too," David said, sitting on the back step and patting his knee. Bruce came straight over, jumped on his lap, and put his head on David's shoulder, just like he always did to Dad.

"He was really connected to Danny and Dean, wasn't he?" David whispered as I walked out the door. "You have to comfort your baby, Dean." David smiled at me. "That's something constructive you can do that will help you both heal."

David stayed only a short while longer. He asked us all to trust the funeral director's judgment and not hold the funeral immediately, until the coroner's work was completed. This would allow the passage of time to erase some of the horrific and sensational aspects.

Mrs. Morgan, for the first time, broke her awful silence. "Thank you so much for listening to our troubles," she said and kissed the old man on the cheek.

Bill Morgan nodded sagely, as did Simon.

A FEW days later, David was back. This was the read back before the funeral the following day, he said, to make sure the facts were correct. "And to give those closest to Danny the courtesy and opportunity to grieve in private before the world intrudes via a public funeral."

At this stage, I was still feeling a numbness and lack of interest in almost everything. Even food tasted like shit. For someone who always loved their tucker, I had neither the appetite nor the will to finish a meal. Everyone was courteous and kind, but the fact of the matter was that none of us had handled such a tragedy close up, and we didn't know what to do or say, except to fall back on the outdated and inappropriate behavior that was part of Anglo-Celtic culture and tradition in this part of the world.

One thing was certain, however—the rumor mill was alive and well, because everyone always thought the worst down here. What they didn't know about a subject, they made up—such were their small minds with not enough to occupy them. It wasn't bad enough that Danny was dead. They were more interested in how and why. Troubled, I mentioned it to both Dad and Mr. Morgan, who asked me how I'd like it treated.

"Tell the truth," I said.

"I agree," Mr. Morgan said. "Otherwise there's no hope for other young blokes in the future."

As it turned out, the celebrant wasn't about to shirk the social issues. He made sure all Danny's brothers were there, along with their wives and girlfriends, before he began.

The old guy told us the horrible task ahead for him was sadly a familiar one.

"Danny suffered from depression, in my opinion," he said. "To me it's quite obvious, I'm afraid."

My head snapped up, and I challenged the information. "But there was no indication that he was sick in any way," I said indignantly.

Mr. Morgan agreed.

"That's the problem with these cases," the celebrant continued. "As we know, hiding one's sexuality is common enough in the country areas because of the challenge it presents to Australian masculinity. But depression is a mental illness that presents an equal if not greater challenge to Australian men. Admitting you're a gay or even bisexual man today is much easier than it was, even down here in paradise." He smiled, not making fun of the district but reminding us gently how much he loved the country areas and country people. "But actually admitting you're mentally ill is, I know, far more confronting. Men go to amazing lengths to hide it, particularly from themselves. When questioned directly they deny it, fearful of the impact on their reputation and, it seems, the public perception of their family.

"Only rarely does one notice the mood swings, the irritability, and little episodes called flashbacks, which most of us ignore but which get internalized by these people. Over time the feelings of inadequacy build up, like the layers of an onion. One episode piles on top of another, and then something happens, rather like the straw that broke the camel's back, and a tragedy occurs. In this case it was the text message from his former girlfriend, and he snapped. I'm so terribly sorry—" He looked around the room and reached for my hand. "—but you must realize there was absolutely nothing anyone could have done to have prevented this tragedy. Nothing. In life," David continued steadily, "we can only do our best, and you've all done that for Danny. None of us are mind readers, none of us are practicing mental health professionals. We're just ordinary people, living, loving, and going about our daily business. Nothing we can do or say will bring him back. I wish I could, but the first step in the grieving process for you all is to recognize that he's gone and to let him go."

We sat there in the Morgan dining room, stunned by all the information, trying to process it. What David was telling us to do was move on with our lives. It had happened, it was over, and Danny wasn't coming back. But more importantly it was pretty obvious why he'd done this, and David was telling us not to blame ourselves because we did nothing to contribute to Danny's decision.

"Focus on his life tomorrow for an hour or so, then move on with yours," he said. "There is no alternative."

DANNY'S FAVORITE music rang out. We put "Kiss Tomorrow Good-bye" by Luke Bryan up front because it was the saddest title, but the lyrics weren't quite so bad, and almost everyone there remembered Danny playing air guitar and singing it in his most awful voice.

I looked around the old theater and estimated there were about 500 people there. Quite an achievement for a community that struggled to say a good word about him when he was alive, particularly when they had also tried to take me down to their fucking level at the same time and failed miserably.

There was no sign of Suzanne or any of the people in her group that Danny had really loathed, particularly Dale Fairweather and Jimmy Coxon. With all the sadness and pressure I was under, I was still mindful that this was Danny's day, and so, with a little help from the police, they didn't dare show their ugly faces.

True to his word, David managed to turn the event into a celebration of the years Danny had rather than a mournful affair, and before we knew it, the ceremony was over. Mr. and Mrs. Morgan held a hand each as we walked him out of the old theater and into the weak winter sunlight.

The Morgan and Prentice families gathered around me, with my other family of Toby, Macca, Paul, and Dougie also by my side as the hearse drove away, and we shed a few tears again. But it was over—this dreadful end to the most beautiful part of my life was finally over, and I knew I had to focus on what was left.

CHAPTER 12
ALONE AGAIN, NATURALLY

EVERYONE KNEW of our partnership status at university. He hadn't met a lot of people there, but those he'd spoken to were impressed, and like a good grapevine, the sad news was everywhere when I finally returned to my studies.

The avalanche of letters and cards that found their way home was extraordinary because they were in addition to all the texts and e-mails.

Paul appointed himself my private secretary so I didn't have to stress more than normal, sorting them into genuine, hurtful, loony, and spiteful heaps, protecting me from the worst of them.

Counseling was available as an in-house service at uni, and at Mum and Dad's insistence, I decided I'd better at least put in an appearance.

I actually felt quite good, considering, but David, the celebrant, the wise old thing, told me to expect a delayed reaction.

It happened as I prepared myself for my third session with Mrs. Burns, the therapist recommended by Henry University.

I had my doubts about her in the first instance. She'd lost a son in similar circumstances to Danny, and in our first visit, she kept on referring back to him and her own journey of recovery, which I found left me in an abysmal frame of mind afterward. She also made this weird noise—a *choof choof choof*, for all the world like the old steam-driven chaff cutter that was always around the agricultural shows. Mrs. Burns made that noise both when she was laughing, which was seldom, and when she was crying, which was most of the time, and I found her hard going to say the least.

By the time the second session came around, I realized I needed something more uplifting. What poor Mrs. Burns had done was to reignite all my guilt and hurt over Danny's passing instead of showing me a path forward. Out of courtesy I finished the second session, but as the third session approached, I felt this deep melancholy and overwhelming malaise, which challenged my normally positive frame of mind.

I had trouble getting out of bed in the mornings and got tearful easily, but what set the alarm bells ringing for Macca, Toby, Paul, and Dougie was that I went off my food, and they demanded I do something about myself.

Fuck it, this has got to stop.

I rang Mrs. Burns, poor thing, thanked her for helping me but declined to continue. She sounded as if she'd cut half a tonne of chaff before breakfast. I also spoke to the student support group coordinator to inform him of my decision and immediately felt better. At least one source of my worsened condition was removed.

I went to lectures. Sarah helped me catch up, even visiting at home, making sure I didn't fall behind, and appealing to what ego I had remaining.

But my motivation had disappeared, and I just missed him.

Even before our reconciliation, he was only a phone call away, or a text message. But now there was nothing.

I missed the silly little things, like walking Bruce at night before bed, and, of course, Bruce missed him as well. Even though Toby didn't like dogs "living" inside, some nights I would hear him crying, and I'd let him into my room.

But the force of whatever was hurting me continued to manifest itself in all sorts of unpleasant ways, and I knew I was being a real bitch to live with.

I rang the only person who had made sense to me through this bloody nightmare—David Canning, the celebrant.

HE WASN'T surprised at my call, but he warned me he wasn't a qualified counselor, just that he and Peter, his partner, "had seen a lot of life." He insisted I bring Bruce with me, which I thought a little strange, so we rocked up at this house in one of the better suburbs of town.

An interesting place, surrounded by beautiful greenery, which gave the place a country feel, a very relaxing atmosphere.

He appeared in the driveway. The gray beard, the specs, and those twinkling eyes just welcomed you into his world.

Bruce went silly over him, squealing like a bitch, jumping into his arms again, head on his shoulder just like a baby.

A fully grown Kelpie is not a lightweight, but David cuddled him, and he responded, obviously remembering David and certainly pleased to see him.

Peter, his partner, looked on in amusement, not surprised.

"He has hundreds of dogs around here who adore him," Peter said. "He walks our dogs every day and has pockets of treats for everyone. He was very taken with Bruce during your sad time. He reckons animals and humans have the capacity to help each other heal, you know."

My head jerked up as I remembered David's words at the funeral. I felt guilty because I certainly hadn't paid enough attention to my faithful friend. He was just always there, and I'd made the same mistake that other silly humans had made from time immemorial—not recognizing that animals had feelings too. There was no doubt poor Bruce was missing Danny something fierce. There had been a bonding there with us as a couple, and with one half of the couple gone, no wonder he had been so bereft.

The tears ran down my cheeks as I watched David skylarking with my dog. He put Bruce on the ground and watched him walk over to me, wagging his tail and looking guilty because he was so enjoying himself.

I sat on the front doorstep, and he hopped up on my knee, placing his head on my shoulder, and the dam burst, and I bawled my eyes out.

David and Peter let me finish, and then we went inside where there was a wonderful smell emanating from the kitchen.

"We rang Toby and told him you wouldn't be home for your evening meal. A full tummy always helps."

I didn't argue. After my little outburst, I'd started to feel a little better, and suddenly my appetite returned. Peter watched like a mother hen as I devoured everything in sight. His roast chook was stunning, with all the vegetables on the side. Then bread and butter pudding afterward, only better than Mum makes, not that I'd ever dare tell her that.

The three of us sat around chatting afterward. I realized these guys were operating as a team when David asked how I felt and if they'd contributed in any way to alleviating the pain I'd been feeling.

"I'd totally forgotten about Bruce," I said, and David nodded.

"He's both a painful and joyful reminder of the past." David smiled. "But what we're really talking about is your future, isn't it?"

I nodded. The old bloke was determined to get my agreement to everything, one step at a time and in the right direction.

"When I see the chemistry between you and your dog, it reminds me of your brilliant future," David said quietly. "You have a unique gift with animals. You can communicate with them at all levels—you walk into a room, and you can do anything with them, anything at all. There is implicit trust, and while veterinary surgeons, like human healers, should stay emotionally removed from patients, your gift will make your career all the more rewarding, I believe."

I wanted to argue with him, but I realized he was right. I did have something my fellow vet students didn't have, and unless I pulled my finger out I'd waste it. Suddenly I was thinking of the future again. *Thank you, David and Peter, you blokes are game changers.*

CHAPTER 13
A DEVIATION

AFTER THE initial visit with David and Peter, I seemed to find my equilibrium restored as well as my sense of humor. I decided my judgment had been correct, after all. What I had needed was a few laughs, common sense, and some great tucker to make me feel better, which I certainly did.

For the first time in many months, I actually looked forward to uni and felt I finally had a future and a career to look forward to. I immersed myself in Veterinary Nutrition and Animal Toxicology, rewarding Sarah for all the time she had invested in me. She welcomed me back from whence I'd been and introduced me to the new man in her life, Richard.

Richard was simply divine—an even-tempered, uncomplicated guy who adored Sarah, and there was no doubt the feeling was reciprocated. At this early stage of their relationship, it was obvious that they had met their soul mate, and as a result, Sarah's life fanned out ahead of her. Career, marriage, kids: it was all there because she and Richard were very much on the same page. I didn't feel jealous, just a little wistful that my life, by happenchance, was now empty again.

I'd naturally not cultivated the casual contacts I'd made before Danny and I became a couple, so I had to start again. I'd been perfectly happy with a quiet lifestyle, just the two of us, and apart from Toby and Macca's little family group and their friends, we'd been content with each other's company.

Not that I was looking for any sort of relationship. I was still so hung up on the tragedy that had visited my life, including those dark days, that I just didn't feel at all horny. In fact, I'd not had a meaningful erection since.

The second visit to David was therefore, by necessity, a more serious one.

Peter sensed my somber mood and left us to talk while he performed his normal magic in the kitchen.

"So what's on your mind, Dean?" the old bloke inquired.

"I think I've come to terms with the issues of guilt quite well," I said, "and I accept there's nothing I could have done to have saved Danny. None of us could have known what was going on in his mind. So, sad as it may be, Danny is now history—a huge part of my early life, but part of the past, and that's cool. But what's hard is moving on to the next stage."

I thought carefully about what I was about to tell David Canning, but he made it easy as he always did.

"You're having trouble because you feel absolutely no attraction toward anyone else?" David said softly.

I nodded and elaborated. "Not only that, but I haven't even had an erection since Danny died. It's like everything has shut down, and I don't know how to get it going again.

"My friend Will came to visit. He and I were very close, never boyfriends, but we were fuck buddies for a while until he dropped out of veterinary science, moved to Melbourne, and shortly after that Danny and I became a couple. He's been concerned for me, and so he stayed last weekend. It was so embarrassing. We slept together, and I just couldn't do anything. Thinking about it later, I suppose I didn't want to do anything because it reminded me of Danny. So I went to Darren Clarke yesterday, and he says there's nothing wrong with me that time won't fix. But it would be nice to have everything in going order again, even if it's just me playing around with myself." I grinned.

The old bloke smiled back. "It's lovely to hear your sense of humor creeping back in, Dean. Darren is a great GP. Being a gay man himself, he's had plenty of experience dealing with men's issues. Did he say anything about the emotional self driving the physical?"

I nodded, and he continued. "Imagine your emotions being a tank of fuel in a car. In your case, when you lost Danny that tank was drained dry. The engine won't run—it simply can't do anything or go anywhere without the tank being topped up again. It's fortunate for you that not only do you have the most amazing birth family through your parents and sisters, but you also have an equally amazing second family up here. Those people are refueling your emotional tank for you, and you probably don't even realize what's happening. One day soon your tank will be full to the brim again, and you'll roar off into the sunset, all systems go."

I looked at the old fellow compassionately. As much as I appreciated him, he was probably full of shit—as was my doctor, spinning me a story to make me feel better.

He caught the expression on my face and knew exactly what was going through my mind.

"You young people always think this has never happened before, never happened to anyone else, and I wish you were right, but you're not," he said grimly. "It will sadly happen again to other people, Dean, because human nature is what it is. And yes, that's why Darren Clarke and I get pretty close to the mark most of the time. So when we say you're on the road to recovery, we're both confirming what we've seen in the past. However, sweetheart—" He smiled, taking my hand and making me feel a bigger prick than ever for doubting his word. "—Mother Nature has some strange ways at times. Just don't be surprised how it all comes together."

I COULDN'T help but notice the pretty girls at uni this year. A number of them stepped out of their comfort zone after Danny's passing. Sarah had spread the word, and because Danny and I had circulated at a few social events, my orientation had never been a secret.

One of the most persistent was Georgia, a distant friend of Sarah's who was genuinely upset at my situation. She told me I deserved better and needed a chance to move on properly with my life, a sentiment I had to heartily agree with, particularly after my last visit with David Canning.

After some more pestering and a particularly stressful day, I caved in and allowed her to take me on a "date," as she put it, a nice-but-filling el-cheapo meal at a local Italian restaurant. It was so pleasant just to go out and relax away from veterinary science and the stress of the last few months. So much so, I completely missed the punch line.

"What did you say?" I asked incredulously.

"I said that a handsome, masculine, well-built guy like you ought to accept that he's transitioned through his gay period and is ready to get on with his life in a more meaningful way."

"That's what I thought you said. I couldn't believe that a nice person like you could be capable of challenging my orientation in such a way."

"Look," she said, "I happen to believe that a man is always a man, and it doesn't matter what path he goes down, he'll always be missing what he was made to do in the first place, to be with a woman, procreate, and further the human race."

"Are you some religious nutter?" I asked. "Because that's bullshit. Look, I realize everyone has a view which is theirs alone, and who am I to argue with that."

"Yes, particularly if he's never been to bed with a real woman."

I stopped, my mouth hanging open, the invitation hanging in midair.

Georgia was a city girl, certainly without the down-to-earth attitude of country kids, but there was no doubt she was pretty without being overtly feminine, a trait I couldn't stand. I always found I liked women who had something to say for themselves, not the bimbos who got by on their looks alone.

I judged Georgia to be somewhere in between, and there was no doubt she was pretty. Hetero guys would probably have called her hot, but I found that term almost offensive. To me she was just an attractive girl. I looked at her now through different eyes. She certainly had big breasts, a little heavyset in the figure perhaps, but she had good well-shaped legs that certainly offset any discrepancies. The only thing that worried me was her attitude to my sexuality—a flag I'd proudly waved all my life so far and wasn't about to stop now—and I told her so, and that I considered her remarks both unintelligent and homophobic.

She smiled sweetly, apologized profusely, and said she'd been attracted to me for such a long time and she'd allowed that to get in the way of our friendship.

"All right," I said, "I'll try for your sake, but you must understand if anything happens it will be purely physical and nothing else, okay?"

"Of course," she purred, and before I knew what was happening, we were walking into her little flat, a one-bedroom affair about five minutes away from the university, within sight of the ICHP and the infamous public toilets—about which Georgia obviously neither knew nor cared, but the irony didn't escape me.

As if he'd been waiting on cue, Traitorous Dick rose to the occasion. In all the conversation over the last hour or so, I realized I'd totally forgotten my erectile dysfunction, and he was ready and raring to go. I thought if I was quick enough I could pull my gear back on and make it up to the toilet block, which would no doubt be in full swing at this hour of the night, but that would be ungentlemanly, so I relaxed and let her have her way.

"Did you enjoy that?" she asked, and I lied my way around it so she wouldn't be upset.

But she did get upset as I began to get dressed preparatory to leaving and going home.

"What are you doing?" she screeched. "Where are you going? I'd planned to cook you a lovely breakfast tomorrow morning."

"I'm going home to feed my dog, do some more study, and prepare for tomorrow's practical," I replied truthfully.

"But what about us?" she wailed.

"Huh?" I responded, having by now some idea what was going through her brain.

"I've given you something no one else has given you," she said and began sobbing. "Here you are, a self-professed *gay person*," she said, spitting the words out, "and I've begun your reeducation back to a normal lifestyle, and you treat the exercise as a joke. Go on, then," she sneered, "take yourself back to your horrible family of queers, and I'll just have to manage by myself."

I nearly spat the dummy on the spot, but further conversation would only aggravate the issue, so I just smiled thinly and walked toward the door. If this was straight sex, then she could keep her secrets, because she certainly didn't have any worth keeping.

I DIDN'T dare tell anyone about my little escapade. Macca had certainly lived a heterosexual lifestyle before he met Toby, and Paul and Dougie had obviously dabbled. How else had Paul produced his daughter, even if it was under duress?

But I thought discretion was the better part of valor as I knuckled down to my studies.

These guys were my beautiful extended family who had stood by me through all my difficulties, and they didn't need to worry about why I'd put my dick in a pussy when my orientation had been so clearly gay all my life.

About two weeks later, I ran into Jill Fraser, another acquaintance of Sarah's whom I knew through some of the university functions.

Jill was the consummate tomboy and a great sportsperson—in fact, she had been a member of the Australian gymnastics team at the last Olympics. She always had an opinion and wasn't afraid of arguing her case, which endeared her to me immensely. It was a difficult position to take at a place like Henry University, where there was the academic/populist view and no middle ground at all. She couldn't give a shit who she offended, and she said so, which delighted me.

So I was all ears when she sought me out in the student dining hall, sliding into a seat beside me.

"So what has my lovely gay boy been up to?" she asked. "Jumping the fence with our Georgia, I hear?"

My face must have dropped like a stone. Jill smiled at my discomfort.

"Georgia has been shooting her big mouth off all over the university," she chortled. "But don't worry about her—she's never minded me going down on her." Jill laughed, holding her sides at the look of amazement on my face. "She's a psychologist's wet dream, our bloody Georgia—loves sex with the ladies but has a real kink for gay men. Loves trying to convert them, then gets shitty when they run a mile like you did."

I saw the funny side at last as Jill told me how she'd waited until Georgia was in full cry with as many people as possible gathered around, bagging me for my supposed lack of performance and how she felt so devastated by the experience.

"I screamed out that I thought she was a two-faced slut who preyed on gay people, particularly someone vulnerable who had lost his partner in the worst possible way. Then I gave everyone chapter and verse on *her* kinky sex life, and her audience deserted her. I don't think you'll be troubled with her anytime soon."

I knew where this was leading and didn't discourage it. We met again after lectures, and I followed her home. Once inside she wasted no time, but not before she gave me a lecture.

"I have no expectations of this," she said, "and there are rules. I don't belong to you, and you don't belong to me. I'll show you what sex with a woman can be like, given I'm bi and you're a gay man, but there is absolutely nothing else, right?"

"Time to go home," she said afterward, coldly living up to her policy of noninvolvement.

"Okay," I said easily, dressing myself as she walked me to the door. "I'll see you later?" I leaned in to kiss her good-bye, a typical friendly Jill kiss that I'd done many times before.

She deliberately turned her head to one side and my lips brushed along her cheek. The physical intimacy had sadly changed everything, and I was just a little peeved, stupidly expecting our sexual adventure to bring us closer together, not the opposite.

LIFE MOVED on at home. Toby, Macca, and the boys respected my privacy, but they knew something was different because I think I became a little remote.

Bloody Bruce knew too. He was even more demanding and would have slept inside if Toby had allowed him. I actually took him to uni a few times, chaining him up to the car in the shade with his water, walking him at lunchtimes.

But I did manage to enjoy myself, particularly the social aspect. Jill and I would occasionally go out together to functions, the movies, and parties, never just the two of us, always part of a group.

I marveled at the ease of it all. It was just a given that I was Jill's companion and she was mine, and no questions were asked because that's what at least 90 percent of humanity did. Two people of the opposite sex went out together.

So different to my previous partnership, which was well-known and welcomed but always seemed to require explanation and analysis even in the university environment.

Man, I can understand now why some gay guys go ahead and marry chicks. This is all so easy, because with an understanding girl like Jill, a bloke could enjoy an almost stress-free existence. But it could all turn to shit if the little wife isn't sophisticated enough to embrace her husband's lifestyle.

YEAR-END CAME up quickly. There was a heavy workload, and I sometimes found it hard to stay awake even in the mornings. I was aware I should contribute more to my home environment. I hadn't cooked for them all for such a long time, and I felt the demands on my time were dragging me in different directions all at once.

Summer holidays, Christmas, and New Year rushed past. I went home to Mum and Dad, and ran Prentice Farm Supplies for two weeks in January so Mum, Dad, and my sisters could have a break. Simon and Julie were great company, and we went out together.

When Dad and Mum returned, I went straight back to Macca and Toby. Macca was having enormous difficulties keeping abreast with the workload. Typical Australia, everyone focused on holidays, yet there was plenty of work around, and no one wanted to do it. Macca had bought a third van. There were roadworks everywhere, and his reputation for service meant they always called him first. Toby was feeding us as Macca, Paul, and I worked from daylight to dark for several weeks in a row.

Dougie ran the florist business, as the owners were on holiday, so our lovely next door neighbor, Mrs. Browning, helped Toby care for Jenny while we were flat-out like lizards drinking.

Toward the end of the month, things began to slow down a little, and Macca found another permanent operator, who began work immediately.

Within a week, the other guy was back from holidays, and I returned to my work with Brett Walker, the practice as frantically busy as ever.

Bruce was always keen to go to the clinic. He bloody knew at breakfast where I was going because of the clothes I wore. If I had on work boots and pants, he was at the car, waiting. There was no point wearing university clobber if I had to shovel shit or perhaps get covered in gore as I helped Brett operate in the theater.

Bruce became the face of Brett's practice. Customers loved him, and even the patients loved him as well. His normal predatory behavior toward cats had been obviously modified. He seemed to understand they were sick, and he was like an old mother to everything that came through the doorway.

As much as I tried to ignore the facts, there was only one human Bruce disliked—Jill Fraser. He snarled openly at her and sulked when she was in the car. When she arrived back from the summer break, I sensed something had changed, and my dog, ever the bloody mind reader, also knew something was afoot.

I soon found out. "I'm pregnant," Jill said, matter-of-factly, as we sat down in her lounge room. "Oh don't worry," she said scornfully, "it's not yours, you should know that, Mr. Supercareful."

I closed my eyes, feeling unwanted, used, and totally pissed off that she'd been screwing around when I'd been monogamous. The fact that she was bi and I knew she'd bedded a few girls on campus never worried me, leaving the door open for me to play around with guys, but I hadn't. My course load had been increasing every semester, and I simply hadn't time to fuck around. "So what are you going to do now?" I asked her, feeling like a stranger in her company.

"I've talked to my parents," she said casually, "and they've agreed to support me totally. I'm going to have the child, so I'll stay at uni until I'm at least eight months. This won't affect us, will it, gay boy?" she said sweetly, almost in the one breath.

But out of nowhere, I grew some balls once more.

Maybe it had something to do with my attitudes toward monogamy, and maybe I felt I couldn't trust her, but I knew it was over.

"Jill," I said kindly, realizing I didn't need an enemy so close to home, "it's over, you and I. You're a very special person and a good friend, but you need to concentrate on the health of you and your child. Obviously you need to spend as much time as you can with your boyfriend."

"What boyfriend?" she snapped. "I don't have one. If you mean the kid's father, then he's just a root anyway, someone I've known for ages. Nothing at all between us except sex, and he's nearly three hundred kilometers away, and I need sex now." She smiled grimly.

"You guys in the arts have absolutely no idea how demanding veterinary science is," I said seriously, cutting to the chase. "I know what's ahead, and if I want a job at the end of my studies I have to work for it."

She glared at me because she knew she needed to do a lot more than just swan through university in subjects that, without her Dip. Ed., would give her little prospect of becoming more than a teacher's aide. And now with a baby in her future she'd be relying on her family's money for many years to come. I didn't stop to argue my point further. I felt tired of what had become a drama, and I just wanted to go home.

I gave her a "Jill kiss" on the cheek and walked out her door, leaving her standing there with her mouth open.

CHAPTER 14
A FEW LAUGHS. IT'S A JOKE, JOYCE.

I DIDN'T have to say anything at home. Toby, Macca, Paul, and Dougie just loved me like they'd always done, and at last Bruce was happier—or he was after I had the car cleaned inside and he couldn't smell her!

I slipped back into their social life effortlessly. I'd always been invited, but now I made an effort to properly participate, studies permitting, and the following Saturday night was such an event—a barbeque at home for about thirty people.

They assured me some new people would be attending who would hold my interest, and after work at the clinic on Saturday morning, I was put to work making mountains of salads.

The first to arrive were Geoffy and Lisa Stevenson, and they managed to set the tone for the evening, that of utter hilarity. I suddenly forgot about my miserable mindset and the feeling of rejection from the collapse of my so-called relationship with Jill. Even Danny seemed a distant but now mostly pleasant memory. Instead I listened with delight to Geoffy and realized my sense of humor had finally returned. Their three sons had turned out gay. The eldest, Craig, was partnered with his old school friend Teddy Lamping, and their twin sons Andy and Chris were partnered also—with another set of twins! The Stevenson boys were all butch, manly looking and sounding blokes working in the building industry, while their father, the only heterosexual male in the family, sounded like a screeching drag queen. He camped it up, laughing one moment and crying the next, while his wife just rolled her eyes. Geoffy had been gently imbibing, a few harmless glasses of red before they left home, so I quickly cooked a plate of food and handed it to him, Lisa smiling her grateful thanks. Then Lisa and Geoffy's family arrived—Craig first, Teddy following, lugging a bassinet with their firstborn inside, a little boy only a few months old, and finally the twins, just a little quieter than their father but with their eyes full of mischief.

Teddy wagged his finger at them and they quietened down immediately, their brother-in-law striking terror into their hearts, and their partners looking relieved.

I always liked the Stevenson family, and Lisa and I had become good friends even though we were from much different age groups. Tonight she was in a reflective mood, and I listened politely. Suddenly I realized she knew all about Jill and me, and it was equally obvious she understood that I'd probably suffered some criticism because I'd "jumped the fence," albeit for a short time.

"Geoffrey was a bi man," she said gently, "but he was an honest one. Back in the days when no one ever discussed this stuff, and before we even went out together, he told me about his preferences, and it didn't shock me because I grew up with a gay elder brother. He's gone now." She sighed. "A stupid drug overdose, such a waste. But he was my brother, and all his friends were just lovely, and they opened my mind up like no other experience a teenage girl could possibly have. So here I was with this self-confessed bisexual man whom I really, really liked, and it turned out he liked me as well, so before we went a step further, we decided we were going to be monogamous to give the relationship a chance.

"Just a few months later we realized we loved each other, and you see the result around you, Dean," she laughed. "A mad but devoted husband, three beautiful sons, and my first grandchild. What more could a woman want!"

I couldn't help but laugh with her, but after delivering lesson one, she wasn't about to stop there. I knew bits and pieces of the more recent family history, but not being a gossip queen and not having a need to know, I hadn't bothered myself with the details.

"We nearly lost everything," she said, looking vulnerable, and I reached over, lifting her hand from her wineglass and holding it.

I knew where she was going and that she'd just realized the facts could be uncomfortable for me, but I reassured her, and she continued.

"We didn't properly discuss sexual orientation with the kids, in fact we really didn't discuss sex at all, because Geoff and I hoped everyone would be nice and heterosexual so they'd have uncomplicated lives, not like their father and not like my brother. Craig was the apple of our eye. He did everything perfectly. We hadn't the faintest idea anything was wrong. He had a girlfriend who moved in with him, and the family building business was thriving because he was a hard worker, a good businessman, and so good with people. Then it all unraveled, and he tried to take his own life, but his brothers had been watching, and we got him to the hospital on time. We tried everything to shake him out of his depression, but nothing worked until Craig decided to go to New York to visit his best friend who had just finished his master's degree there—Teddy," she said, a tear running down her cheek.

"It just goes to show, it really doesn't matter what your orientation is, if you love someone, it's all that really matters. As it turned out, Craig is about as gay as anyone could be, and so is Teddy, so it wasn't a stretch at all," she said, laughing at her unintended naughtiness.

"But the twins were different, and Geoff and I, to be really honest, didn't know how to handle them. It took Teddy with all his patience and love to sort things out. Just look at them now," she said with obvious pride. "Andy, we believe, has always been far more straight than even bi, and Chris was definitely gay. But they were *very* close. They even slept together in the one bed. Andy would go out with a girlfriend, but he would dump her home early so he could get home to Chris. If they are apart too much they drive you mad texting each other. Geoff and I couldn't find common ground, and even Craig, whom they worship, couldn't get through. Living a dysfunctional sort of lifestyle, totally reliant on each other admittedly isn't all that bad—but never giving each other a chance to develop individually worried us.

"As it turned out, miracles do happen, but to manage those miracles takes a special person, and that's Teddy. He introduced Leigh and Todd to Andy and Chris and then told them all what he expected of them! I always hated conjoined houses, but I changed my mind when I saw what Teddy and Craig suggested to the boys. Leigh and Andy in one side and Todd and Chris in the other, with a door between the two homes, and they're thriving! Andy and Chris are still naughty boys, but Leigh and Todd give them just enough rope, and then they reel them in," she chortled.

"The point I struggle to make, Dean, is that with all the sadness you've endured, there's always someone out there who loves you. But never, ever marry anyone you don't love."

THEN MY favorite policeman walked in—Steve Norris, and his partner Aaron. Together they were a formidable team. Aaron's divorce had been amicable enough, and he and Steve now had custody of his two little girls, who burst through the side gate like banshees, looking for Jenny. Now she had two little mothers who proceeded to rock her to sleep, taking over from a relieved Dougie.

I looked on fondly, remembering the night Danny died and how Jenny with her childlike view of the world brought us all back to earth again. Now was such a time again, and my reverie was broken by Toby, who slipped his arm around me, recognizing we were both a bit clucky.

"When are you and Macca having kids?" I asked.

"About two years from now when we can be sure Paul and Dougie have a sustainable income stream." He smiled. "We've had such a dream run with this lot, hardly a harsh word since they arrived, and just look at what they're making of themselves."

He pointed to the middle of the group, where Paul and Dougie were quietly listening as the Stevenson twins held forth. Then it was time for little Jason Stevenson's bottle, and Teddy showed the girls how to burp his little son. But Jason delivered both ends, and I watched the naughtiness fade in the eyes of the Stevenson twins as the cloying smell drifted across their noses and their normally ruddy complexions turned ashen.

THERE WAS a bang at the gate as it burst open, and Peter Briton danced in, followed by his partner David Canning, our trusty celebrant and all-round good bloke. Peter also had obviously had an early start for the evening. David, I knew, refused point-blank to drive when he'd had even one drink, so they'd taxied over, Peter in fine form.

"Oh," he shrieked, "what a pack of bitches, all of you pissed, why didn't you wait for me?"

"Well, you certainly haven't waited for anyone, pet," said Geoffy, and the slanging match was on.

"Just as well they don't take offense at each other," a male voice said beside me.

I turned to look at him. About thirty years old, and I realized he'd arrived with David and Peter. Obviously the means by which my interest would be held for the evening!

Barry introduced himself, and he was just gorgeous—a bit rugged and a bit of a bear. During the course of the evening, I struggled to work him out. It seemed there was a vacuum in his cranial cavity until you actually listened to him. He sounded so fucking dumb initially but saved himself from the blond brigade with a great sense of humor, self-deprecating but shrewd. I realized later the dumb act gave him time to analyze other people.

I knew I had to have him. It had been a while since I'd had any sort of sex, but Old Dick definitely told me he still liked blokes, and how. The drought was about to be broken. I loosened my belt to give myself a little more room, but long before the last of the partygoers had gone home, we slipped into my room and locked the door.

It was pandemonium for a while, each of us trying to get as much of the other as possible in the least amount of time. Finally, as I reached for the condoms to take the next step, I sensed something was wrong. "What's going on in that handsome head of yours, sugar?" I said.

He hunched up at the end of the bed, looking conflicted. "Sorry," he whispered, "I've got something to tell you."

For once in my life, I shut my big mouth and listened. All semblance of his dumb act evaporated as he spoke steadily and quietly. "I really, really like you, Dean." He smiled thinly. "I don't think in a million years we'd ever make a married couple, but I think we could be magnificent fuck buddies and best friends."

I nodded, agreeing totally.

"What I'm going to tell you I've told no one else, but I feel I can trust you already," he pleaded, and I thought I knew what was on his mind. "I was diagnosed HIV positive five years ago," he said, his eyes downcast, a mirror of his misery. "I've never had any sort of anal sex, top or bottom since then, just oral. I was raped by a married, supposedly straight friend of my cousin. She would die if she knew the facts, so I didn't tell anyone. Not my parents, nobody except my doctors, and I've internalized this ever since."

I looked at him with compassion but hopefully not pity. "What happened to your attacker?" I asked, curiosity demanding I know more.

"He died of the illness. I named him through my infectious diseases physician, but before they could contact him, he was really ill. Only on his deathbed did his wife discover what his illness was. He'd refused treatment and lived in a state of denial until he passed away. I can only assume he used condoms with the little missus. I wasn't that lucky, and I had no choice—he was a big African man, and he wasn't taking no for an answer."

"Bastard," I responded, and Barry agreed. "So what's your viral load?" I asked.

"Undetectable."

"So there's almost no chance of you passing the virus on even if you had unprotected sex?"

"Exactly. I went on to medication immediately after diagnosis, which has limited the damage to my immune system, thank heavens, and my prognosis is really good. But try telling that to any member of the general public. The stigma is real. To admit you're positive in this community would be the end of everything, even among other gay people."

"Particularly among many gay people," I replied. "But not me. I studied the disease in some detail because of its original transmission from animals to humans."

Barry slipped his legs down, standing up and reaching for his clothes.

"Where do you think you're off to, princess?" I grinned.

"Off home. I guess I've outstayed my welcome."

"You stupid fucking bitch, what for?"

"I made a mistake, sorry, I shouldn't have mentioned my troubles to you."

"Get your beautiful arse back on this bed immediately. Have you cleaned yourself out?"

"Um, no, I didn't think I'd need to."

"Well, the gear's in the bathroom here. It hasn't been used since my late boyfriend used it, but I'm sure you know what to do. You've got five minutes counting from now."

His face lit up with joy. He hadn't misjudged me, after all. If the huge boner on display was any indication, he was looking forward to a good old root.

THE NEXT morning he staggered into the kitchen, where Toby was at the stove, Macca walking in soon after. I was already sitting at the breakfast bar enjoying my first cup of coffee. "Good morning, sunshine." I grinned at him, and he just smirked.

Macca looked at him and asked if he was okay and that maybe he looked a bit tired.

"You'd be bloody tired if you'd been fucked so hard your fucking teeth rattled," he snarled.

Macca and Toby roared with laughter and a friendship was born. I had a great mate and fuck buddy, and Toby and Macca's home had a new visitor and a source of much humor.

CHAPTER 15
TROUBLE IN PARADISE

MY WELL-PLANNED, bookish, hardworking existence quite suddenly imploded. Barry was adamant that my education wasn't complete unless I had experienced everything that life could throw at me. I tried to be serious about my future career and my veterinary science studies, but he said my life education was just as important, and while I was able to maintain an erection, the two could exist harmoniously side by side and even complement each other.

"You're full of shit," I commented, and he laughed, but I also realized he had a point.

"Sitting at home on a Saturday night watching free-to-air television, how fuckin' productive is that?" he said with a wicked smile. "You could be studying anatomy at one of Melbourne's saunas, perhaps doing a thesis on the male appendage."

So we went cock hunting together, and if either was unsuccessful, the other filled in for the night. There were no set rules. There was no expectation we would end up in bed with each other, but we were aware of each other's feelings at all times because that's what real mates did for each other.

The local beats and Grindr made up the slack. Barry was an expert in both areas but took some silly risks with both the unlawful and physically dangerous aspects of his "community service," as he called it. Notwithstanding, I couldn't believe the haunts Barry took me to, and many were in broad daylight, which made me acutely embarrassed and scared shitless at the same time.

Lectures finished early one day, and my phone sang its silly song. It was Barry.

"Come for a walk," he said, "for exercise."

I was stupid enough to get sucked in and looked on in disbelief as we walked along the path by the river. Carstairs Common ran alongside the river. Because it was a flood plain, building wasn't allowed, so the local council had laid down bitumen walkways for citizens to walk their dogs, themselves, or in the case of some, display their little treasures in the secluded cul-de-sacs and undergrowth that bordered the pathways. Some of the treasures were, in fact, gigantic, and we looked on as guys openly played hide the sausage, some inviting us over to join in. Barry sensed my discomfort, and we declined the offers, walking back toward the entrance and nearly falling over one of my university lecturers buried up to the hilt in one of the town's best-known real estate agents, Grant Slater. We nodded our pleasantries, and I ran off with Barry laughing behind me.

"Wonder what Mr. Slater's missus would say if she knew?" I wondered aloud.

"Probably join in, pet," Barry giggled. "That's what this town's like. Everyone maintains a façade of decency and niceness up front when in reality it makes Peyton Place look like a kindergarten. But what about the teach?" He grinned.

"Well, Clinical Laboratory Medicine will never be quite the same again," I laughed, "but it really doesn't worry me."

"Yes, I know." He smirked. "Not exactly God's gift to humanity, is he?"

"Yeah, he can keep his secrets," I laughed, and Barry roared. My education was progressing nicely.

IT HAD been getting worse since the party, raised voices in the sleepout at times, and we all worried that Jenny might pick up on the tension.

And tension it was. Paul and Dougie glared at each other over breakfast most mornings and snapped at each other constantly.

Polite questions from the remainder of the house got a surly response and no real information, and eventually Dougie moved next door, renting a room from Mrs. Browning. He continued to spend most of his spare time on our side of the fence, however, and insisted on caring for Jenny as he'd always done, the only difference being she slept in her cot alone with Paul in the sleepout at nights.

I felt really sorry for Toby and Macca. They had taken these guys out of the gutter, put food in their bellies and a roof over their heads, and motivated them to continue in the right direction, raising their baby daughter with love and affection all around them. And it had worked until now. Paul was well on his way to a business career, working part-time for Macca, and Dougie was fully involved and enjoying the creativity of the florist's trade.

But it so obviously wasn't the dollars and cents invested in Paul and Dougie that my cousin and his lovely partner felt badly about, but the impending failure of their family structure, and they needed help as much as Paul and Dougie.

It was clear to me they felt guilty—that they'd failed Paul and Dougie in some way when the opposite was the case.

I thought long and hard about what I should do, if anything at all. It's usually conventional wisdom and manners to let couples sort themselves out—it's their business, after all. But something told me Toby and Macca were paralyzed by fear of defeat. That if they pushed the issue they could push Paul and Dougie over the edge without any hope of reconciliation, so they just moped around the place looking and no doubt feeling useless.

Barry was also about as much use as tits to a bull. He just shrugged with a grin and reminded me that relationships just weren't his strong suit, but if I needed his help, I could count on him. And I knew I could, because he loved Paul and Dougie too.

After having endured a Mexican standoff for long enough, I talked to the only person I thought could offer some sound, commonsense advice—David Canning. He'd been closely involved when Steve Norris had rescued the boys and knew our little family intimately.

"Ah yes. The little family that everyone expects to be perfect, just like hetero families are supposed to be. Think about it, Dean. Those two were concentrating on survival when they were dropped on Toby and Macca. In fact, I think it took them some time to realize they didn't have to worry about that aspect of their existence anymore. So they've gone literally from rags to riches, always focused on little Jenny, which I must say is commendable, but never on themselves. They're still only *kids*, Dean. They've never had time to even date each other let alone manage a love affair—think about it. Sometimes love just isn't enough." He smiled thinly, almost talking to himself. "When the veneer wears off, we have to manage what's left, which is a relationship, and that's what's happened to Paul and Dougie. As their lives have changed, so have they. They've become different people with vastly different expectations from what they held previously."

"So what you're saying is that there's no hope for their relationship, David?" I asked politely, my spirits totally deflated.

"I didn't say that. In fact, I was watching them one morning at home just after their disagreement became public. They're trying to strike out on their own, but in my humble opinion that'll never happen because it's obvious they still love each other."

"But it's been three months, and they just seem to be getting worse," I said, feeling at a loss at David's words.

His eyes gleamed as he slid his powerful arm around my shoulder and hugged me.

"You care about people, Dean. That's why Peter and I love you so much. You've copped so much shit in your life, yet you worry about other people."

If the old guy had wanted to make me feel good, he'd succeeded.

PAUL WAS like the reluctant debutante. He whined and wailed, but I was adamant. We were going out the following Saturday night together, and there was no further argument. I thought how he'd lost his way in the last few months. When Danny died nearly two years ago, Paul had taken over as my secretary, answering the condolence cards and e-mails. Yet now he was just bumping along the bottom, quite demotivated and useless.

I'd decided to drive to Melbourne rather than take the train, and he sat slumped in the passenger seat, staring mindlessly out the window as I tried to keep him occupied.

"Sorry, Deano." He grinned. "I don't know how you put up with me, I'm not much fun."

"Oh, you'll have fun tonight, I can guarantee that."

"But a bloody gay sauna. How can that be fun?"

"It's very sophisticated. It has a bar and restaurant, so if you don't feel like cruising we can always sit around and just enjoy the scenery—and there's plenty of that. You need to get out of this awful rut that you're in."

I almost shouted the words at him, then looked across and realized I'd nearly pushed it too hard. He was, I judged, not far from being tearful, and that would fuck the evening up completely.

We changed in the very modern locker room, and he seemed to lighten up a little. I took his hand, and he allowed me to lead him to the showers, where I pushed him in and let him go, hoping he'd find the guys there appealing.

I showered quickly, running back to my locker where my phone was ringing madly. I answered it, smiling to myself, and met Paul as he emerged from the shower area, his towel not able to disguise what was a beautiful body. I watched as several pairs of hands gently squeezed him in all the right places, and he finally smiled.

At last. It's been a bloody long time since anyone has shown their appreciation for the poor guy. Let's hope he goes home in a more positive frame of mind.

"Would you like a coffee, Paul?" I asked, knowing his alcohol consumption was almost nonexistent, and he nodded with thanks.

I returned with two cappuccinos and watched as his eyes began to roam around the talent, which was increasing by number and quality as time progressed. I smiled as he seemed to hone in on smaller fair-haired guys with tattoos and piercings, particularly the ones who seemed to have a bit of attitude to go with it. I could see the bulge growing under the towel, so I quietly slipped my hand under the table and squeezed it.

He laughed at me—another beautiful smile. "You keep that up, Deano, and I won't be responsible for me actions."

Good. Couldn't be better.

My phone beeped again with a text.

"Christ," Paul said, "someone's keen to catch up with you tonight. You'd better say yes before I do."

I didn't reply but just beckoned him with my finger. "Come on, all the good trade is in the dry sauna. I've been watching."

He looked at me with a puzzled expression and followed me as I led the way, opening the door and gently pushing him inside. There were only three people in there. One of them was a smallish tattooed guy with a couple of piercings and a really hot body. I quickly and quietly closed the door, which opened again suddenly as the two other guys walked out, leaving just Paul and his new friend in there together.

Barry joined me at the window, which gave us a clear view. Paul's back was to us, but Dougie turned his head, and the expression on his face went through surprise, recognition, and finally sheer delight when he realized who'd just sat down opposite. We couldn't hear what they said to each other, but they weren't stupid and would have worked out in a flash they'd been set up.

They didn't even turn toward us, knowing we'd be watching. Instead they jumped to their feet, towels falling to the floor, and reconnected on a higher plane. They only had eyes for each other, hugging, kissing, and becoming totally emotional.

A huge bloke walked toward the door, intent on interrupting, and Barry sprang at him, dragging him away and apologizing before he could open the door. Barry explained our reasons very succinctly.

"Just give them a few minutes, will you please, mate?" he asked.

But the resident bogan started to get stroppy, and I cracked. "Look," I said, "there's our two lovebirds in there. You're not going to get anything from them, so why don't you fuck off for five minutes?"

He looked me up and down, about to issue a challenge, then saw the determined look on my face and decided to quit while he was ahead.

After a few more minutes, we left and went quietly back to the restaurant, knowing the heat would drive them out eventually.

THEY CAME back to the restaurant as Barry and I were enjoying a drink. I'd decided to have a red wine and Barry a cola because he'd offered, very nicely, to drive home. We decided they also needed a glass of something to celebrate, and I bought them a small bottle of champers, which they sipped at, both pulling a face at the taste.

"You'll never make queen status if you can't vaporize champers," Barry laughed, and they shook their heads, definitely high on Mother Nature's sweetness, which was obviously more important than the sour taste of alcohol. They hadn't stopped chattering to each other, and I suddenly realized that tonight for them didn't seem to be about connecting sexually but just talking to each other.

Jesus. I was panicking. *We've interfered in their lives like a pair of busybodies and reintroduced them, but what do we do now?*

I thought quickly, knowing the sauna had rooms on the third floor, which were clean and private. I suggested they might like an hour or so there before we headed home. They nodded gratefully, and like good parents, Barry and I waved them away to do their own thing.

Barry looked at me suggestively. "Wanna play mommies and daddies while we wait for the kiddies? I'll be mommy."

CHAPTER 16
A RECONNECTION WITH THE PAST

EVERYONE HELD their breath, but Paul and Dougie's reconciliation seemed to hold together, and there was relative peace at home. It helped that they'd sat down with Macca and Toby as their adoptive parents and finally let it all hang out.

Then, after talking to me, they rang David Canning and spent several sessions with him and Peter, just talking through the issues, listening to David's common sense and just being loved and overfed by Peter.

Without their knowledge, there had been a little collection among the group. The Stevenson family, Steve and Aaron, and even Barry and I helped, but so did all the others. Toby and Macca made up the balance—more than enough to send them away for a holiday, just the two of them, down the coast to a B&B we knew, owned and run by two lovely lesbian ladies and their dogs.

Everyone understood why. Not only was it to give them some precious time to themselves, but to Macca it was also a reward for their "bloody persistence," as he put it. Our Macca was a closet romantic.

There was one facet of their little holiday that needed further negotiation, however. They accepted that the time away together was exactly what they needed and at the right time, and they even swallowed their pride to allow other people to pay for it all. But the one thing that wasn't negotiable was Jenny. No way were they leaving home without her!

Ten days later they were home again, the complete lack of any pressure or tension showing on their faces. Both of them had put on weight, which made them look hotter than ever, and even Jenny's progress was noticeable. For the first time her words were decipherable, marking a decisive stage of her little life, her face beaming as her dads told her how clever she was.

But there was something else I couldn't quite put my finger on. It was to do with their attitude toward each other, a calmness and serenity that hadn't been there before.

A sob escaped me, and a tear trickled down my cheek when I spotted the rings on their right hands. How Danny would have loved this moment as Toby and I launched ourselves at them, congratulating a couple who, after some social engineering and a lot of love, had suddenly grown up and taken the only course they'd ever really wanted to. The word spread. Macca left the job he was on, David and Peter arrived, and before we knew it, all the bloody Stevenson family was there. And Barry, normally the last person to get excited over such news, swapped shifts at his work, and a gigantic party was suddenly in full swing.

I WATCHED Paul and Dougie, arms around each other, the absolute center of attention as they deserved to be, and I felt the same dreadful sadness creep over me again. Not only would Danny have loved to be here because he so loved Paul and Dougie, but we would have been headed in the same direction—engagement, marriage when it became legal, and kids.

But he wasn't here. He never would be again, and I mourned for him all over.

It was Macca who picked up on my mood and calmed me down, dragging me over to Barry, who immediately realized I was in a bit of trouble and ordered me inside to my bedroom. With unspoken tenderness, he coaxed me back to the present day, and we made love in the most beautiful way and for all the right reasons.

Barry, ever the consummate bottom, had a way of taking over in the bedroom even after the event, and it was lovely to feel comforted and loved by him in his own special way. We were both realists. It was a relationship with no rules. We gave each other total freedom with our sex lives, yet we had grown steadily closer over time. I wondered, after today's event, if life with Barry was a possibility in the future. He was good-looking, articulate, trustworthy, and of excellent character. It would never be what life with Danny would have been, but Barry was a different person, and I guessed I was too, after all that had happened to me in my short life.

I knew already that a vet's life was a busy one and I'd be permanently tied to a practice, either my own or working for someone else. The lifestyle certainly didn't allow much freedom. Days were long, and animals needed care after hours just like humans. A vet's partner would need to be very understanding and especially supportive. I'd seen both Tim Rodgers from my hometown and Brett Walker, my current boss, cancel plans at the very last moment to attend an emergency. That took a particular kind of person to make an active choice between their own career and their partner's. Was Barry that person? I didn't know. I suspected he might be—he'd been grumbling lately about "inconsiderate young people," and he was only thirty-two!

I was enjoying my cuddle and feeling loved when my phone rang. Speak of the past, and it suddenly reappears. It was Simon Morgan, of all people. I sat on the end of the bed and talked to him. Julie was fine, his mum and dad were fine also, as were the rest of the family. I'd kept in touch with them all, not out of a sense of duty but because I liked them. Furthermore, I knew that to a large extent I'd replaced Danny as the son and brother they'd lost, and while at times we became emotional on my visits, we were very comfortable in each other's company.

Simon had to attend the national conference of the real estate franchise for which he worked and would be in town from the following Thursday through Sunday and asked if he could stay with us. Julie had plenty to occupy her at home, he said, and he was looking forward to spending his fairly generous accommodation allowance on us, taking us all out for a nice dinner.

I checked with Toby and called him back, looking forward to catching up on Thursday evening.

Barry, to my surprise, didn't want to hang around, claiming he had housework that hadn't been done for months and I should spend some quality time with the brother of my late boyfriend. I smiled to myself. The only housework he'd be involved in would be cobwebbing at one of the cottages or maybe checking the steam output in one of the Melbourne saunas. But I took him at his word so I could focus 100 percent on Simon. Simon and Julie remained one of the constants in my life. They'd been part of my life ever since I could remember, fighting for Danny and me when we were a couple and helping me clean up the emotional detritus afterward.

Even when I came to Henry University, they were in touch by e-mail or phone at least once a week, and when I went home, they were the next stop after Mum and Dad. It seemed they'd been girlfriend and boyfriend forever—I guessed about ten years or so—and had been cohabiting for most of that time.

SIMON WAS ever the gentleman, insisting we all go to dinner with him—Macca, Toby, Dougie, Paul, and myself. Missing were Barry with his mysterious domestic duties and Jenny, who was fast asleep in her crib with Mrs. Browning watching.

Toby had booked a table at a really nice pub we frequented when we had both time and money to spare, which wasn't often, so the night was really a treat. Paul was driving, so we threw caution to the wind a little, allowing Simon to "indulge himself" as he put it, because he wanted to congratulate Toby and Macca's kids on their engagement! Macca thrust his chest out, full of pride, and Toby beamed. Paul and Dougie thanked him for being so thoughtful, and I marveled how a straight man from my home patch could be so inclusive and generous.

We had a marvelous night with far too many drinks. Toby had really let his hair down. Dougie winked at me as Toby pushed Macca into their bedroom, and the door slammed as they said their hurried good-night.

"I'll show you to your room," I said to Simon as I grabbed some fresh towels from the linen press.

"Ah, that's a bit silly, isn't it?" Simon replied. "Why don't I bunk in with you? Then Tobes won't be on laundry detail after I'm gone. You don't mind, do you?"

"No, of course not, as long as you don't bloody snore." I grinned back.

It was sensible, as I now had my own little shower, which would ease the traffic in the main bathroom the following morning as everyone prepared themselves for the day ahead.

I couldn't help but notice how Simon had developed. In his spare time, he helped his father and brothers around the farm, and it showed. His shoulders seemed bigger, and his biceps were more noticeable. He turned his head to smile at me as he stepped out of the shower, and it hit me almost forcibly—Danny had always turned his head the same way with the same goofy grin when eye contact was made.

Simon understood, however. "Remind you of someone?" he asked gently, and I nodded, feeling like shit but knowing I had to get over it.

It must happen all the time in their family. I thought of Simon's mother and father and realized I'd be letting them down if I allowed myself to wallow in self-pity, so I picked up my towel and strode into the shower, washing all my problems down the drain.

When I came out, Simon was already in bed, his head on the fluffy pillow. There was no doubt he was a good-looking guy. At that angle he only looked like himself, and I sent Old Dick a message not to embarrass me, because the slightest hint could have triggered him into action, and I needed to stay friends with Simon and Julie.

I hopped under the covers, smiled across at him, and turned off the bedside lamp, wishing him good night as I did so.

"Don't I get a kiss good night?" he said, the question hanging in the air, demanding a response.

I grunted something unintelligible and leaned across the bed, aiming for his cheek. He suddenly turned, and our lips meshed as if made for each other. His tongue found its way inside my mouth, trying to make friends with me.

That was it. Dick sprang into action and stood tall, looking for further instructions.

I quickly switched the lamp back on, clearly embarrassed. "What's going on?" I demanded. "What about Julie? She'd kill us."

Rather than looking guilty, Simon looked amused. "I'm here with Julie's blessing."

"But not to fuck around with me you're not."

"That's exactly the understanding," he said, sitting up in bed, taking my hand in his and using his free hand to stroke Dick, who was by now rampantly hard and leaking love juice. "Jules is with her girlfriend this weekend."

I looked on stupidly, not comprehending.

"Maggie Martin, Maggie Prendergast that was."

I remembered Maggie. She'd been ahead of Danny and me at school and later married Michael Martin, whose family were the largest wool growers in the district.

"Yeah, well, I suppose it's nice she's got a girlfriend to stay with while you're up getting your rocks off."

Infuriatingly, Simon just grinned. "Julie has always been bi. She and Maggie have been an item since their school days."

I was aware my mouth was open, and Simon bloody laughed at me.

"So where do you fit into this scene?" I asked, completely dumbfounded.

"Our relationship has thrived because of Julie's lover," he said. "It would probably go south very quickly if Maggie's husband ever found out, but at the moment it continues to enhance what Jules and I have already, and I suspect Michael has one very horny lady to deal with after Jules has revved her up!"

"You're not jealous, then?" I asked anxiously.

"Nah, quite the opposite. We're even closer because we understand each other so well. If this had come as a surprise, we wouldn't have lasted ten minutes, let alone nearly ten years."

I'd become somewhat deflated trying to absorb all this information, but Simon started stroking me again and then kissed me quite passionately, causing Dick to rear up and show appreciation.

"I've always been fascinated with you, Dean," he said, looking longingly into my eyes. "I've never been with a guy before, although I've certainly thought about it, and particularly with you. When Danny died I wanted so much to comfort you then, but a sense of decency stopped me in my tracks. Julie has kept me going, I guess, but we do talk about everything, and she knew we'd go nowhere if I didn't get this outta my system. I'm sorry, but when I put it into words it sounds sleazy, doesn't it, and that's the last thing I wanted."

He loosened his grip on Dick, and I finally saw the funny side of it and laughed. Simon looked crestfallen until I slipped my hand under the covers and found ample evidence of his interest in me, so I dived on it and took it down so far it was an anatomical feat. My further education through Barry had given me an edge as a participant, and I decided bloody Simon would get his right now and forget about the implications.

Simon was naïve but a good student. It was refreshing to find someone whose sole interest in bed was to give me as much pleasure as possible, and I loved it.

It was strange. There were things that reminded me of Danny, like his smell, and other stuff that was brand-new, like the kissing. But the thrill of teaching someone was exciting.

When I entered Simon for the first time, I thought he'd wake not just our household but the entire suburb. But it wasn't pain that drove his vocal cords, it was sheer delight. Simon *loved* being fucked. Whatever preconceptions he'd had about gay sex, his expectations were obviously exceeded. I'd gone gently at first, but when I discovered his predilection for cock, I fed it to him harder. He squealed and shrieked and actually slid right out of bed and across the floor as the result of one mighty thrust from me.

I did our Simon three times and blew him in the shower before breakfast. Surprisingly, in the kitchen he looked absolutely stunning, not a hair out of place, all dressed up for his conference.

Macca was studying the news on his iPad, and Toby was talking about nothing much, while bloody Dougie just smirked with a knowing look. This caused Paul to shoot him a glance that would have wilted gum trees.

Simon thanked us for a nice brekkie and went cheerily on his way, the elephant in the room not acknowledged.

I was suddenly the villain, which gave me the shits.

"Look," I said to the room in general, "I'm as surprised as you are. I had no idea this was going to happen." And watched their bloody eyebrows rise like garage doors.

Only Toby sprang to my defense. "Cuz," he said, "I agree, the straight ones are impossible to pick sometimes, but this one has gone pretty close to taking advantage of your friendship as well as compromising his own domestic arrangements. I mean, he's always been so nice to you and so supportive of you always, and you weren't to know."

"Well," I said with a smirk to match Dougie's, "he was a great fuck."

And the room erupted. Macca, who could be a touch judgmental because he'd grown up in a rather sheltered environment, nearly wet himself, Paul and Dougie rolled around the old lounge suite, and my cousin laughed at all of us. We were a team, no question about it. We all knew we couldn't possibly keep secrets from each other, even if those secrets stayed within the four walls of Toby and Macca's house.

That Friday at uni was one of those days where I wondered if anything had sunk in at all. Sarah, as always, was my savior. She took me down to the dining room, bought me a coffee, and we went over our notes together. Anesthesia class had always been difficult for me to grasp, and without Sarah's kindness and expertise, I would have been in trouble. But she knew me too well.

"Something going on at home?" She smiled at me with those beautiful eyes.

No bloody wonder lucky Richard had fallen immediately in love with her. She was beautiful and she was smart, and because we'd always been close, I told her.

"Enjoy it while you can," she advised, "but don't let him use the 'I'm Danny's brother' credential, sweetheart, because it's bullshit. It's not up to you to be his fucking counselor, even though you could turn entire football teams if you tried. I mean, you turned one of my ex-boyfriends. He's never been the same since you got your claws into him!"

I had to laugh at her. She could wind me up like no one else, but there was implicit trust between us, and the proof of our friendship was that Will remained in frequent contact with both of us.

SIMON HAD arrived home early from his conference. There was an official dinner that night, but he'd begged off, using a migraine as an excuse. I knew he was in line for an award, but even that didn't deter him from his mission—me.

Toby looked at me and raised his bloody eyebrows again, but I tried to put a positive spin on it—at least I was getting laid. The only downside was the by now obvious emotional baggage that went with it, both on his side and mine, because I'd suddenly realized I'd rather be in bed tonight with Barry, not Simon. It was something that had been gnawing away at me for some time, a realization of just how close Barry and I had become.

Nothing was said, it was just that our two minds had begun to think as one. We never pretended to be monogamous, and Barry loved the cottages. And then there had been our trips to the saunas in Melbourne.

The last visit was strange, however, for both of us, because neither of us found anyone we fancied. So we slipped into a room by ourselves and had a great time together. On the way home in the train we'd laughed at how we could have saved our money and fucked at home instead. We realized that our friendship had deepened, the only problem being neither of us knew if we wanted to progress it further.

One thing was certain, however—every time we went to bed together it was better than the time before.

SIMON LOOKED on with amazement at the gentle expression of domestic bliss around him. Paul and Dougie had arrived home, and Mrs. Browning had already fed Jenny, who cuddled quietly in Dougie's arms, sucking her finger. I started the vegetables, thrusting a glass of wine into Toby's hand. I was overdue for kitchen duties, and Paul began to ready the meat for the barbeque.

Out of nowhere came Bruce, his harness in his mouth. He dropped it at Simon's feet, wagging his tail furiously, obviously remembering Simon but very focused on his immediate needs.

"Oh, does he want a walk, does he?" asked Simon.

"No, mate" came Macca's voice from where he stood covered in the day's grime. "He's just got this leather fetish."

Simon wrinkled his brow in disbelief as Macca slipped the harness around Bruce's shoulders as if the dog were a horse, leading him outside to where a stylish-looking miniature sulky sat. He clipped the shafts into place, and Jenny's transport was ready. Now fully awake, Dougie sat her in the contrivance and strapped her in.

"Hup, Bruce!" Macca commanded, and Bruce sailed up the driveway like a pacer at the Inter Dominion.

Poor Simon shook his head as Bruce trotted around the backyard with dexterity, barking with excitement and clearly enjoying it as much as Jenny was.

Dougie ran alongside the sulky, his shirt riding up his back revealing a myriad of tattoos, and I'll swear I saw Simon lick his lips.

Dirty bastard. I realized I'd probably unleashed a sex-crazed monster in Simon. I wondered idly if he thought we wanted to fuck him in a gigantic gang-bang just because we were gay. Such immaturity seemed sadly typical of the "straight" guys who came over to the dark side for the first time.

Just then there was a *toot* in the driveway, and I recognized the sound of Barry's little diesel Mazda.

"G'day," he strode through the door, kissing me lasciviously on the lips, his tongue doing gymnastics in my mouth, pushed open to accommodate the intrusion. I introduced him to Simon, who glared at him, and the penny dropped. I remembered the phone call a few days ago when he'd done the twenty questions on me about my love life. Thinking he and Julie were still worried about me, I responded as truthfully as I thought necessary and told him I had a fuck buddy called Barry. And while that was technically correct, to Simon it must have looked like it was more than that.

What didn't help, of course, was the manner in which Barry was welcomed by the others. Paul and Dougie had always adored him and had grown even closer since he'd helped me engineer their reconciliation. Barry and Toby swapped insults like two old fishwives, and Macca knew at some stage Barry would be squirming on his knee "talking about the first thing that pops up." Bruce caught sight of him and roared across the yard to say hello, sulky still attached, Jenny squealing with delight and/or terror, with Dougie in hot pursuit.

"Oh fuck," I muttered, wondering if I could just disappear for a few days, but I must admit it did crystallize a few things for me.

Simon and Julie hadn't disappointed me necessarily, but they'd shown me they were more human than I'd thought. I had no doubt the next cab off the rank would be a text or call from Julie asking me to hop in the middle of their bed when I was home next, and that left me cold. Out of nowhere they'd gone from protector-savior mode to predator mode for their own reasons.

What appealed to me at the moment was an uncomplicated life where Barry, my best mate, and I could continue having a blast and above all, continue caring for each other—simple as that.

"You stayin' the night?" I whispered to Barry quietly, well away from Simon's gaze.

"Not tonight, princess, I can see you've got your hands full. Does he trot across the hall or do you?"

I actually blushed. Barry was much more aware of what was going on around him these days. I'd trained him too well.

"Actually he invited himself to share my bed 'to save Toby the housework,' and I fell for it," I said, realizing how gullible I'd been. "For once I didn't see it coming, but I think he's in over his depth."

"What about you?" Barry asked.

"No way. He may be Danny's brother, but he's just another straight boy trying to prove something. To be honest, I'd rather you stayed."

"Why, because I'm better sex?" Barry grinned.

"Yes, that as well."

"I know what you're saying, but if you kick him out of your bed he'll be embarrassed and you'll have lost a good friend. I'll be around for a lot longer than he will, so don't worry about offending my tender sensibilities, pet. So tell me all me all about it—has he got a big one?"

"YOU UPSET with me?" Simon asked as we walked into the bedroom.

"Why would I be upset, Simon?" I replied with a smile. "Anyone can see we're closer than ever these days."

It worked. My attempt at humor hit the mark, and he laughed.

But the undercurrent remained. There was a possessiveness toward me that worsened because of my "relationship" with Barry.

He made an attempt to discuss what was on his mind, but I resisted with an unoriginal but truthful excuse. Tomorrow was Saturday, and I had to be at the surgery at 7:00 a.m., which meant I would be out of bed at six, showered, dressed, and with breakfast, ready to go by six thirty.

Simon nodded. He was a country boy, after all, and he understood.

I sighed to myself as I watched him undress because there was no doubt Simon was a stunning example of the male species. He reminded me so much of Danny in so many ways because of the common genetic pathway. But I realized with a shock that Danny had been more worldly than Simon. At least he finally accepted his sexuality, whereas this bloke was quite naïve, like a kid in a candy store trying everything and not quite sure why he enjoyed it all.

I didn't have to remind him about preparation, however, as he looked like he'd been very thorough. When he walked past he saluted me with his baton as if he was about to conduct his own orchestra, which was probably accurate, except it would be my baton doing most of the work.

My fatigue seemed to melt away. I sent myself a mental note that, tomorrow being his final night, I'd better pace myself a little, but Dick had other ideas, and he was a hard act to follow. Simon looked at Dick and swallowed him whole, and suddenly it was a repeat performance of the night before.

I quickly took him, and he screamed with even greater abandon.

I could imagine Dougie wanting to sell tickets for the performance, and I knew the inquisition would happen tomorrow—if not at breakfast, then at some time later on. I could trust our team, nothing was sacred, and I think Simon fascinated them. Macca seemed to understand and cut him a bit of slack. Toby, like me, had known him forever, and Simon was still a mystery to us. Never had there ever been the slightest hint that Simon might be gay—or bi at the very least—yet here he was, legs in the air, screaming enjoyment as I ploughed his arse like an autumn paddock.

THE ALARM screamed at me, yet Simon slept through it all. I completed my ablutions and breakfast, and before Bruce and I left for work, I kissed Simon on the cheek. He was raring to go again, but knowing I had to leave he just smiled at me, rather seriously for someone who had only a few hours to wait before it happened all over again. His conference seemed to have taken a back seat to the evening entertainment, and not once had he mentioned Julie or had any contact with her since Thursday. "See you tonight," I said, waggling my eyebrows suggestively, and he laughed.

CHAPTER 17
RACING AND RAY SIMMONS

I HAD wondered idly why Brett Walker, my lovely employer, had wanted me so early this Saturday morning. We were in the Land Cruiser and driving toward the western side of town before he came clean.

"I've never been much of a marketer," he said across the cabin at me, "but every now and then an opportunity falls in me lap, and I'd be a fool to pass this one up."

Brett was the very last person to keep secrets of any sort—he was always too busy helping sick animals to worry about that stuff.

"You have any idea where we're going?" he asked.

I shook my head, still mystified.

"What would you say if I told you that Ray Simmons is considering bringing all his local vet work to us?"

I gasped in spite of myself. Simmons Racing was one of the biggest thoroughbred complexes in Australia, and Ray Simmons had an enviable record as a trainer with two Melbourne Cups under his belt and several Caulfield Cup winners. He was a bloodstock breeder in his own right, usually heading up the national yearling sales with some of the finest stock available. He must have had an army of veterinary equine specialists crawling all over the place, even on race days, but here we were driving out to Simmons Park as if it was a common occurrence.

I thought, before I opened my big mouth, that a piece of business like this didn't happen overnight unless there was a very good reason, so I smiled at my boss and said simply, "Did someone fuck up?"

Brett laughed and nodded. "Yeah, it appears so. He had a bloke from Melbourne living at Simmons Park who developed a nasty cocaine habit and couldn't be bothered looking after the horses after hours. And as we know, Murphy's Law says that's when a problem is most likely to happen."

I smiled, remembering the night calls with Brett and my old friend at home Tim Rodgers, who unfailingly did the right thing and generated so much goodwill they grew their customer base as a result.

"There's more," Brett said, "which is unfortunate, because as the guy's habit took hold of him he got very stroppy with the horses and took the whip to those that displeased him, and for no real reason. Ray Simmons heard about our team from his own daughter, who is quite a successful rider involved in eventing at a pretty high level."

"Georgia Simmons?" I asked.

Brett nodded. "The one and the same. Georgia told her dad how some of the half-wild horses that were sent to us for treatment went back to their owners quieter, better behaved, and much happier than when they came to us, so on her word alone her dad wants to talk to us."

We turned in to an old-fashioned double brick entrance with wrought-iron gates that looked in such good order they probably even worked, the sound of the Land Cruiser's diesel echoing in the beautiful English trees lining the driveway.

As we drew up in front of the stable complex, a man of average height but with the most stunning head of beautiful steel gray hair emerged, and I recognized Ray Simmons instantly from his media profile. His face lit up as he and Brett shook hands warmly. Brett then introduced me and finally Bruce, who had jumped out and was busily watering a nearby tree.

"I think you'd better keep him in your truck," Ray advised. "Some of my charges get a bit aggressive and could hurt him, and he might stir them up when I've spent all the last week trying to calm them down."

His shoulders sagged. Ray looked like he'd done a few rounds with a prizefighter. From what I knew of the man, he was very much a self-made person, always calm and really connected to his horses, old-fashioned to the core but a very successful and consistent trainer, probably Australia's best. Yet here he was, apparently searching for answers, trying to calm his horses down after his former vet had started whipping them when he was off his head on coke.

"Mr. Simmons," I said, "I may be speaking out of turn here...." I struggled for words, but I knew I could help and so did Brett, who saved me from making a fool of myself.

"Dean may be a student still," he interrupted, "but he's exceptionally competent, and he'll be working full-time for our practice the instant he graduates next year. Dean has a deep connection to animals I've seldom seen before, even in the veterinary profession. He and that bloody dog of his are an amazing team, that's why I suggest you let them inside and see what happens."

I could see something clicked in Ray Simmons's mind. A superb race-day tactician, he realized he had little to lose and everything to gain. He had millions of dollars' worth of racing stock that were upset, nervous, and skittish, not going anywhere much until they realized their stable here at Simmons Park was once again a safe haven for them. So he agreed to indulge me—and Bruce.

There were some wild eyes staring at us and bared teeth, but nothing seemed to faze Bruce, as I expected. I followed him as he padded down the walkway in the middle of the building, watching every horse. I'd seen him at home when he wasn't much more than a pup, helping round up a mob of Uncle Ted's sheep. Out of hundreds he'd pick out maybe half a dozen that were flyblown, then cut them out of the mob so we could catch and treat them. Years later, without prompting, Bruce had developed an empathy for the patients at Brett's surgery that was extraordinary.

Brett's practice focused heavily on equine surgery, ongoing care, and rehabilitation, so Bruce's continual exposure to horses had become part of his doggy life, and mine as well.

He stopped opposite a stall where a filly was snorting and pawing the straw underneath her. She was young, I judged a two-year-old, and Ray nodded.

"She had her first race at Ballarat last week. Ran third but should have done better. She stacked on a real turn at the start and got left a good six lengths behind."

I put my arm out and asked them not to go any closer, because for some reason Bruce wanted to say hello. She lashed out with her left hind leg, but my dog was faster. He dived under her, and she slipped and nearly fell on him. Brett went pale, and I had visions of broken bones and an enormous veterinary bill, with us paying. Before anyone could do anything Bruce was in her face, licking her nose, and she was obviously so shocked she didn't know how to react further.

We all stood there, transfixed. A strapper leaned on his pitchfork with fear etched on his face as we waited for what seemed an eternity for disaster to eventuate—except it didn't.

Ray looked on in disbelief as Bruce made himself comfortable near the manger, and the filly, Twilight Rose, stood there softly "talking" to Bruce with a soft mumbling and gentle snorting. I'd seen it before with old Top Flight, the stallion whom Bruce had become close to, but neither he nor the other horses had been quite as aggressive as Twilight Rose.

I judged the time was right, and before Ray could speak, I walked over. She stared balefully at me but just shook her head and mane as Bruce made eye contact, obviously telling her I was friend, not foe. I stroked her neck, and she practically smiled at me. Bruce wagged his tail in affirmation. Another one reduced to a state of utter calm.

"Well, I'll be fucked," a normally polite Ray Simmons said. "None of us have been able to get near her for days now. She was always highly strung, but that mongrel bastard picked on her more than all the others, and there's no doubt she was upsetting the rest of them."

A small crowd of people gathered around and, rather than upsetting Twilight Rose, their presence now seemed to stimulate her. She whinnied quietly to the other horses and the humans gathered around. I undid the rope, and with my finger hooked through her halter she, Bruce, and I toured the stables, with her "talking" all the time. Brett couldn't wipe the grin from his face—mission accomplished!

I was aware Ray Simmons was watching me as well as Bruce. After we put Twilight Rose back in her stall, he asked if he could talk with me privately. Embarrassed, and wondering if I'd done something wrong, I looked at Brett, who smiled his lovely reassuring smile and waved me toward Ray's office. I was ushered in and a chair offered.

"It's all right, mate," Ray said. "I asked Brett a question about you, and he told me because it was personal I'd better ask you myself."

Fuck, if it's personal it can only mean one thing, and if he's that conservative, then he can go fuck himself.

Ray smiled at me, rather gently, which confused me even more.

"You see, Dean, you remind me of someone very close to me, and if he'd been here, I think the result would have been somewhat similar. He would have used different methods, and it would have taken him longer, but in the end, he would have restored the horse's confidence just like you have. My younger brother, Clancy," he explained. "He's not here because he's running our Hong Kong operation successfully, together with his Chinese partner, Lim."

I gasped and then smiled, because Clancy Simmons was also well-known as part of the Simmons dynasty, but that side of Clancy certainly wasn't public knowledge.

"I realized a long time ago through watching my brother grow up that life can be cruel to gay people, even in these enlightened times. It appears my gaydar is still intact, but I wanted you to know your orientation is an asset here, not a liability. If I could fill this business with women and gay men and leave ego-driven hetero males out of it, I'd be a happy man, because I'd know the horses would be safe, well looked after, and all I'd have to worry about was training them."

My phone beeped at an incoming text, and I apologized, but Ray told me to attend to it while he spent a few minutes with Brett, who took my place in the office.

My eyes popped out of my head. The text was from Simon:

on my way home, babe decided to leave 2 day because if I didn't I'd never go at all. rang tobes thanked he & macca 4 their hospitality. I know u could never luv me like u did Daniel my problem not urs. gotta fix things at home instead of trying greener pastures. never had 2 nights like that and prob never will again but will remember it always. don't forget we're still best mates hope I haven't stuffed that up Si xxxx

I breathed a sigh of relief. I didn't have to give him the message—he'd taken the hint, and I had my single status back again—sort of.

I sent a text to Barry:

coast is clear get ur nice arse over 4 dinner prepare 4 any eventuality hope ur not 2 tired from doing housework @ cottages

The reply came back almost immediately:

sounds good what do u think I am a slut? don't answer that energy level 100%

CHAPTER 18
BARRY

I WAS nearing the home stretch. Final year was looming, and I knew I had to stay focused on my studies, but my part-time work with Brett Walker was now more demanding than ever thanks to Simmons Racing becoming a client. Brett put on another full-time vet plus two part-time workers, but he was still falling behind.

It was me who suggested another student, but Brett was wary—he didn't want to deal with staff retrenchments if the level of business diminished. But as the weeks rolled by it became obvious that was never going to be the case. An ever-rising tide of domestic pets and their owners inundated us, as our reputation had spread far and wide.

But instead of being delighted, Heather Walker was alarmed. Brett, Alistair—the new vet—and myself weren't getting enough rest, and it became obvious something had to give way.

After talking to Heather, I took the law into my own hands and introduced Sarah to Brett.

"This is the other student I was thinking of, and she's a lot smarter than I am," I laughed.

"I'm not," Sarah laughed. "But Dean and I work well together, even at our studies. I could do with some extra cash, and the experience would be amazing." She looked at Brett with a big grin, outspoken as ever. "And I've got an amazing boyfriend, so you can tell your wife I'm harmless. It's not that I'm not interested, I'm just too bloody tired."

Brett looked at her as if he didn't hear what she'd said. Then he laughed, rolling his eyes back in his head.

"You're as mad as he is," he said, pointing at me. "I think we'll get on well together."

With Sarah on board, it all suddenly clicked. She ironed out the peaks in workload and allowed us to service Simmons Racing properly.

Ray Simmons was a delight to work with. Even though I wasn't qualified, he insisted I was there, with Bruce, helping out. The horses knew us—not just Bruce and me but Brett, Alistair, and Sarah, and they began to respond. Two weeks after we'd restored Twilight Rose's confidence she won at Caulfield, blitzing the field, accelerating away from the pack at the finish like a jet and causing a sensation in the racing world because she looked unstoppable.

After the Simon incident, Barry and I grew closer, but time was at a premium. Barry had been promoted at his work and was on duty many weekends, while life for me was simply seven days a week, studying and working at either the practice or Simmons Racing. Everyone thought I was trying to fit too much into my life, wondering when I would have a nervous and/or a physical breakdown, but none of them had seen my bank account. There had been an embarrassingly large deposit paid in by Simmons Racing after Twilight Rose had won her first race, and Brett had insisted on giving me the fully qualified veterinary rate.

Barry and I were partners at a few select parties and functions, but most of all we were there for each other. Some nights I spent at his little apartment, usually with Bruce sleeping in a nest of old blankets in his laundry. Other nights Barry stayed with me at home with Toby, Macca, and the boys. Jenny was a firm favorite with Barry, and I always took that as a good sign of the person within. He genuinely liked kids.

We agreed to be monogamous because there was neither the desire nor the time to go cock hunting. We were both so tired we usually slept away any time off to prepare ourselves for the next day. There was something there—it wasn't hearts and flowers, we weren't deeply in love or emotionally involved, but we felt whatever it was—even just friendship—deserved a try, just to establish if we could do the suburban picket-fence thing long-term.

MY LOVELY old car finally let me down. Its transmission had been making odd noises, and after checking all the basics, it became clear it needed work. Once, when life was simpler, Danny would just take the car away and service it, and it ran like a Swiss watch afterward. I wasn't a complete fool with mechanical things, but I recognized motor vehicles were beyond my capacity.

Barry wasn't much better. Even though he was one of the ecological progressives who drove a diesel car, his mechanical knowledge was even scantier than mine.

Thank heavens for Macca. He drove my car around the block, then with a white face parked it to one side in the driveway with a pan underneath to catch the transmission oil that had begun to pour out underneath. Less than an hour later, it was at the car "hospital" with Macca's mechanic friend, and a reconditioned transmission had been ordered.

I finished late that afternoon, walking out to the car park like an idiot, patting my pockets in an increasing state of panic, finally realizing I had my house keys only and even if I'd found the car keys they wouldn't have been much use anyway. I was about to reach for my phone when a *toot* sounded from Barry's Mazda, and I walked over with a grin on my face.

"Just as well someone's on the ball," I laughed, hopping inside and throwing my bag on the backseat.

We drove slowly past the infamous cottage at the entrance to the university grounds. Usually the car park there was packed with workers calling in for some public service on the way home to the missus. Tonight, however, it was nearly deserted.

"There's old Norm's car," said Barry. "She's entertaining the troops again."

I laughed at my mad mate. He was very protective of Norm. After Norm's wife died around twenty years prior, he finally did what he'd always wanted to do and became a dedicated beat queen instead of a part-time one. So at nearly eighty years of age Norm was in high demand! When Barry had frequented the beats, he swore Norm got more than he did. The old guy would never take no for an answer and somehow avoided the violence that could erupt if the wrong person was asked a leading question. Norm was a delicious character. As he grew older, he complained his memory for names and faces was diminishing, but he could always tell who a person was by looking at his cock!

Suddenly Barry stopped the car with a jerk. "Look," he said, "a bloody unmarked cop car."

He gunned the engine in the Mazda, which sounded like a Kenworth when he revved it up, and sped into the car park.

"See the bastard there?" he hissed, pointing at a big Ford with barely noticeable red and blue lights set into the panel behind the rear window.

The car was empty, and we feared the worst—that the cops were already playing decoy inside, and Norm may be in serious trouble. I was about to say that I thought it unlikely because Steve Norris had put a stop to all that dreadful stuff, but Barry wasn't listening to reason.

We sped inside. There was a lone figure at the long urinal, a tallish, dark-haired, quite handsome-looking bloke, and only one cubicle with the door closed. "Norma," shrieked Barry, "Lil's here, Lilly Law."

The door of the cubicle cracked open, and an immaculate white-haired Norm stepped out calmly and went over to wash his hands. Noticing the fellow at the urinal, he smiled gratefully at Barry and quietly left. Only the copper and ourselves remained.

Rather than leave quietly, Barry decided he'd have his say.

"Nothing better to do than frighten old queens?" he asked, staring at the young copper, who looked more scared than either of us.

I was aware the atmosphere had changed. Barry and the guy looked at each other with the type of glance I hadn't seen for a long time, yet I remembered what it meant so vividly. I bolted outside and left them to it, with a sinking feeling that the lovely laid-back relationship between Barry and me was changed forever.

He came out looking distracted and slid behind the wheel.

"You get his number?" I asked, and he shook his head, his body language negative.

"Get it now," I commanded.

The guy was unlocking his car. Barry looked at me strangely and then almost fell out of his seat, running over to him. Obviously it was still a work in progress, their body language more like a ballet as they pranced around each other. I watched as they studiously typed their numbers into their phones and tested them, finally turning to look at me.

Christ, they're so predictable. I got out of the car and walked over, introducing myself with Barry looking on, still unsure if he was in trouble.

His name was Greg, and yes, he was a policeman. I suggested they go to Barry's place and get better acquainted—after Barry dropped me home, of course.

I broke the awkward silence on the way home, placing my hand on Barry's leg and rubbing it gently. "We both knew this could happen, didn't we?" I said, and he nodded. "Don't feel guilty. Nobody should ever contradict nature, and it's obvious that it's instant attraction on both sides."

"Jesus, Dean, I've just met the guy, and you've got me in a wedding gown already. He could be an axe murderer, for Christ's sake, or he's got the little missus at home. Either way it could be disastrous."

"The funny thing is I've never heard Steve Norris mention this guy by name, so I guess he has to be in the closet."

I kissed him on the cheek as he almost reluctantly backed out of the driveway into what he obviously thought was an uncertain future.

I LINED my extended family up at breakfast the next morning and told them the facts of life. They laughed at me, teasing me because after a chance meeting with someone else, I was just so certain Barry had found himself a keeper.

Only Macca listened quietly. He knew I'd probably be hurting just a little, and he told me so, away from the others. I thought how wonderful Macca had been over the years. His concern for me had never wavered, and he wasn't about to stop now. Steve Norris had once said Macca had probably saved the lives of at least ten young people as a telephone counselor, just telling them how it was but making it clear they were never alone, that he bloody cared. He gave me comfort, reminding me how I'd accelerated Barry's personal development since our friendship had begun and if it hadn't been for my influence, Barry wouldn't have found the confidence to even think about a relationship with someone else.

It was certainly sweet sadness for me because I'd seen the look that passed between Barry and his new friend—the same look that had passed between Macca and Toby, Paul and Dougie, and my beautiful Danny and me. It was easy to be maudlin about it, but if I was honest with myself, what I really wanted was for Barry to be happy, even at my own expense.

Looking back on our association, both of us had held something back without quite knowing why. Right now nature was busy telling Barry why, and I guessed at some stage I'd find out.

THE ACADEMIC year was actually winding down. I couldn't believe it. My remaining studies were elective over time but flexible and realistic to accommodate a practicing veterinarian, actually working full-time without the crushing hours of study as a backdrop to my existence. Brett and Heather Walker were flying, the practice was booming, and Sarah and I were formally offered generous employment contracts.

Barry was a hopeless case. It turned out that Greg was indeed married, and within a day or so Barry was a frequent visitor at home again, but he pointedly always went home to his pad afterward, never revealing what his story was. He'd become so withdrawn we hardly knew him anymore. The fun-loving insanity on legs that was Barry had gone missing somewhere since meeting Greg.

It had become impossible for me to nursemaid him except to ensure he was safe and well, but now the academic pressure had lessened, I began to focus on him again. I missed our comradeship, and if I was honest, I also missed the sex but was prepared to do anything to make him smile again.

Finally, after dinner one night I stole his keys, and Barry, never being overly fond of walking anywhere, decided to tell me what was going on—or walk home.

With a sigh he sat down with me in the garden and admitted he and Greg had cooled it to the point where they were just in contact but not really seeing each other. Over the past few months, they had both acknowledged there was a powerful attraction between them, but Barry refused point-blank to even sleep with him until Greg was a single man again.

I looked at him askance. "Do you mean to say you've not got him between the sheets yet?" I asked in disbelief.

"No, never, and I won't while that poor girl has no idea of his sexuality. I guess I've hung in there because he's asked me to place myself in her position, that she deserves a proper and full explanation and that he wants to ensure she comes out of this as gently as possible. We've had a good time. Gone to the movies, quiet picnics in the country, all that sort of stuff. I guess I haven't pushed it because I know sooner or later he has to hear the truth about me, and of course I'll probably never see him again anyway."

"You have no way of telling how he'll handle the news," I said. "But I think you should tell him straightaway. I have a feeling he's hesitating because you are, am I right?"

Barry studied his feet, raised his eyes, and nodded sorrowfully. "But what if it doesn't work out?" he said sadly, his eyes misting over.

"You love him, don't you?" I said, and he nodded again, vigorously.

"Then you have to hope for the best outcome, remembering that it usually takes time for people to come to terms with HIV, and especially if that person is to be their long-term partner. To be honest, I reckon you'll have a battle on your hands, but you don't have any alternative, do you?"

Barry sighed and agreed.

"Get it over and done with. But give him time to sort his head out. Sooner or later he'll have to come out to his family, come out at work, and eventually introduce you as his new missus."

Barry had to laugh in spite of himself. His eyes sparkled, just like the Barry I knew so well.

"You've always got me for a friend, and actually you'll be quite unique."

"Why's that?"

"Met in a toilet and formed a marriage of convenience."

Barry looked at me, amazed that my sense of humor was still functioning. Then after deciding I wasn't sending him up, he laughed—and laughed.

Wiping his eyes, he grinned at me. "So do you reckon I'll ever get married, then?"

"Yes," I said, answering the question that to me was obvious yet wasn't to him because of all the roadblocks that lay ahead of his romance and seemingly made it insurmountable.

"Why would the guy even bother, Dean?" Barry whined. "It's all too hard for guys like him, just too difficult, too much public ridicule, too complicated."

"Because, you stupid tart, Greg loves you. He's just waiting for you to make the next move." I grinned back. "My mum reckons love will always find a way, just get your lovely arse into gear and get on with it."

CHAPTER 19
GRADUATION

I WAS absolutely pissed off with the pair of them. I knew the split had finally happened with Greg and his wife, the dust settling on a nasty public episode, but life does move on, and the root cause of Greg's 360-degree change in lifestyle direction was moping around like a petulant and despondent child. In fact, the pair of them rather reminded me of Paul and Dougie when they'd spat the dummy at each other.

I knew Greg had finally come out to Steve Norris, whose counseling skills and humanity transformed Greg's attitude. But I could only guess at Greg's other dilemma. Having found his life partner, he now had to decide whether he wanted to spend the remainder of his life with an HIV-positive person.

I guessed that Greg had kept Barry's sero status totally confidential even from Steve or the support group because that knowledge could ruin a person's life. The ignorance and social disconnection was a sad fact of life for a person with HIV. Yet the reality was that with today's modern drugs, patients lived almost a completely normal lifestyle, and there was almost no danger to their partner if they used basic precautions and took their meds as Barry had done. Let's face it, Barry and I had been banging away for around two years or so, and the worst I'd caught had been a bloody cold. But we'd always had commonsense rules—always wear a condom, never fuck when drunk, get tested regularly, and regardless of where we did it, always have the meds in a little bag for the next morning.

So Barry was well practiced and smart in handling his affliction, but he always knew it would limit his chances of meeting and settling down with Mr. Right. We both knew that if he and I had really become serious it would have solved a lot of problems for him, but he never wanted to become a victim, and he valued our friendship too much to commit further, as did I.

So my lovely best mate was now playing ball in a big paddock, and if his new partner decided not to step up to a partnership, I doubted Barry would ever really recover from the disappointment.

It was postfinals and before graduation. I was in town, running some messages for Macca, when I spied Greg, in uniform, handling a small traffic accident. Somehow the planets must have been aligned. He'd been on his way to lunch when he had to adjudicate at this bending of fenders, and when he looked up, after folding his notebook, there I was. The look on his face was sheer pleasure, and so I was invited to lunch at a little nearby café. He and I had talked a few times, and I liked him. He'd been brave, telling his wife the truth but releasing her so she could recover and hopefully move on with someone else.

But we hadn't spoken since Barry had told him the news about his sero status, and was I in for a shock. Greg had been in touch with not only experts from the medical profession, but he'd also talked with several support groups for people with HIV and even sought scientific opinions from researchers on the latest progress. He was on a bloody mission, that's for sure. The problem was he'd told no one about his conclusions except me, and frankly I couldn't give a flying fuck because I'd studied the virus and its ramifications in a similar fashion.

I excused myself from the table and almost ran to the toilet, pulling my iPhone out when safely inside.

When I returned to the table, he was preparing to leave, apologizing for having to eat and run.

Jesus, what can I do to keep him talking?

I begged him to extend his lunch break a little. "Surely you can't run back when you spent nearly half an hour on that accident. Steve's not that difficult to get on with." He grinned at me, the poor bloody naïve prick, agreeing that perhaps he was due for some extra time and that in spending time with me he was "doing his bit for community relations."

So I sat there and talked my head off, complete bullshit of course, and poor bloody Greg just looked at me as if I was a bit loopy. But when the shadow fell across the table and Greg realized who it was, he forgot about everything.

They stared hungrily at each other just as they'd done the first night they met—the sparks were almost audible, and it was quite obvious where it was going as they lit up the little café like Guy Fawkes Night.

Yes, I knew my relationship with Barry had changed forever, and there was a certain lingering wistfulness on my part, but I reasoned I had gained yet another friend for life in Greg.

I kissed them on the cheek and excused myself, ringing Steve Norris and giving him a heads-up. He confirmed Greg wouldn't be required back at work that day and told me to leave the details to him. I watched Greg pick up his mobile and swing around in his seat with a broad grin on his face, shaking his finger at me from my vantage point on the other side of the street.

I felt good about myself. Greg and Barry were always intended for each other, all it took was a good push along. Afterward they told me I was unselfish and a whole lot of other complimentary stuff, but the fact was nature always intended they be together. I just hurried the process up a bit.

AT LAST my moment had come as we paraded down the aisle of the main auditorium in our gowns and mortar boards, looking like a bunch of silly dicks.

Except I realized it wasn't about me but about those who had supported me and loved me through good times and not so good times. For them I'd been a work in progress, and here was the result of their labors—a qualified veterinarian already employed and busy as buggery.

They were all there—Mum, Dad, and my sisters, plus Uncle Ted, Aunt Helga, and my cousins, and of course my "other" family: Macca, Toby, Paul, and Dougie, together with Jenny.

Barry and Greg rocked up, probably their first public outing together as a couple. Again I felt a fleeting moment of loss, which was quickly replaced by satisfaction—they looked like they belonged together, it was obvious.

I gasped as I saw what must have been Danny's entire family walk in the door. I don't know who was doing the milking at home that day because the Morgan clan was all here. How amazing that after all this time they still saw me as part of their family group. Simon and Julie waved, and I waved back. The complication that Simon might have created in our lives hadn't gone anywhere, but I was still on my guard.

Yes, it was lovely that they made the effort. It demonstrated that the links that held us together were as strong as ever, regardless of how far I had moved on. I wondered if those links would persist down through the years ahead. I knew I would never live and work back where I was born and bred. My future so obviously lay here in this big town, working with Brett Walker and becoming even further entrenched with Ray Simmons and his horses.

I was suddenly filled with a feeling of deep regret—Danny should have been here today. He would have been so proud of me. He never needed to go into competition in our partnership. Danny instinctively knew what I needed to function on a daily basis, and we had shared domestic and work tasks without question. Allowing me to focus on my studies had been our little family priority at that time. The tragedy that had taken him away from me had abated over time, of course, but today it came rushing back, leaving me floating around without any visible anchor, physically or mentally.

SARAH WAS reading my mind again. She became quite alarmed that my past history might get in the way of a promising future, and within seconds they were there, she on one side and Richard on the other, a comfort that someone knew what was going through my mind. It was as if I'd set off a distress beacon, because Macca was also there shortly afterward. Toby knew well enough to let him go, and finally I calmed down enough to talk to everyone.

Sarah and I had decided months before that we were going to combine our activities on graduation day, our families hiring a function room at a local hotel.

I moved around slowly, Macca handing me a nice red he knew I really enjoyed, and I calmed down, allowing the Morgan clan to offer their congratulations. Mr. and Mrs. Morgan were effusive. I told them I was amazed that the entire family had made the effort to put work on hold, put on their best duds, and drive all this way just to see me walking around like a prize dick in an academic gown!

It was Simon who quietly took over from his parents.

"You see, Dean"—he smiled—"when Danny passed away, as I think you already understand, you became the surrogate son and brother, and that's simply what we do for family. Your success has been our success."

"So I've had some discussions with your dad over a few drinks," Bill Morgan continued. "Between the two families, your HECS fees have been covered, so you start your working life without any debt."

My eyes started to water. I couldn't believe the kindness and the substantial contribution made—many thousands of dollars. I hugged them, and we cried. The memories had become raw again, but the kindness and caring nature of ordinary people made me feel better.

Macca handed me another red, which tasted even better than the last, and I moved over to Mum, Dad, and my sisters. Dad wouldn't tell me how much he paid and what the Morgan's contribution was. That was the subject of the agreement he had with Bill Morgan over a great many laughs and a substantial amount of Irish whisky, which old Bill imported by the case.

But Prentice Farm Supplies was booming. There had been some good seasons, and the hobby farmers were multiplying like rabbits, increasing Dad's client base and volume throughput and finally giving my parents something for their eventual retirement. My sisters were there with Jamie and Terrence, their boyfriends, and I suddenly understood why they'd elected not to go on to higher education. Both the boys came from farming families, and the road ahead for Emma and Megan was simple and straightforward. They would be farmer's wives with a tribe of kids, doing the normal country thing—playing Russian roulette with the seasons and just hoping to survive and prosper. There had been an embarrassing incident with Emma's former boyfriend, who'd launched a drunken homophobic attack on a fellow football player, supported by his best mate, Megan's boyfriend. So my sisters dumped them instantly, as did the football club. Clearly attitudes had changed.

First Jamie and then Terrence phoned to apologize to the girls on behalf of the footy club, and within weeks they were dating. I thoroughly approved. They both seemed genuine, modern guys, and they doted on Emma and Megan.

CHAPTER 20
NEIL

IT WAS a typical late Friday afternoon in winter as Sarah and I finished surgery and began to bed down what patients we had overnight in our little hospital.

As we stepped outside into the courtyard, a lone figure leading a dog toward the car park turned and looked at me. The light was beginning to fade, but there was no mistaking his blue eyes—so blue the color seemed to wash over his face, a very handsome dark face at that. Fortysomething and swarthy, I thought automatically, Dick doing the talking as usual. *And a hot daddy at that.*

He was about twenty meters away, and I was transfixed. His masculine beauty was just breathtaking—I could find no other description in my addled brain to describe my feelings.

Sarah grinned at me. "Whoa, down boy, he's straight. But I suppose that's never stopped you before, has it?"

I continued to stare as he smiled the most brilliant smile at me, finally turning toward a smart-looking Mercedes SUV, opening the rear door for his dog to get in and then waving as he drove off.

"Actually," she said gently, "his family and my folks have known each other, like, forever."

"What's his name?" I queried nonchalantly, and she laughed at me.

"Dean, darling, he *is* straight. That's Neil Andrews, and he certainly needs understanding in large doses at the moment."

I looked over at her and raised my eyebrows, allowing her to continue.

"He's had a rough time of it the last few months or so. Margot, his wife, passed away with cancer. He and the family nursed her at home until the last few days, and she went into palliative care, where she passed away. Poor woman was only in her early forties."

I listened with a degree of compassion, even shock. *The poor bastard.* But I couldn't get the image of his face out of my consciousness. Somehow I just knew he was really special.

"They're an unusual family in one respect," Sarah continued thoughtfully. "He and Margot met at high school, and she fell pregnant, and Justine, their daughter, was born. When Neil turned eighteen they were married, and nine months later, John, their son, arrived. So two kids, and their parents weren't even twenty.

"Then years later Justine met a bloke at university. He moved in with her, she fell pregnant at eighteen, decided to have the baby, and her little son, Jack, arrived. *Then—*" Sarah said theatrically, and my mouth fell open.

"She didn't do it again?" I said.

"Yep," Sarah laughed. "She then had Sophie, but unfortunately it was all too much for the father, and he pissed off, leaving Justine and her mum and dad to raise the two kids. Then John married Pam, and they have a tiny daughter, Angela, so our Neil is a grandfather of three."

"So they're certainly a family of early bloomers," I laughed.

"Oh yes," Sarah said, a mine of information. "But it must be genetic because Neil's mother, Marjorie, was only nineteen when Neil was born, and of course she's only in her early sixties now."

I did the maths in my head and nodded. "So that would make him around forty-four?"

Sarah nodded and didn't say anything more. She knew me too well.

I FINISHED up at work as the vet nurses ran the mop over the floors and Alastair finished his last consult. Brett and Heather Walker were on a well-deserved holiday with their kids. With three of us, we were constantly busy, and the days, while stimulating, were tiring, even for relatively young people such as Sarah and me.

Wishing everyone good night, I wearily climbed into the Land Cruiser and drove home, Bruce sitting next to me like a person with his seat-belt harness on.

Toby had mentioned they had a guest for dinner, an old friend, and it would be just the four of us as Paul, Dougie, and Jenny were out.

I showered, dressed, and fed Bruce.

Hearing voices in the dining room, I walked around the corner of the big buffet and stood there, mouth open but unable to speak.

His eyes were the color of the Blue Lake at Mount Gambier, washing across his dark features and lighting up the room in the same way he had two hours earlier at the clinic. And he was smiling at me—a smile of recognition and, I thought, interest, because in the midst of my confusion I knew I held all his attention, as much as he held all mine.

Dinner was almost ready, but Toby made sure he performed the introductions first, with Macca grinning like an idiot, fully aware of the effect Neil Andrews had on me. I helped Toby serve the meal, my bloody mind in turmoil. All I could think was that Sarah's gaydar was badly broken. Either this bloke was so deep in the closet he didn't know himself, or maybe Sarah was just so close to the family she hadn't seen what was clearly there. I decided to be discreet, however, and hopefully well-mannered enough that I'd get to hear his story if he chose to tell it. In the meantime I had trouble breathing, let alone eating, so I stupidly reached for another wine. Macca had opened a nice little Merlot, and we vaporized the first bottle so quickly, I sprang up and found another.

As the meal progressed, I learnt that he was indeed a gay man, tried experimenting at college, the girl fell pregnant, and he married her. But she always knew he was gay because he told her. It turned out they were a great team, but she was a realist, pointing him in the direction of the Melbourne saunas shortly after their second child was born, and he found he could manage his life this way. That's where he'd met Toby and found someone who was a great friend and didn't judge him, and no, he laughed, he and Tobes weren't the slightest bit interested in each other physically.

"Margot was my life," he said. But she made him promise to move on with his life after she died, and that was the end of the information trail.

"Drink up," I said, about to pour him another merlot.

"Oh no, no, no, I've got to drive home, and Mum will be expecting me. I've moved in with my mother since my wife died," he explained.

I quite rudely held out my iPhone. "Well, give Mummy a call and tell her you've had one glass too many and you're staying the night."

He looked at me, astonished, as Macca and Toby scurried into the kitchen and quietly closed the door.

"You can sleep in my bed," I said. "That way we can cut down on the housekeeping."

I was breathing properly again, I noticed, but Dick was rampant. I leaned across the table and kissed him, but noted with satisfaction that he'd thrown caution to the wind and was moaning a lot and kissing me back.

"I wanted to kiss you ever since I saw you at the clinic," he breathed in my ear.

"Then why didn't you?"

"Oh, can't be too careful in public, you know," he said.

I thought that was a fucked-up attitude but managed to get his attention by nipping him on the lip.

He gave me a sickly grin and rang his mum. Dick was waiting, but I had enough presence of mind and good manners to open the kitchen door and say good night to my cousin and his partner. I gleefully accused the latter of holding his ear to the door. Macca rewarded me with a blush, and they laughed—there'd never been any secrets between us and never would be.

"What would you like for breakfast, Neil?" Toby asked solicitously.

"Oh, I'll just have whatever you blokes have," he replied, obviously on the defensive.

"Bullshit," I said, "he'll need eggs, bacon, grilled tomato, and black coffee to build his strength up."

Macca found the little writing pad on the counter used to order the groceries we needed and poised a pen above it. He looked at Neil mischievously. "Will that be one egg or two?"

"Two would be lovely," Neil said smoothly. "Sounds like I may need all the help I can get."

CHAPTER 21
NEW BEGINNINGS

IT FINALLY dawned on me that whatever I'd been searching for had suddenly found me. Recently I'd been so wrapped up in my studies and then my career that I hadn't given much thought to my future apart from my place in the lives of sick animals and enjoying life with Macca, Toby, the boys, and little Jenny—who wasn't so little anymore and so perceptive and articulate.

My early life with Danny now seemed so long ago. Certainly I'd had little affairs but never considered a permanent partner, although at the time Barry and I thought we had something going.

But when I led Neil into my bedroom, completely besotted, I was at the mercy of my own emotions, unsure what to do next, frightened I'd stuff it up, speculating if it was too soon for him after his wife's passing and a million other things over which I had no control anyway.

But he was a breath of fresh air. He sensed how I was feeling and told me so as we sat on the edge of my bed and talked.

He knew about Danny and made me feel comfortable about my past, a topic that could be covered without rancor or discomfort in the future.

Then he leaned over and kissed me again, and I felt like a giddy schoolgirl. I'd gone from the leader, the instigator, to a willing follower, encouraging him, supporting him, aware that the gentle part of my personality was having a bloody good run down the paddock rather than the brash, down-to-earth person I'd somehow become over the years.

Then it clicked in my feeble brain. This bloke had to be a top! Emboldened, I asked as we came up for air.

"Yes," he said and smiled.

No discussion necessary, because somehow I knew it really didn't matter. I warned him that I'd no experience as a bottom but was willing to try, and to his great credit, he said just to wake up in the morning with me beside him was reward enough, and there was plenty of time for "that" later.

I thought that was one of the most amazing things I'd ever heard from anyone, and to top it all off he was talking about *me*.

Macca and Toby were as good as their word the next morning. Neil and I realized they'd gone to much trouble to cook us breakfast as Macca ceremoniously slipped two eggs onto Neil's plate.

I walked him to his SUV, surprised to find it parked a good distance up the street. "Christ, you should have left your car at home and walked, it would've been quicker. Why did you park all this distance away?"

"Oh," he replied, looking uncomfortable and putting firmly in place part of the complicated persona that was Neil Andrews. "One can't be too careful in this town. If my kids or grandkids discovered the truth about me, it would destroy our family entirely."

"So you parked up the street away from Toby and Macca's because you didn't want to be seen visiting a well-known gay couple, is that it?"

"Um, yes, I guess so."

"Well, you're one fucked-up dude, that's all I can say. When you decide to grow up, why don't you give me a ring," I snarled, and charged away, nearly late for work.

I RAN in the door at work, followed by Bruce, and booted up my desktop to find a message from Ray Simmons. Within minutes I was on my way. Ray was puzzled that two of his mares had suddenly developed diarrhea overnight.

On the phone I'd impressed upon Ray he needed to quarantine the entire stables while we worked out what it was. A virus could ruin his entire racing season, so nothing should be left to chance.

I shut Bruce in the Land Cruiser, much to his outrage. He expected to be in and around the horses as he normally was, so he sat in the passenger seat and looked totally pissed off.

I suited up in protective gear and treated the two mares, who seemed to respond in minutes, but it was another thing entirely to work out why they'd been affected that way. After taking samples, I turned my attention to their feed and had a sudden brainwave, running outside to Ray and his staff.

"Who fed the horses last night?" I asked, and a young stable hand, Melissa, held up her hand, nearly in tears. "It's all right, love," I said, "you haven't done anything wrong, but did they have anything different in their diet last night? Think hard, because it's only these two mares that are affected."

"Oh no," she replied, "but I did run out of mix toward the end of feeding, and I had to open some of the new chaff that arrived the other day to mix with the grain, just like you and Mr. Simmons recommended."

"And how many horses did you feed with the new mix?"

"Only the last two mares," she said, and it hit all of us at the same time.

Within half an hour, the new shipment of chaff was outside the stables, and Ray was reaming the supplier to get him "some stuff that won't give my horses the shits," and the first part of my day was over. I let Bruce out, and he went straight inside, "talking" to all his equine mates, and after a final check on the mares, I was on my way back to the surgery.

It was chaos, of course. Alastair and Sarah had split up my patients between them, so I threw myself into it with gusto, and by about midafternoon we'd cleared the decks and could breathe again.

I walked into the reception area and noticed a huge bunch of flowers there—a stunning arrangement of wildflowers, obviously very expensive.

"Oh," I said, "someone's popular. What's the occasion?"

"We were about to ask you that." Sarah smiled evilly. "They're for you."

I knew immediately they could only have come from one source. Sure enough, I opened the card, and it was a simple message:

Please call me, N.

THE FOLLOWING Friday evening, the Mercedes arrived in our driveway. Neil greeted Toby and Macca and met Paul, Dougie, and Jenny for the first time.

"Oh," I said quite snappily, "parking in the driveway tonight, I see?"

He blushed and didn't respond, while Toby and Macca tried to work out what was going on between us. Then the other side of Neil Andrews emerged, without him being aware of it, I thought. A kind, caring, and utterly romantic person who adored kids. He sat there fascinated, listening to Paul and Dougie's love story, and told them he wished he'd known they'd been living so precariously because he would have helped them too.

He had such a puzzled look on his face as he acknowledged the amazing work Toby and Macca had done with young gay people. I could see he was struggling with the concept of an all-gay household, and similar to Simon Morgan, he couldn't believe how cogent and natural our little family was.

Even to the uninitiated, the two gay couples were relaxed and happy and Jenny was so obviously thriving, very advanced for her age and secure in a loving environment, a profoundly different lifestyle to the nuclear family of just a few years ago.

And then throw in me—a single out-and-proud gay guy—and a dog.

Bruce had been studying Neil ever since he'd walked in the door. Suddenly, even though he was ageing, he hopped onto Neil's lap, turned around, and laid his head on his shoulder, as he did with the other humans he loved, particularly Dad.

Neil looked astonished at first, but then he actually looked flattered as he and Bruce got acquainted.

"You *are* the most beautiful creature, aren't you?" he said, and Bruce's tail thumped on the armchair as they spoke to each other.

I was surprised. Not only did Bruce approve of Neil, but I could see an immediate bond there. I promised myself to remember that, however difficult and socially conservative Neil Andrews might be, there was an exceedingly nice part of his nature evident because he loved animals, and particularly Bruce.

"Are you ready, Dean?" he asked, and I nodded as we waved good night and went out for dinner.

We drew up outside The Elm Tree, probably the most expensive restaurant in town. I looked at him questioningly, and he covered my hand with his.

"I wanted to do this properly," he said. "I got off on the wrong foot, and I need to show you how much you're appreciated, so tonight it's my treat, totally."

He knew the owner, a smart, snappily dressed man, was an entrepreneur who had built his business with good food, good wine, and an understanding of the pretentious behavior of the town's nouveau riche, which hopefully didn't include Neil.

I liked the food. Simple is always best, and it was obviously fresh and well cooked. I managed to make a slovenly pig out of myself, enjoying a magnificent lobster Mornay for the main course. We talked at last without the intrusion of physical attraction and simply enjoyed each other's company. It was neutral ground, so every subject was up for discussion.

He admitted that the death of his wife had stunned him and that his comfortable life had been shattered forever, but through that dreadful experience he could appreciate the pain of others. Even though the circumstances of our partners' passing were different, he understood we had something in common, no matter how grim. He said he realized the healing process takes time and goes through certain stages as one readjusts to life.

I asked him how he made his living, knowing already he was a farmer and ran cattle on the family property on the western side of town. He told me that over the years he'd bought more properties in the same area, and as they were on the fringe of the metropolitan area, they were appreciating nicely. He'd taken the smallest of the properties, tried his hand at property development with some success, and planned to do more in the future. The evening flew by so quickly I was shocked and even a little pleased that we'd somehow connected so well. Neither of us could believe where the time had gone as the owner wished us good night, the very last to leave.

We sat in his vehicle in our driveway, holding hands, not wanting the night to end, when Neil produced the solution, an overnight bag and his toiletries. For once I wasn't the one taking the initiative.

We quietly moved inside. It wasn't that late, but settled couples, no matter how young, don't need much to entertain them if they're in love, and the place was in darkness. He pointed to the shower, and I nodded.

Thank Christ he didn't have to be reminded. He was a cleanliness freak like me.

So while I prepared myself, he used the shower, and shortly afterward I completed the job and walked into my bedroom.

For three tortuous bloody days I'd used the dildo, which normally resided in the chest of drawers, and when I explained to him what was on my mind, he was quite perturbed.

"You don't need to do that," he whispered. "Just do what feels right for you."

"I am," I replied. "This is my gift to us."

He looked quite upset until I clad him in a condom and then sat on him—slowly. It hurt like hell, but after I adjusted to his not insubstantial size, he began to enjoy himself.

Fuck, what had I put other people through? Danny, Will, Barry, Simon, and a whole heap of other guys.

Now the tables were turned, I thought bitterly as my arse both burned and ached at the same time.

He was very considerate, asking if I was okay. But he was a man, and let's face it, a guy with his cock up another human being's most intimate receptacle is just an animal anyway, despite their best intentions, because he feels only pleasure while the poor bloody receptacle often feels considerable pain, as mine was, although it did begin to feel better as time progressed.

I asked him to pull out and smothered everything in lubricant as he pushed into me again.

Jesus, that feels nice, as the bastard hit my prostate and I started to wail like a big sheila.

We rutted like animals. Pain had given way to absolute pleasure, and I wondered why I'd never tried this before.

The thought had hardly crossed my mind when the answer became clear. This was meant to be—it was us. Whatever had transpired with other people had no bearing on what suited us as a couple. By being sensitive to Neil's needs, I'd inadvertently found a profoundly enjoyable way of lovemaking, which enhanced our early beginnings.

HE WAS an early riser, one of those bright morning people who manage to give everyone around them the shits. It took at least two infusions of good coffee for me to become even remotely intelligible, although I was always organized, making sure I was out and about early enough to compensate.

"Thank you for last night," he whispered. "I've never enjoyed myself so much. It was amazing."

I managed to grin at him and agree, trying to get my brain to cooperate long enough to say something sensible and was quite proud of my early-morning insightfulness.

"Yes," I said, "the sex was wonderful too."

His face lit up like a bloody searchlight, but there was also some uncertainty there, and I wondered if he'd ever truly understood life's most precious emotion, the true regard of one human being for another.

EVERY DAY we saw each other. The following weekend I had the luxury of two full days off, and he had plans for me. To my surprise he asked me to pack a bag because he was taking me home with him. He even understood I didn't travel alone, and Bruce rode in the load area of the Mercedes, looking a touch insulted.

I recognized the area because it was on the same road that ran past Simmons Park. I guessed Ray's place was just a few minutes away as we turned into a nondescript driveway next to a large and obviously empty building.

Neil pulled the Merc in next to the building and beckoned to me, unlocking a solid-looking door and leading me inside.

Neil said it had been temporary madness on behalf of his late father, who had, in his later years, decided to become a mushroom farmer. Problem was, the project needed at least another three sheds to be properly viable, but his dad passed away, and no one had the heart or the interest to continue. Neil pointed out the drainage system in the concrete slab and the controlled-atmosphere air-conditioning throughout the growing area, then pointed me toward the area behind the entrance, which had three decent-sized rooms used for grading, opening into a spacious area in the front of the building, reminding me of the reception area at the clinic.

My mouth dropped open. "You're a cunning bugger, but a clever one. Who put you up to this?"

He laughed. "To be truthful, I've only just thought of it myself after meeting you, and I promise I've spoken to no one else, but with very little work it could be converted into quite a fine veterinary clinic, couldn't it?"

I could hardly contain my excitement. In my head I could see the sorting rooms converted into three consulting suites, and the open area at the front to a reception and waiting room. Overnight accommodation in pens out back would be easy, the drainage system allowing the whole area to be hosed out and kept clean.

"Something to occupy our thoughts, isn't it?" he said, and I nodded, my mind whirling with possibilities, because the building and its location fitted perfectly into a business scenario I'd already discussed with Brett and Heather Walker.

He put his arm protectively around my shoulders, one of the surprisingly nice things Neil Andrews did well. "Don't work yourself into a tizz." He smiled. "You're supposed to be relaxing this weekend. Come and meet Mum."

THE HOUSE was the original family home, and since Margot's passing, he'd moved back here with his mother, which suited both of them. His daughter, Justine, and her kids, Jack and Sophie, had his old house, while he'd helped John and Pam build their new home just down the road.

"And their little baby is Angela," I said.

Neil looked surprised. "You're well informed," he said.

"Sarah, who else?"

I thought Neil was going to have an apoplectic fit.

"Oh," he said, "oh no, Sarah mustn't know about us, that would be most unwise. They're lovely people, but they do talk a lot, you know."

He must have seen the glint in my eye and decided discretion was the better part of valor, knowing I wouldn't tell his precious secret to anyone. But he'd managed to give me the shits again, and I told him so.

"Build a bloody bridge, Neil," I said.

"A bridge?"

"Yes," I snarled, "and get over it."

At least Bruce was doing okay for himself. He'd made friends with Sandy, Neil's old cattle dog. Neil was surprised because any male dog was usually a threat to the resident male's territory. But Sandy and Bruce were like puppies, playing around and being quite stupid.

"Bruce is gay," I said to Neil. "And it looks like your dog is too."

The look of horror on Neil's face wasn't worth the remark as I sighed inwardly. This was obviously going to be a long process.

MARJORIE ANDREWS was a doll.

The fact that she was a great-grandmother in her early sixties obviously hadn't slowed her participation as a member of the human race. A country girl first and foremost, there was a total lack of pretentiousness, which I loved, despite the fact she was probably a wealthy woman in her own right. But there was also a sense of sophistication there, not at all elitist, but our Marge just seemed to be aware of everything around her.

"I read a lot, Dean," she explained. "Both old-fashioned hard-copy books and online. I keep in touch that way. How on earth can we advise the young people in our families these days if we don't know what's going on in the world?"

I smiled at her and agreed, telling her what a breath of fresh air she was, while Neil squirmed in his seat. Sarah had told me that Marge could be out on the tractor baling hay one moment, and within hours she could be a picture of elegance, hosting a dinner party for a visiting cultural delegation from China. It was clear Marge's outspoken views on the arts, politics, and life in general embarrassed Neil.

And she knew about us, I could see, with Neil trying to butch it up, her eyes gleaming with the naughtiness of it all. Marge's sheer enjoyment of life was infectious, and now she had an excuse to stir her son remorselessly in the future.

"This is your room," Neil said. "Right across the hallway from mine. You can use the en suite in my room. Mum uses the main bathroom."

I rolled my eyes in exasperation. "So what do I do in the morning?"

He looked at me with a question in his eyes.

"Do I wash the sheets myself to get rid of the spunk stains after I've wanked off at least three times?"

He caught my meaning, no doubt because of the menace in my eyes. "Oh no, you'll be sleeping in here with me. I'll just set the alarm for about 6:00 a.m., and you can return to your room. Look," he said, "there's another matter I forgot to mention. It slipped my mind altogether."

I wondered what else could come along to fuck up what had initially appeared to be a nice weekend.

"Yes, well, I quite forgot that I'd promised Valerie I'd take her to see this rather daring European film tonight, so I'll be missing for a few hours. Do you mind keeping Mum company while I'm out?"

"Who is Valerie?" I asked in all innocence.

"She's my lady friend," Neil replied, looking a touch uncomfortable.

"Your girlfriend?" I asked incredulously, and he nodded.

"Oh, we don't do anything," he said, "we're both in Rotary, and it's convenient for us to have a partner for couples' nights."

"So on top of everything, Neil, you expect me to compete for your attention with a girlfriend. You have to be joking. Why don't you just drop Bruce and me home on the way, and we'll call it quits."

To my amazement, he burst into tears, the most unlikely reaction I expected from him, whether I was putting him under pressure or not.

"Please give me some time to adjust," he whispered. "I've never had this type of relationship before, and I just need to get my head around it. Believe me, you are already the most important person in my life, and we've only known each other a few weeks."

I shrugged, the bared emotions and the logic getting to me.

But there was a compensating factor. I got to spend a night of spirited discussion with Marjorie Andrews, and that was something to look forward to.

CHAPTER 22
THE ANDREWS FAMILY

WHEN NEIL returned home, Marge and I were still at the dining table, ever so slightly tipsy but certainly not out of control. There was too much to talk about, and I needed to keep a clear head so I could enjoy her intellect.

We cleaned up the dishes, kissed Marge good night, then walked Bruce and Sandy down the driveway with much celebratory leg cocking and showing off. "You might be right about those two." Neil laughed. "They do seem to like each other."

I wondered idly if Neil had drawn the obvious conclusion. That perhaps our canine companions were simply a reflection of their owners. At this stage of the evening, I'd even forgiven Neil's bloody girlfriend and fucked-up lifestyle because Old Dick had a mind of his own, and we literally ran back to the house, focused on one thing—and one thing only.

We flung our gear off. I almost ripped his shirt from his body, his smooth, dark skin and trim body gleaming in the moonlight through the window. A body that in my opinion could well have graced any bodybuilding magazine, a total turn-on for me, and I found I wasn't breathing properly again.

And while comparisons are odious, I realized how mundane my previous sex life had been. Everything he did heightened my physical feelings and enjoyment, and it wasn't hard to work out that the experience did the same for him.

MARGE WAS an early riser. Breakfast was on the table as we walked into the big warm country kitchen. She smiled as I tore into the food. I love my tucker, and after the workout I'd had the night before, I was starving.

We were on our second cup of coffee when the door burst open and the remaining generations of the Andrews family flooded the kitchen.

Justine was beautiful. She and Neil looked like brother and sister, and the relationship seemed similar, as they teased each other, comfortable in each other's space.

Her two kids stopped in their tracks as they spotted me.

"Hello," I said, "who are you?"

There was a deep chuckle from the little boy who appeared to be about four or five years old.

"I'm Jack," he said, in a voice that shocked me. For such a tiny fellow it was loud, clear, and could have penetrated armor plate at a hundred paces.

"I'm Sophie," his sister said with similar vocal qualities but without the volume.

I looked over at the adults as they held their sides at my expense.

"It's a genetic trait," Marge laughed. "Every few generations in the Andrews family one pops up again, this time two in the same family."

Then John walked in with Pam and little Angela in a bassinet. I'd seen photographs of Margot, and he was most like her—fair hair, slim build, and nice glasses. And Pam was a tiny dark-headed thing, full of energy.

They all looked so young to be parents. Despite Sarah forewarning me, I was mesmerized. They were so young in years, but as I listened to the conversation, I realized Justine and John had grown up very quickly.

The conversation naturally drifted to the business proposal. My presence could be easily explained that way, and there was an enthusiastic response, particularly from Pam, who was a trained veterinary nurse, and I mentally ticked her off as the first new employee.

She caught up with me after lunch as they were on their way home.

"We'd be a great team, princess," she giggled, looking over her shoulder, making certain she couldn't be overheard. "I had to stop work when Angela was born, so if your project goes ahead, the timing would be perfect." She looked at me, and whispered, "There's still some fucked-up people in this world, darling. Neil's very old-fashioned as you probably know, but Marge and I always work it all out, no worries."

I laughed at her beautiful audacity and confirmed her gaydar was spot-on.

She smiled at me. "I have a gay brother, and I've been around, but Justine and John are a touch naïve. Nothing that can't be remedied in time. Lovely to meet you, welcome to the family."

THE FOLLOWING week Brett and Heather returned from holidays, and after some rough quotations from builders and a sorting out of the finances, it was almost a done deal. Of course, it helped to have a cousin who ran the loans department of the only bank we wanted to deal with, making sure our proposal got immediate attention.

Six weeks later we were ready to begin the renovations. The successful builder was engaged, and it was all systems go.

Brett and Heather together would hold 30 percent of the new business, Neil and I 30 percent individually. Sarah wasn't a businessperson and initially refused outright to participate financially, but I bullied her, and with Richard's help she took a 10 percent share, which meant she would eventually get some return for all her hard work. It would make her feel part of the business, because I insisted she and I would run the new clinic together.

I would service the Simmons Park account because it was only five minutes away and I was already a part of Ray's team. Brett would only get involved if surgery was required on any of the horses.

So we had our first directors' meeting, and because we now straddled the town in a direct line, east to west, we decided, for marketing and communication reasons, to call our place the West Clinic and the original property the East Clinic. Sarah and I would run West Clinic, Brett and Alastair, East Clinic.

The great imponderable that was so hard to estimate was all the domestic pet business coming from the new suburbs out this side, and some of the established areas as well, so we had a very conservative business plan.

The following months were probably the busiest of my life. Not only were we flat-out at East Clinic, but I was helping supervise the renovations at the new place and putting together a marketing plan targeted at the developing suburbs. Then I began attending some of the bigger race meetings with Ray Simmons because he wanted me there with the cream of his horses, making sure they were as fit and as well as we could make them.

Finally, the mayor declared West Clinic open in a simple ceremony that was well reported in the daily press, and from day one the business went ballistic. The days often started before daylight, and Sarah and I finished work when we finished. Pam ran the front desk with enthusiasm and helped out in the surgery, Marge was always there with meals, and Neil just fussed and worried even though the cash flow was stupendous and far exceeded our expectations.

I'd been so busy I hadn't thought about me very much, and it was a combined approach from Marge and Neil that finally brought me back down to earth.

I'd been driving across town to Macca and Toby's sometimes late at night and always early in the mornings. It made sense, they said, to move into the homestead.

I naturally had mixed feelings. I wouldn't have to drive to work or drive home again, and I was moving in with my lover, although that was a double-edged sword because Neil had a lot of growing up and adjusting ahead of him.

But the family and I got on well together, and I was already helping in the parenting role with Jack and Sophie, which I enjoyed.

But behind me I would leave a home environment that represented a huge part of my own personal development, the connection with all Toby and Macca's friends, and the close family ties I felt for Paul, Dougie, and Jenny. It was the place where I'd been blissfully happy and settled with Danny until he died. It was where I'd met Barry, bedded Simon, and it also represented the time frame where I'd found I had some compatibility with women, even though my sexuality remained what it was. But it was the place, after all, where I spent my university years, helping prepare me for what consumed almost all my waking hours now and probably into the future, just trying to be a good veterinarian.

I extracted a promise from Toby, Macca, Paul, and Dougie that we'd have a meal together once a week, and they all agreed, knowing it wouldn't always happen, but at least we'd all try.

CHAPTER 23
ROTARY

WEST CLINIC grew and prospered at breakneck speed to the amazement of our shareholders. I realized much of this success lay in the teamwork we'd developed. Sarah and I trained our support staff so customers weren't left unattended even when we were busy, so repeat and referral business was driving the turnover.

Within the first month, we established an animal crèche for sick and abandoned animals, and on weekends whole families would arrive because it was like a minizoo, and the kids could interact with a variety of animals from budgerigars to lambs. Neil usually did little tours of the premises with those people, and many of our visitors became clients.

The local radio station contacted me for help—there was a need for a talkback segment with veterinary advice on Saturday mornings, and would I be interested for a small fee? I talked to Brett and Heather, then rang the station back. I'd do the segment for no charge if we could promote both East and West Clinic, and if the station could allow me some flexibility by broadcasting from the clinic rather than the studio when we had emergency surgery or similar. Brett would take over when I wasn't available, such as big race days with Simmons Park.

The following Saturday I nervously sat in the hot seat as the local radio jock peppered me with questions, eventually going to talkback. The third caller was a male voice complaining he had a sick pussy, and what would I advise? Adrian, the jock, caught my eye as I recognized the camp voice of Geoffy Stevenson, the so-called straight father of three gay boys, the most loyal and beautiful family anyone could have as friends. It reminded me I hadn't been in contact with so many of my friends for months, due to the establishment of West Clinic and Neil.

I quickly responded to Geoffy without naming him. "Sweetheart," I said, "I think your pussy has had too much of a good thing. So I suggest you have a really close look at its diet." I dropped my hand, and Adrian cut the call, forcing me to control my mirth because the next caller was on the line.

Justine suggested we open a memorial park for pets. She told me that, through her own experience, when someone left your family circle through death, whether animal or human, there was usually an unspoken need to visit a place where there was a cogent reminder, whether a grave, ashes, or just a plaque.

It took months to get planning approval. Practices like ours had various ways of disposing of euthanized animals, including cremation and mass burial, but we were the first to take the formal step whereby we gave owners a choice.

We had part of a paddock near the main road rezoned for the process, with a separate entrance, and the project took off like a rocket, thanks to Justine's persistence.

The trouble clouds began gathering shortly afterward. Richard almost forcibly removed Sarah from work for a holiday, and we had a replacement from East Clinic, a new employee who was a lovely bloke but bloody useless. I knew by the time I trained him to replace Sarah, she'd be back at work, but I had to persist. Marge and Neil worried, and I could feel myself about to burst with the tension and pressure. In fact, everyone kept their distance because I was bad tempered and probably a touch unpleasant to be around, but eventually the workload slowed a little, and Sarah returned to work.

I decided to keep Sam, the new fellow, until I could have a short break myself, and I was amused to see everyone around me heave a sigh of relief.

I WAS too tired to go anywhere. I planned just to stay home and sleep in, actually have some meals without rushing and have them on time.

Neil was on his guard, knowing I couldn't resist walking the one hundred and fifty meters to the clinic just to keep my finger on the pulse, and he warned me I was approaching nervous breakdown territory at alarming speed.

This was the really beautiful part of Neil's nature—the caring and nurturing was always there, particularly for those closest to him, and he could become quite bossy and persistent until he was sure I was doing okay.

"Tonight," he said, "you're coming with me to Rotary."

I looked at him as if he'd stepped out of a spaceship.

"Rotary," I shrieked, "that's for retirees, do-gooders, and fucking wankers."

Even though I'd insulted him, he found his sense of humor from somewhere and laughed at me. "It's actually a service club with a very diverse age range and demographics," he said seriously, and I felt like a heel, knowing I'd effectively boxed my way into a corner with my bitchy remarks.

So I agreed to go, thereby keeping the peace.

We had to collect Valerie on the way. Not surprisingly, Neil still felt the need to preserve his image in public, particularly at Rotary, but what I wasn't prepared for was Val herself. She was just lovely. Tallish, late forties, and with great dress sense, she was everything an academic wasn't supposed to be. We chatted away like old friends all the way to the venue, a popular pub close by in the western suburbs. As I held the door open for her she smiled gratefully, thanking me and commenting how lucky she was that two lovely gentlemen were escorting her tonight, and she hoped that would continue. I heard a cough and glanced across the bonnet of the Mercedes in astonishment. Neil's face was flushed, his male ego in tatters because I'd clearly upset the status quo. I shrugged to myself. I was enjoying Val's company, she was an interesting person, and I wasn't about to allow Neil to spoil my night with his silly possessiveness and mood swings.

He even attempted to seat me at another table, except Val wouldn't hear of it. She was enjoying my company as well.

The meeting was in a spacious private room away from the noisy bistro and gaming area. The publican, Gerry Spicer, really wanted the Rotary business and had become a member quite recently, sparing no expense with the level of service and surroundings.

The meeting opened, and immediately afterward guests were welcomed. Neil introduced me as his business partner and referred to West Clinic as a much-needed service in the area. There was a general nodding of heads acknowledging me, the media having been really effective, and word of mouth having done the rest. Besides, I recognized several of our customers there. I waved to them, and they waved back.

I felt the eyes on me before I saw them. Two tables away a rugged-looking midthirties guy was staring at me, but my gaydar remained silent. He came over and introduced himself.

"My wife works with your cousin," he said genially. Then the penny dropped.

"Curtis Fleming," I said. "Of course, you and Diana came over for dinner one night."

"What a great night too." He grinned. "Bloody Macca loves a glass or fifteen of red, doesn't he?"

I smiled, and Curtis continued. "What an amazing household that is," he enthused, and I was aware that the remainder of our table had stopped talking and tuned in to the conversation. "Never have I seen such kindness and humanity in two people as Toby and Macca, and those two young blokes they rescued with their baby just shows what can happen when people forget about their hang-ups and focus on other human beings. I'd love to have Toby and Macca as guest speakers one night, and they should bring those young blokes with them, what are their names again?"

"Paul and Dougie. And their little girl is Jenny."

"Oh, they sound so interesting," Valerie said. "Could you organize them for us, Dean?"

"With pleasure. I know they've already spoken at two other Rotary Clubs. They'd be delighted to spread the message about their counseling and work with young gay people."

Everyone at the table nodded in agreement with the exception of Neil, who appeared to be trying to disappear under it.

No one noticed but Val and me. She winked outrageously at me, and it was then I realized she'd known Neil's little secret all along, and that he and I were a couple. Clever girl, but she was a woman, after all. *No one should underestimate a woman or a queen. We see things invisible to mere mortals.*

I was surprised that, toward the end of the evening, I found I'd actually enjoyed myself. The agenda wound its way to a natural conclusion, and I had a chance to talk to most of the forty or so people attending as we had a "fellowship" session afterward. A convoluted way of saying having a drink with your mates.

But it was an opportunity at last just to stop and think about things other than work, which unfortunately, I had to admit, had taken over my life. These people were warm, welcoming, and downright friendly. They all loved a drink, that was quite obvious, and took turns as designated drivers, but if they managed to get really pissed, then Gerry Spicer took them home in the pub bus—all of this set against a background of service to the community, which I thought was pretty cool. So they focused on those less fortunate and rewarded themselves by having a great time together every Tuesday night, which in itself was a real commitment.

It wasn't long coming. As we stood to leave, the treasurer, Bill Sadler, asked if I was interested in joining, and I surprised myself by agreeing with some enthusiasm.

We dropped Val home. She kissed us good night, refusing to allow either of us to escort her to the door. I knew the game had changed, yet Neil hadn't noticed. I felt sorry for him because the path he was progressing, ever so slowly, was one so many of us had traveled over the years. He was simply twenty years behind everyone else. I resolved to keep on trying because he was a good and honorable person, and the depth of emotional longing, at least on my part, was very real. So I found a new lease on life when we got home and rewarded him the only way I knew how. When he kissed me, I bloody near lost it. It wasn't just sex, it was far more. We both knew it by now, but I knew it was too early for him to talk about it.

THE MEMBERSHIP committee interviewed me at home. I asked Marge to be present, trying to negate any questions that had the potential to embarrass Neil. I was correct—the committee were gentlemanly and didn't even ask if I was partnered. They caught the look in Marge's eye and kept the discussion on my background and birth family, my education, and West Clinic. They were fascinated with my involvement in the thoroughbred racing industry through Ray Simmons, and sneakily asked if perhaps Ray could be a guest speaker, which I assured them wouldn't be a problem.

My induction was set for two weeks' time. But I was truthful —working up to sixty hours a week didn't leave much time for community service. The committee accepted that and asked me simply to do what I could, and if that meant being a "knife and fork" Rotarian until the business was less demanding, so be it.

CHAPTER 24
EVERYTHING TURNS TO SHIT

LIFE SETTLED into a more pleasant routine. After discussion with the other directors, I decided to keep Sam on permanently, and my workload eased as a result, allowing me to manage the business more effectively, leaving more time for relaxation.

I looked forward to Tuesday nights. My Rotary membership brought with it responsibility for providing guest speakers, which I relished.

First of my presenters were Macca and Toby, with Paul and Dougie as special guests. To give Neil credit, he didn't attempt to influence my choices. He knew I was committed to the cause. Anything that would help open society's eyes, get them on side, and lower the rate of suicide in the under thirties always had my attention. Macca didn't disappoint. He was brilliant, with a PowerPoint presentation dealing first in facts and figures and, importantly, the reasons behind them. I looked around the room and saw horror etched on the faces of my fellow members before he moved on to the more gentle human-interest aspects, taking time to stress how fortunate he was to have Toby as his partner and how, through mutual friends, they'd realized they had much in common. Then Paul took over, with Dougie by his side, and they told their story, their presentation peppered with shots of Jenny from the day they arrived to live with Macca and Toby until the present time and including me as part of the family group. There wasn't a dry eye in the place. Everyone stood and applauded, and I turned the meeting over to questions. There were some intelligent remarks—the marriage-equality legislation was currently before parliament, and everyone wanted to know if both couples were getting married.

"Yes," said Macca.

"Of course," said Dougie. "Paul proposed two years ago."

I'd been watching for signs of negativity, and it wasn't long in coming. I sighed inwardly because I knew some attitudes took longer to change than others and some people remained homophobic forever, seeing no need to change at all.

The question came from an early-forties high school teacher, Grant Davis, who should have known better.

"The young blokes I teach don't know what they are," he said. "Once upon a time, boys were one way or the other, now they seem confused. How are they supposed to determine their sexuality these days?"

It was my lovely cousin who took up the cudgel. Toby rose to his feet, giving the guy the benefit of the doubt but refusing to move away from the purpose of their presentation. "Grant," he said, "we're not here tonight to discuss causation of sexuality. We're here to talk about the vulnerable kids in the community who've experienced homophobic remarks and behavior and who feel so much on the margin of society they can't find a place for themselves, so they take their own lives. Those kids usually come from the smaller country towns and settlements, but sometimes they come from this place as well. Your students sound well-adjusted, Grant." He smiled. "If they can actually talk about their sexuality publicly without feeling threatened, that's a hell of a step forward."

Grant slumped in his seat. His mate, Nigel Travers, a florid-faced stock-and-station agent, put his head down, and they sniggered together like idiots.

THE OTHER members ignored their behavior, but I knew at some stage I'd face some sort of shit from the goons. In the meantime, there was more applause as I thanked the boys for their "insightful" presentation, and our president, Henry Jones, invited our guests to join us for a light supper.

Neil had looked straight ahead during the presentation, his face impassive, while Valerie had been on her feet, applauding. He caught the look in my eye and decided he had only one course of action remaining or go without sex for an indeterminate period. He walked over to the boys and congratulated them, making no secret of his friendship with Toby.

Maybe our relationship may not be as one-dimensional as I thought. This is certainly progress.

On the way home, he seemed to regress somehow, answering Valerie's remarks with single-syllable replies. It wasn't until we closed the bedroom door that he was back to normal and became quite emotional and passionate, steadily driving both of us to earth-shattering orgasms—three times in an hour and a half.

TWO WEEKS later it was Ray Simmons's turn as our guest speaker.

There was great excitement from the gamblers and racegoers in our midst, and quite a few partners turned up because Ray was so well-known.

Ray was famous for his straightforward nature. He always said it the way it was. His knowledge, experience, and honesty put him in a special place in an industry where such candid behavior was rare, and consequently he spoke with such authority that ordinary people never questioned his opinion.

I could see there was a more relaxed atmosphere than two weeks prior when Macca, Toby, Paul, and Dougie held the floor. This presentation wasn't as challenging or even embarrassing in the slightest. Even Neil appeared more relaxed.

Ray spoke about his family first. He was one of five kids, living in rented accommodation at one of the training complexes where his dad had been a stable hand and later manager. "It was a hand-to-mouth existence," Ray said. "My mother often went without so we kids had enough, and there were no luxuries of any kind. It didn't do me any harm to come from those poor circumstances. It helped me stay in touch with the basics and stay grounded, you might say. The last thing I'd want anyone to think was that I'd inherited Simmons Park from my family, which is simply not true. The only family involvement is my brother Clancy.

"He and I worked hard to build Simmons Park together. He is my only sibling to share my fascination and love of horses, and he's my closest mate."

The lights dimmed, and I noted with satisfaction that he'd put together a really high-quality picture show. Ray traced his progress as a trainer from his humble beginnings to the present day, weaving his philosophy into the presentation. "Contrary to what many people might think," he said, smiling, "together with dogs, horses are companion animals to humankind, and if you want their cooperation throughout their working life, including race days, you have to treat them as equals."

The room fell utterly silent as Ray expounded his theory.

"Horses, dogs, dolphins, apes—their intelligence naturally varies individually just like we humans, but if you treat them with a patronizing attitude because you think you're superior, they never respect you, and your working relationship will be flawed before you start. Dogs are interesting too. The pack mentality has stayed with them down through the ages, but they are immensely flexible and so intelligent they sense their place in the domestic pack in which they find themselves and adapt accordingly."

Ray paused and looked at me, smiling, and I suddenly knew where this was going. So did Brett and Heather Walker, whom I'd invited specially, and who were smiling at me.

"I hope I never become too old to learn," Ray continued. "Because in thirty years as a trainer I'd never witnessed anything as remarkable as I did around three years ago, when I first came in contact with Dean and Brett."

Ray went on to describe what had happened in his stables and how the horses were traumatized. Suddenly the screen came alive again, and there was Bruce licking Twilight Rose's nose as she looked bewildered. The next shot showed her nuzzling Bruce, and the final shot was of Bruce, me, and Twilight Rose walking through the stables together. When Ray explained to his audience what had happened, there were the usual knowing smiles normally reserved for nutcases and gong-bangers, but Ray stopped them in their tracks.

"Twilight Rose has won every race since," he said, "and the performance of every single animal in those stables has improved out of sight since Dean and Bruce settled them down. If you think that's a coincidence, then I've news for you, because horses are a lot smarter than we silly humans give them credit for."

He was obviously very convincing. There was no smoke and mirrors with Ray Simmons. If he said that was the way it happened, it certainly did, such was his reputation.

"So that's the story of Simmons Park. There's actually a lot more if we include the Hong Kong branch."

Everyone sat up in their chairs, because while Simmons Park Hong Kong wasn't a secret, very little was known about its daily operation.

"It's very much a family operation, just like here." Ray grinned, and a picture appeared of Ray, his wife Sharon, and their two kids, Georgia and Luke, both of whom were involved in the business.

"My younger brother, Clancy, runs our Hong Kong operation most successfully, together with his Chinese partner, Lim. In fact, it's the jewel in the crown, so to speak, because they're such a great team, and Lim knows the local scene so well."

I nearly pissed myself with mirth. I could see my fellow members straining to make sense of "Lim," a really funny name even for an Asian girl. Then the final picture flashed up, and it was perfectly clear that Lim was a most handsome man, standing shoulder to shoulder with the equally handsome Clancy and two little kids, whom I guessed were around eight and ten years of age.

Ray's calming voice continued. "Clancy and Lim adopted Lee and Nanci from an orphanage in Guangzhou," he said proudly. "They're actually brother and sister.

"Their parents were killed in an accident, and unusually for Chinese kids, they have no known relatives because they came from a great distance away. Those kids are so like their new parents," Ray said, his words full of pride. "All four of them have the same gift with horses that our Dean has. They can turn a horse with a difficult background into a winner in a matter of weeks if the animal has potential. That's one of the reasons they're doing so well."

I looked around the room at the glazed expressions on everyone's faces as I moved a vote of thanks to Ray on behalf of the Western Heights Rotary Club.

Ray looked at me and winked. "Sorry to do that to you, Deano," he whispered, "but it's time everyone got the message, don't you think?"

I was almost too scared to look at my other half. When I did, I could see he was struggling. He stared at me as if I'd written Ray's presentation for him, when in truth I knew absolutely nothing of the content. Valerie was ecstatic and ran up to Ray to shake his hand and congratulate him, as did most of the members.

I watched Grant Davis, the homophobic schoolteacher, and his mate Nigel Travers, the equally stupid and homophobic stock-and-station agent, sitting transfixed as if someone had hit them under the ear with a blunt axe, or taken their bag of sweets away from them. The bloke they thought was the epitome of maleness had a gay brother, and I couldn't have been happier at their discomfort.

THE NEXT morning Neil and I arrived for breakfast together. I poured his coffee from the old percolator, just the way he liked it, as Marge's eyes followed me with amusement. I poured her a cup as well. But the Andrews family were all bloody freaks. They didn't need coffee to wake up as I did. They sprang out of bed and were immediately mentally alert and ready for anything, where it took me at least two hours to be coherent.

Consequently Marge was speaking to me, and her words weren't registering, but I noted that Neil's body language had become instantly defensive, so much so he seemed frozen in his chair as I apologized to his mother.

"Sorry, Marge darling," I said with a grin, "but you know what I'm like in the mornings. What did you say again?"

She laughed at me, just so relaxed and lovely. "I simply asked when you blokes were going to have pity on a poor old washerwoman like me and just put out one set of bed linen instead of two. You never spend more than a few minutes in *your* bed, Dean, from one week to the next."

Neil had gone to a pasty shade of white. It was clear Marge had simply decided it was time to talk about the elephant in the room whether Neil was ready or not, and I realized she'd done so because of me. Something told me that she knew a great deal more about the subject than she was willing to admit to at this stage, but she pressed on.

"Sweetheart," she said to Neil, "you're such a good son and a great man, but it's important to me that you and Dean relax and live your life as a couple, not like you're ashamed of who you are. I'm not ashamed of you, neither is Dean, but you're missing out on the full enjoyment of your lovely relationship because you've kept it a secret."

"It's not the sort of thing we should talk about," he said. "We have to remember I'm a father and grandfather, and that brings with it certain responsibilities."

"Yes, it does," snapped Marge, "but the responsibility of being honest with your family far outweighs *your* sense of what's right."

Realizing she had more of a fight on her hands than she'd expected, she continued with determination. "Neil, you're an equal, functioning member of society with every right to expect equal treatment to heterosexual people. You're not a bloody pariah. You should be feeling good about yourself, not the opposite."

There was no admission or denial from Neil. While this little showdown had been coming for a long time, he looked shaken, and I couldn't help but feel sorry for him. He looked straight ahead, his face impassive, probably trying to pretend it hadn't happened. But indeed it had, and the look on his face said it all. His life was about to change from this point onward, and his place in society and within his own family group would never be the same again.

"How did you know, Mum?" he whispered, rather stupidly, his question simply illustrating how naïve he was in hoping to conceal something as important as this.

"Darling, I guess I always have," she said gently. "It wasn't much of a stretch, because your father was the same way."

Neil reacted as if lightning had struck him, his face going completely ashen with shock, his lips moving but making no sound.

"That can't be!" he shouted, finding his voice. "Dad was a fine man. He'd never do anything like that."

"Well, you're a fine man, dear, and you're as gay as Christmas, so why would you doubt my words?"

Marge sat back in her chair with a gentle smile on her face, and it was about that time I thought perhaps I should quietly sneak out the kitchen door and open the clinic half an hour early, but Marge read my mind.

"No, Dean, dear," she said, "this is critical to our family's future, and you've been part of this family for some time now. Why don't you get Sarah to open up for you?"

I nodded and sat down again, but as I did so, I squeezed his hand to let him know I was there for him. His lack of response shocked me, and I wondered just what was going on in his mind.

"Your father was a good man, Neil," Marge said, "and I loved him, but he wasn't as honest as you because I only found out the truth after you were born. At least you were honest with Margot before you were even married."

"How did you know that?" he said weakly with a look of terror on his face, finally understanding his secret life hadn't been secret at all.

"Margot and I had lots of discussions on the matter over the years," Marge said truthfully. "But it was only between ourselves. The children were never included.

"Your dad was something else," she said grimly. "He tried to deny everything, but I wasn't a fool, and I moved him out of our bedroom immediately—you were just a baby at that time. Finally he realized I had irrefutable evidence and asked me if I wanted a divorce, but after thinking about it, I declined his offer because it would have ruined our lives. It was a very different social environment back then, as you can probably imagine."

I smiled at Marge and nodded, holding her hand this time because this was also a life-changing event for her as well as her son.

"We told you that we slept separately because Dad snored, but it was because we elected never to be intimate that way with each other again, given the circumstances in which we found ourselves. Your father had Dick Flannery as a lover for many years, and I had Gerald Grimshaw," Marge said matter-of-factly. "Both married men, but they enjoyed the extracurricular activity. They've passed on now, so I guess the family secrets are still safely hidden from sight. Mind you, I've had a few assignations since, but now your father's not here, so I suppose it doesn't matter, does it?"

I simply couldn't keep the smile off my face, which Neil saw, and he snapped at me. "It's no laughing matter. This is all disgusting, if you ask me."

"But dear," Marge said, "I'm not asking you. I'm telling you the facts of life, and if I've been delinquent it's because I haven't mentioned it sooner, but you and Margot were quite well settled with your little arrangement, and I frankly saw no need to disturb the status quo."

"What do you mean?" yelped Neil, looking defensive.

"Your little forays to Melbourne to the gay saunas, of course. Margot discussed that with me ages ago, and I thought she was so sensible. Margot was also a saint, Neil. She could have taken a string of lovers, she was so beautiful, but she never worried—her main concern was that you should have a proper release for your natural urges."

Oh fuck. How is he going to handle all this?

I excused myself at last and fled to work. At least it was only two minutes away, and I could surround myself legitimately with veterinary health matters and let the remainder look after itself.

I could tell Justine and John were more than a little puzzled with their father's recent behavior, so I told Pam what had happened and swore her to secrecy, knowing she'd talk to Marge anyway.

I HAD a feeling Neil was really struggling with his feelings this time, and I tried my best to comfort him. Sex didn't have the normal calming influence. If anything, he was verging on rudeness much of the time, as if it were all *my* fault.

I began sleeping in the other room to give him some space, but nothing seemed to work for him. He was rude to everyone, but I noticed he increasingly picked on me at every opportunity, even in front of other people, which was most out of character for Neil because of his inherent good manners.

We struggled through the next weekend. I slipped back into bed with him, and for a day or so, he seemed to respond to kindness and attention, until the Monday afternoon when I had a short break between consultations, and he came bursting into the surgery.

"I've been dumped!" he shouted, his face red and twisted-looking, anger dripping from every word.

"What do you mean, dumped, love?"

"I've told you before," he shouted, "don't address me with endearments in public. It's disrespectful. And, for your information, Valerie has told me she won't need me around anymore because she has a new love in her life and he'll be taking her to Rotary every week."

"Well, I wouldn't be too worried about that, Neil," I said. "At last you and I can go somewhere as a couple and not worry about pretending. In any case, Val is entitled to her life, and if she's found someone to love, then good luck to her. Val is a very nice person, and I for one look forward to continuing the lovely friendship we've forged since I've been in Rotary. Val has always known we've been a couple, Neil, and she's incredibly supportive of us. I hope you don't say anything nasty to her because I would be very fucking pissed off, understand?"

He looked at me as if I'd just emerged from a lunatic asylum, turned on his heel, and marched away toward the house.

We ate dinner in silence. I knew Marge was worried, and I tried my best to console her afterward as we cleaned up the dishes while Neil sat bolt upright, staring at the television as if it was about to explode.

I EXPERIENCED the silent treatment again as we drove to Rotary, and surprise, surprise, he didn't want to sit with me, and so I gravitated to Val and her new beau, Roger. He seemed a really pleasant fellow, had been a member of Rotary in the past, and because of his friendship with Val had decided to rejoin. Peter and Wendy Carmichael were also at our table. They were close mates with Val and also great favorites of mine and had, Wendy assured me, a very gay group of friends and acquaintances. They'd married late in life, were childless by design, and were both mental health professionals. Wendy was a clinical psychologist working for a private organization, and Peter worked somewhere in the public hospital system as a mental health nurse. They were possessed of a wonderful sense of humor, sending themselves up continually, telling everyone they had a really "mad relationship" and endearing themselves to the other members by being such caring yet totally unpretentious people.

Wendy's eyes were everywhere, finally finding Neil and bellowing out that his presence was required at our table and refusing to take no for an answer. Suddenly I knew Wendy had deduced Neil was having a bad time, and there was no way she was allowing him to feel any less loved than he'd been in the past. I smiled gratefully at her intelligence and watched Peter also take Neil under his wing, speaking quietly to him and introducing Roger.

Thankfully Neil was quite pleasant and even helpful with advice, helping clear the way for Roger to rejoin Rotary.

I breathed a sigh of relief. Neil's angst seemed to have dissipated, and he even laughed and joked, his mood improving with every glass of wine. Suddenly I realized he'd had far more alcohol than he should, and I deftly removed his keys from his pocket as we walked out the door on our way home.

There was outright abuse this time, and I could feel my blood pressure rising as he carried on and on about what a thoughtless cunt I was and how I'd taken advantage of his hospitality and good nature. I guided the Merc home and parked next to the backdoor, manhandling him into the bedroom, stripping his clothes off, and throwing him into bed, without his customary evening shower.

Thankfully he was asleep in seconds, and I crept away to my own bed, hoping a good night's sleep wouldn't elude me, but sadly it did. I tossed and turned all night and was showered, dressed, and out of bed at an ungodly hour for me, moving quietly to the kitchen so I didn't wake Marge.

I needn't have worried. She was already up with the coffee brewed and some eggs in the pan. "Sit down, darling," she said, "and have some breakfast."

She looked sorrowfully at me, her eyes full of apology. "It looks like I've ruined everything for you. I really thought you'd forced him to grow up, but it appears he's just as much a child as ever. I must admit I don't know what to do," she said, tears slowly rolling down her cheeks.

I sprang to my feet and hugged her. Seeing Marge give way to emotion was a new experience for me, and I found it upsetting. I told her she was the most beautiful mother any person could have and that we were all so proud of her. "The fact is," I said, "that it really wouldn't matter what anyone said or did. Neil has to work this through for himself. We both know that, don't we?"

She nodded bravely, and I took over at the stove, cooking her breakfast for a change and making sure she ate it.

I HAD a particularly depressing morning. There were several animals to be euthanized, never a pleasant task, and regardless of how we rationalized the procedure in our minds, it always affected us. Sarah and I tried to help each other in these cases.

Neither of us spoke much about the other elephant in the room: Bruce had aged suddenly over the last few months, and I was fairly sure he wasn't all that fit. Two months ago we had put Sandy down because of pure old age, and Bruce was naturally missing him, the absence of his mate upsetting as he padded around the property looking for him.

By coincidence, only a week later Uncle Ted and Aunt Helga suddenly appeared at the backdoor on their way to spend the weekend with Toby and Macca. In the back of their dual-cab ute was the runt of a litter, a tiny little Kelpie bitch named Millicent, after the town in South Australia where the sire originated.

I couldn't help myself, of course. She was very small for a Kelpie, but she made up for her diminutive size with her hyperactivity. She couldn't sit still for an instant, but she was just beautiful, and I fell in love with her. So Millie came to live with us.

Jack and Sophie loved playing with her, and Boots, their little fox terrier, decided he was in love with her too and shadowed her everywhere. It was clear she didn't have the special qualities with horses Bruce had, but she was bright, boisterous, and such a loving creature that she fit in beautifully. She sensed Bruce was elderly, and to my amazement, she quieted down when she was around him, totally affectionate, and Bruce responded. I saw some joy come back into my old dog's eyes, and he looked for her when she wasn't around.

Millie did have an affinity for other sick animals, however, and while Bruce in his senior years usually hung around the back veranda so he was close to Marge and the warm kitchen, Millie was hard at work in the waiting room. Her instinct for herding, as with all Kelpies, was inherent. One of her first performances was to drive a dozen hens through the open door one day while our customers looked on in amazement, particularly when one of the hens simply couldn't wait any longer and laid an egg in a corner of the room!

This, I realized, was one of the reasons West Clinic had grown so quickly—kids and their parents loved the rural atmosphere. Bruce first and now Millie walked freely in and out of the waiting room and surgeries, and it was obvious to Sarah, Sam, and I that we shouldn't change a thing. Boots the fox terrier frequently escaped from custody, but Justine always knew where to find him. He would take a shortcut across the paddock—he could cover the two hundred meters or so in less than five minutes—just so he could spend time with his girlfriend. Thankfully he was neutered, but Millie wasn't. I realized I'd verged on being irresponsible and had Sam do the procedure immediately, with me assisting. Sam, I realized, was becoming increasingly confident because Sarah and I had stood alongside him, making a friend out of him instead of just an employee. There was almost nothing he couldn't do if we weren't around, and that was a great comfort because I would eventually need some more time off, and I knew Sarah and Richard wanted to start a family.

I WAS finishing up in my office when there was a tap on the door and Neil entered. I knew immediately he didn't come bearing glad tidings. His face was without expression, which was unusual for him. Neil was usually either happy or sad, no in-between. I said nothing, I wasn't about to make it easier for him. In fact, I was royally pissed off that he had been behaving so badly for so long over an issue that the general population found boring these days. Neil and I had been together for around nineteen months or so. In that time he'd avoided almost all discussion about our future, and for some obscure reason still felt badly about himself—worried at best that if his sexuality became public knowledge people would think less of him, at worst that it would cause a huge scandal, affecting the good name of his family.

Marge had been totally unperturbed on that level. She and I knew little Pam was just so smart and wise but also that she could be trusted to keep the information to herself. I had to admit I really didn't know if Justine and John knew the score, or if they did were cool with it, and that really was the only reason that Neil had to persist with the crazy attitude he'd adopted.

I was tired of it all. I'd been raised in a family where I'd been taught to embrace the truth and be prepared to live with it always. While I'd initially been circumspect in public, it really didn't matter who my partner was, and as long as I loved them and they loved me back, it was my business alone. That freedom was amplified when I attended university and lived with Toby and Macca, and where for a time I'd played both sides of the fence. But never, until now, had I been forced to live in the shadows and pretend I was something I really wasn't.

My attention focused on Neil, who by this time had dissolved into tears.

"I'm sorry, Dean," he sobbed, "but I just can't handle a gay relationship. I think we should just be friends, you know, with benefits, look after each other that way. I really can't handle anything else."

I know I should have been more understanding, but Neil's behavior over the last week had built up a deep resentment and I exploded.

"So that's it, is it, Neil? All a matter of image for you, putting on a brave face just like your late father, total dishonesty and a misguided ego trip, with no thought for anyone close to you, let alone me, you selfish bastard."

Suddenly a thought hit me, my guts turning to water with the tumultuous events surrounding me. "What's going to happen to West Clinic?" I barked. "I suppose you're going to walk away from your commitments there as well."

Neil looked thunderstruck, shaking his head wildly. "No, no, no, that's your business. The Andrews family wouldn't ever walk away from what you've done here. Not only is it a goldmine, but it's providing direct employment for the family and a learning curve for the grandchildren. It's extraordinary, and we wouldn't want to change anything."

"Fine, Neil," I said coldly, "then I'll see you every three months for board meetings. I'll take the day off work tomorrow and move my stuff back to Macca and Toby's if they'll have me."

"Oh, Dean, you can't. Mum would be distraught," Neil wailed. "She would be devastated. Won't you reconsider? I mean, we can continue pretty much as before."

"Yes, as long as we kept it a secret, Neil," I said sadly. "Which will take us absolutely nowhere as a couple. You just don't get it, do you? When two people love each other, they usually plan for a future together that is compatible with their lifestyle and each other. The way things are, I'm going one way, and you're going the other." I drew a breath and ceased my tirade for a few seconds, focusing on what I had to say so he understood me completely.

"Neil, I didn't think I could love anyone again after Danny and love them as completely as I've done with you. And yes, I've overlooked your obvious shortcomings, hoping you'd sort yourself out, but you haven't, and you won't. Your family are all lovely people, and I adore them. What you have managed to do is insult all our combined intelligence because you need to play games about who you are."

I looked at him. He appeared to be a lost, even frightened soul, as he searched for something more to say, but I'd been hurting for a long time now, and I was aware my tonality and demeanor were as cold and unforgiving as my mood and mindset.

"Neil," I spat, "why don't you fuck off now and leave me alone. You're just a waste of fucking space."

He turned on his heel and walked out, the once-strong shoulders and handsome features slumped in sorrow, a look of defeat on his face. I sniffled a bit, but bit my lip as I faced up to the next chapter of my life. I'd done it hard in the past, and I knew I had some difficult times ahead. It was no earthly use in lying down beside the road and feeling sorry for myself. I had to get up and get going again.

CHAPTER 25
SEPARATION

I FELT a little better after I spoke to Marge, and of course she understood. We had a leisurely dinner together, talking the issues through once more and agreeing that I'd had no alternative but to bring the relationship to its sorry end. There was no sign of Neil—the Merc was gone. So I packed an overnight bag, rounded up the dogs, and was on my way to Macca and Toby's.

I'd rung Toby earlier, and he wasn't surprised. My bed was there, and Macca met me at the door with a glass of red, helping me forget the shitty events of the day. I gave them all the facts. We never held anything back from each other, and I wasn't about to start now.

It was quieter than normal, and I suddenly realized my timing was spot-on because Toby and Macca looked—lonely.

Less than two months ago now, Dougie had gone next door with a cup of tea to wake Mrs. Browning and found her in her bed, sleeping the eternal sleep.

We'd all attended the funeral. She'd been an exceptional example to the community at large, the final years of her life having been spent as part of a big group of gay boys, and she'd admitted she'd found her calling, babysitting several of their kids and Jenny in particular. She'd been there for me when Danny died, mothered Paul and Dougie, and remained a huge supporter for them all through their troubles, never doubting for a moment that they would make up and resume their life together as nature intended. In turn, Paul and Dougie never forgot her kindness, and I remember thinking at the time how Mrs. Browning had, in addition to Toby and Macca, so capably filled the void left by the disinterest of their own parents.

Stephanie Mitchell, solicitor to the queens, had drawn up Mrs. Browning's will only six months prior, in which she left her only relative, a drug-dependent daughter, a significant amount in a trust fund, tightly controlled and administered.

What came as a complete surprise to everyone was the balance of the estate, which was worth close to two million dollars. Mrs. Browning left Paul and Dougie the house and contents. Macca, Toby, and I were the other beneficiaries, with a heavy suggestion that it was high time we started our own families!

I'd said nothing to Neil. At the time he wasn't even interested in a proper partnership, let alone becoming a parent again, but I guessed correctly that Toby and Macca would now take the logical step, particularly now that the first part of their family group had grown up so beautifully and moved next door.

In the morning Paul and Dougie were there, of course, including Jenny. There was a small crèche at Dougie's work, and most days she was there. She was so pleased to see me, and I chastised myself for not paying more attention to her upbringing. It had taken a crisis in my own life to be around her again, and I made a silent promise I would pay her more attention, particularly now Mrs. Browning wasn't around.

The boys hugged and kissed me, fussing over me like two old mother hens, which was pretty cool. In their lifetime they had been penniless and on the street, and now they were worrying about other people, like me.

Toby and Macca grinned but didn't say anything, and I thought how Mrs. Browning would be so proud they'd continued to bloom and grow.

Paul and Dougie didn't play around, their own peer group considering them something of an oddity. They claimed to have seen enough of life to be content with what they had, yet my situation was the first subject they brought up quietly when Toby and Macca weren't in the room. They made it clear they were prepared to make an exception in my case because they loved me and wanted to lessen my pain.

"Don't you dare feel bad because Neil didn't want you, Dean," Paul said. "Because we want you. You can sleep between us every night, and we'd look after you in every way possible."

"And we'd find a few new ways too," Dougie said seriously, and we laughed at each other, understanding full well they meant everything they said. It was hard for them because I knew, just like Macca and Toby, they liked Neil too, and this was their way of telling me they loved me in a special way.

I arrived at work to find Sarah there early. She didn't look all that well, claiming she'd eaten something that didn't agree with her. I nodded, then looked at her closely again, about to suggest she have the day at home to recover. But something wasn't quite right... I couldn't put my finger on it until she'd left the room. I raced after her and spun her around.

"You're preggers, aren't you?" I laughed, and she nodded, sniffling into her handkerchief.

I gathered her into my arms. She was nearly three months gone, and I'd been so absorbed in my own affairs that I'd totally missed all the signs. Sarah had been my friend since my very first day at university, loyal, supportive and caring through all the dramas of my life, and now it was time to support her.

Pam arrived for work and found Sarah and I hugging each other, laughing and bawling our eyes out in turn. Smart little Pam knew straightaway. She'd suspected, she said, a week ago, but didn't say anything because that's just the way she was.

I sat there with my girls, feeling a raft of different emotions. Pleasure and pride in Sarah's news tinged with a gentle jealousy that gay men having babies still faced censure in some respects. It also highlighted my own personal situation and brought into focus my deep longing to have babies of my own.

At twenty-eight years of age, I knew I didn't want to hang about much longer looking for a life partner, otherwise I'd be too old. Time marches up on those who're indecisive, and right now my bloody life sucked.

I'D TAKEN my dogs home to Macca and Toby's. Bruce had to be helped in and out of the Land Cruiser, and Millie stayed close to him all night. He was pleased to see them all. He did his business outside as usual in the morning, and Millie squatted beside him, the epitome of feminine practicality, keeping an eye on Bruce while she relieved herself.

I helped him out when we arrived at West Clinic, and he tottered up the laneway to the homestead, looking forward to some more food, the warm kitchen, and Marge—it was difficult to say who had adopted whom. Millie, of course, followed him, occasionally tugging at his collar to keep him on track. Bruce had mild canine epilepsy, something that had developed with great age. He'd had several convulsive attacks that weren't pleasant for him or those around him, but he always recovered quickly.

I was treating a Pekinese whose only real ailment was obesity and a mentally bereft owner who insisted on treating the animal as if it were a human being. Suddenly there was a hammering on the surgery door, and it burst open. Marge apologized but asked me if I could come up to the house quickly, as Bruce was having another of his convulsive fits. I palmed Mrs. Pekinese off to Sam, grabbed my bag, and walked briskly up to the homestead.

Millie was beside herself, so Marge held her while I tended to my old dog.

There was no way I was going to replicate Mrs. Pekinese's behavior. I gave Marge my bag to carry and picked Bruce up, talking quietly to him. I'd noticed how much condition he'd lost over the last few days, as he was now almost featherlight, a sure sign that he was close to the end of his life. Almost certainly there was another internal complication, like a tumor.

Millie watched me as we walked back to the surgery, where I walked inside and laid him on the table. The convulsions had stopped, but it was clearly time. My beautiful guys gathered around me. Sarah shaved his foreleg while Sam readied the needle and Marge held his head, tears running down her face.

Out of nowhere Justine appeared and held my hand, and Pam just sniffled into her hanky. I had to do the job myself. I pressed the needle into the flesh, and he opened his eyes, smiling at me with that knowing look of his. I slowly pushed the plunger home, and his eyes drooped and closed, and Bruce had gone to the Big Kennel in the sky.

We all bloody wailed, including Millie. Christ knows what our customers thought, but I didn't care. In the space of forty-eight hours my life partner and I had split, and now I'd had to end the suffering of my most faithful and beautiful canine companion. I knew I'd done the right thing. It was what I'd been preaching to owners ever since I graduated, but it still impacted on me like a tonne of bricks.

Gone was my very last link with Danny. I truly felt that life just couldn't get any fucking worse, and if someone had offered me a cup of hemlock, I probably would have thrown it down like a martini and fucking enjoyed it.

CHAPTER 26
JUSTINE

IT HAPPENED relatively quickly. I had a text message from Neil to say he'd be gone for an extended period, probably up to eight weeks overseas.

Nothing more.

It was Marge who confirmed he was traveling with Wendy and Peter Carmichael, who were the quintessential globetrotters and had taken Neil under their wing. I was relieved in several ways. Firstly, because Wendy and Peter were responsible people, and, for the sake of his family at least, Neil would be in good hands, and secondly it would put some literal distance between Neil and me and allow me to resume my life, albeit on my own.

A few days later, Valerie called into West Clinic and asked when I was returning to Rotary. I'd only missed two meetings, but she was persistent as I squirmed in my chair trying to find an excuse.

"Look," she said, "no one will stand in judgment of you—they all know about you and Neil. The only issue for members is a degree of sadness that it didn't work out, so you'll find a surprising level of support. Besides—" She grinned. "—I do have an ulterior motive, because I'm standing for president, and I'll need every vote I can get."

"What makes you think I'd vote for you?" I said cheekily, my sense of humor almost working again.

"Darling," she said very directly, "you wouldn't fucking dare do otherwise."

I'D JUST finished setting a cat's broken leg, with Pam assisting, when my next visitor arrived—Justine.

"Heard you're going to Rotary next Tuesday night," she said, and I knew the bush telegraph was working well.

Rather than dare ask who'd said what to whom, I nodded and smiled.

"Good," she said, "could you pick me up at six o'clock? Pam is babysitting for me."

I knew better than to question a member of the Andrews family on anything, but I was on my guard. Even Blind Freddie would have known about my relationship with her father, and while Neil refused to talk about it to his daughter and son, I wondered if this was an attempt by the kids to become involved or even entangled in what was patently my business alone.

I arrived in good time, and the kids were almost out of control. Jack's voice boomed out the moment I walked in the door, and his sister's shrill tones were equally invasive. Pam put her hands over her ears and pointed upstairs to their bedrooms as I readied myself for storytelling duty.

Jack and Sophie told their mother they loved my stories because they were "different." I did repeat a lot of the old fairy tales but put my own spin on them, always adding animals as the heroes. But it required a good memory, because they would invariably slip off to sleep before I'd finished, and on the next occasion I was expected to continue where I'd left off.

Justine looked amazing, her hair braided in a style that would have looked silly on most young people but looked just right for her. She wore a comfortable skirt with a roll-neck pullover with a smart soft leather jacket, the combination highlighting her good looks.

We'd always traveled to Rotary in Neil's SUV, but as Justine was my guest, I decided I'd better clean up the Land Cruiser. I realized I'd never remove the smell of disinfectant completely, but I managed to make my venerable old four-wheel drive habitable, and she noticed.

"I've never seen this bloody thing so tidy," she laughed, putting me at ease immediately.

Valerie waved us over as we arrived, seating us with Roger and her.

We hardly had our feet under the table before we were besieged by the lovely dirty old men who represented most of my fellow members. They were keen to meet Justine and know her life story, all of them allowing their imagination to run wild. She answered polite questions about her father and the Carmichaels and the status of their world tour. Not once did she make me feel uncomfortable. She was the perfect partner, focusing and supporting my enjoyment of the evening, flirting with the old lechers in good fun, but always a lady to her fingertips.

It came as no surprise that Valerie asked her to consider joining and that our fellow members wanted more of her company whether she was a Rotarian or not.

We rocked in her front door around 9:30 p.m. Pam pulled on her parka for the ten-minute walk home and air-kissed us good-bye.

Justine beckoned me. She knew my weakness well, and we crept up the stairs to the large room where the night-light was on. The two lovely ones were sound asleep, their innocence and unspoiled beauty on display for all to see. Justine and I really connected at this level. She knew how I loved kids, and to be honest, the two little things sleeping so soundly were among the prime reasons I was moving back in with Marge—my things were back in my room, and the Andrews family seemed to feel happier about the situation.

I'd told them, however, that when Neil eventually returned home I'd probably leave again, and they all seemed to understand.

But in the meantime it was important that Jack and Sophie had some constancy in their dealings with adults. Even though we silly grown-ups couldn't get on together, it was no reason to desert these two beautiful little people—quite the opposite. I felt we should all try harder for their sake, so they could grow up without stress and confrontation in their lives, just loved by everyone.

Justine kissed me good night. She smelled of lavender, usually an old lady's perfume, but on her it was just right, emphasizing both her physical beauty and her amazing mental strength.

I had a cuppa with Marge. She was so glad to have me home again, she said, where I should be, and simply refused to discuss the future, which, she pointed out, would resolve itself. I crawled into my bed after a shower, allowing my muscles to relax, and contemplated my life. On one hand, I was lonely and unfulfilled, the intimacy of my relationship with Neil had gone, and if I was honest, I missed it. On the other hand, I was a lucky man. I had three distinct but equally supportive family groups who invested their time and energy in me—my parents and sisters; Toby, Macca, Paul, Dougie, and Jenny; and now the Andrews family, who gave every impression of being more possessive of me than all the others put together, particularly since the bond between myself, Justine, and her kids seemed to be growing all the time.

WE CONTINUED to attend Rotary together every week, and finally Valerie's persistence wore her down, and Justine agreed to become a member. As was the situation in my case, she was very honest about the constraints on her time, particularly when she was busy as a wedding planner in the summer months. In the meantime, however, she was embraced for her management skills and experience as we prepared to organize the District Conference for the following year.

The night before her induction, I asked her why she hadn't waited for her father to sponsor her, as he'd done for me, and she laughed.

"You know what he's like, Deano," she said grimly. "He'd find a way to say no. So I just do my own thing, thank you very much, and he can have his wall-to-wall conniptions in his own time. I'm too bloody busy to have Dad running my life or listen to the sermons about being a nice young woman, because I'm not!"

I laughed at her view of life. She and I were so similar because we both dealt with the priorities first and found the fine detail usually looked after itself.

Importantly, neither of us seemed to worry about public opinion. In fact, we delighted in being as outrageous as possible while Neil was overseas, so we could finally let off steam.

There was no doubt she was a strong woman. What was comforting to me was that I was certain she had my back. For some unknown reason I was the recipient of the same degree of loyalty she afforded everyone else in the Andrews family group, and with her support no one would ever dare push me around.

I WAS finishing up work a few days later when she rang in a panic. "Boots!" she gasped. "He's not breathing properly, and he's frothing at the mouth."

"Lay him on the backseat of the car, clear his airway, strap the kids in, and drive slowly up here. I'll keep the side door to the surgery open."

We somehow possessed the ability to calm each other in times of stress, paying strict attention to the real priorities—in this case, Jack and Sophie.

She arrived a few minutes later with their little dog in her arms, the kids behind her wide-eyed and distressed.

Poor Boots was already stuffed, I reckoned. I pumped his stomach, but it was obvious we were too late. Despite Justine's best endeavors, Boots was the world's best escapologist, and this time he'd picked up poison bait meant for the rabbit population, which had been building up again in the district.

Her eyes met mine. She knew what had to be done, but she didn't know how to handle the kids, so after sedating their little dog, I led them into the waiting room. Fortunately, Sam was still in the building and agreed to take over in the surgery.

I took a deep breath, emphasizing that none of this was their fault, explaining what was happening right now with Boots. I told them the truth—that Boots would never recover, and we had to make sure he didn't suffer anymore by putting him to sleep. The kids with the big voices sat there with silent tears running down their faces. So I took my time with them, knowing full well that part of their innocence had disappeared but remembering what life had been like for me and my sisters, growing up in the country where we were exposed to the best and the worst of life and death in the animal kingdom.

Suddenly I had an idea and phoned Marge. Millie had been all afternoon in the kitchen with her, another reason Boots had wandered away.

Marge and Millie arrived, and Millie managed to make the kids smile just a little as she wriggled and licked her way all over them, so I had my answer and went into the office. Consulting the records, I found who I was looking for.

Within twenty minutes Justine, Marge, the kids, and I were at a breeder's house looking over a two-month-old litter of Jack Russell terriers. There were only two pups remaining unsold, a male and a female, and the kids fell in love with them both.

Justine looked troubled, and I took her to one side.

"They'll want both of them, Dean," she said. "But the truth is we can hardly afford one this month. Things are quite tight for me in the winter months."

"The only thing I want you to worry about is the life cycle of the pups, which is about fifteen years or so. By that time the kids will be in their late teens and more interested in girls and boys, not little dogs. It's a real commitment for you."

She nodded and smiled, probably trying to work out how she could borrow money from her grandmother, when I cut across her thoughts.

"I never intended that you or anyone else in the family would step up to this. I've already got a great deal from the breeder as she's a West Clinic customer, and the pups are a gift from me to the children."

"Dean," Justine said quietly so the kids couldn't hear, "I can't ask you to do this. You've been fucked around royally by the Andrews family, and all you can do is turn the other cheek."

"What part didn't you understand?" I said sweetly, not acknowledging her thinly veiled reference to her father's behavior. "You and the kids are really precious to me, and to see them being brought up so well with all the right values is reward enough. I've always wanted kids," I said seriously, "and Jack and Sophie are wonderful. It's almost like they're my kids anyway."

I stopped and thought about what I'd said. "And, well, there is another kid," I said quietly. "I need your help."

"Of course," Justine said, probably thinking me quite insane, "anything to help."

"Her name's Jenny, and she's a little older than Jack and Sophie. Only recently I promised to spend some more time with her. I've been a big part of her early upbringing, but after I left to come over here, we've not had any time together at all. I think a bit of interaction with Jack and Sophie would be really good for her. She adores animals, and maybe she could have the occasional sleepover with your two. What do you think?"

Justine cuddled me. "I think you're the greatest."

She smelled nice, and Old Dick stirred for just a moment.

"You're staying the night," she said. "There's a meal in the crock pot. After I feed the kids, we'll have ours, and we'll talk."

The casserole was delicious—fresh home-cooked tucker with homegrown salad first, just like the Americans, I told her.

"Oh yes," she said, smiling, "that's where it came from. I had a few months in the Midwest of the United States as an exchange student. Much better to have the salad before the main course—too much flatulence otherwise."

We looked at each other and roared. What a pleasant bit of nonsense after the stressful day we'd had. We toasted each other with a glass of red.

I left early the next morning because all my clean clothes were in my bedroom at the homestead. The Land Cruiser belched black smoke, its normal behavior for a cold start, and I slowly edged my way to the road gate, closed to keep wandering stock out. I left the Cruiser idling as I hopped out and opened it, when a familiar vehicle came in sight, and my heart nearly stopped.

It was John, and I felt the blush rise in my cheeks as he grinned broadly, slowing a little, blowing the horn and waving madly, then speeding and heading for his work in town.

JENNY WAS ecstatic. All weekend she'd gone from one adventure to another, playing "nursie" with Pam in the surgery as we treated the various domestic patients, then out on the tractor and trailer with Marge, feeding hay to the cattle. Then she discovered where eggs came from and was more surprised than shocked.

Jack and Sophie shadowed her, and it was obvious they had the makings of a real team, which delighted Justine and me.

I rang Paul and Dougie as I'd promised on Saturday night. Dougie was always paranoid about Jenny's welfare, but this time he was very relaxed.

"Darling Deano," he said, "why should we worry? Our daughter couldn't be in better hands, and it sounds like your lady friend is very nice too, so just enjoy Little Madam's company while we have a bloody good rest."

It was late Sunday afternoon when I drove in the driveway. Jenny had been fast asleep in her seat but quickly realized where she was. Paul and Dougie couldn't get a word in edgeways as she regaled them with her adventures. She was still chattering as Dougie fed her an early dinner, then was asleep in minutes.

The five of us sat around in Toby and Macca's dining room, Dougie slipping next door to check on their daughter and smiling as he returned.

"Absolutely dead to the world." He grinned. "Thank you, Deano. You've always been there for her, and now, in the middle of all your drama with Neil, you haven't forgotten her. I think that's really special."

Paul smiled at me and nodded in agreement, his hand rubbing my knee. They were giving me the come-to-bed message because they reckoned this was the only way they could make me feel better.

I laughed at them all. So uncomplicated, so loving, and so bloody spot-on with their remarks, because they knew me better than I knew myself.

Macca elected to walk me to the Land Cruiser after I helped clear the dishes. He was probably the only person who'd understood my motivation after Danny died. He was, at that time, even more approachable than Toby because he'd lived as a straight man and understood better than anyone what I'd gone through.

"I'm completely over it, Macca," I said. "The gay relationship thing. It's brought only misery and bloody heartache. First Danny, then Barry, and now Neil. I want to have babies, Macca," I cried, surprised at the level of emotion within me. "I also need to be supported. You can't understand what it's like to be working with such responsibility every day of my life and going home to nothing. I mean, yes, I've got the Andrews family, and I've got you guys, but it's not the same as having someone there who can be an emotional prop when I need it. Someone whose main purpose in life is to be there for me, who looks after all the domestic shit but is also capable of being a sounding board when I've got a difficult decision to make. And I've had plenty of those lately."

I hesitated, but went on in a quieter voice because I knew Macca was already on side and I already knew what direction my life could take in the future.

"I want to get married," I said almost pleadingly to Macca, "to a woman, so I can have babies of my own and a simple, uncomplicated life where I don't have every asshole advising me how to live my life just because I'm considered different."

I stopped, surprised at how I'd given vent to my feelings. But if there was anyone with whom I could have done so without being judged, it was dear, lovely Macca. The look he gave me was full of compassion, yet there was also a hint of censure.

"Deano," he whispered to me, arms on either side of me as I leaned against the driver's door, "life isn't like that, and you of all people understand that well. You don't go and get married just because you want kids or need someone to give you emotional support. You only marry someone if you love them, just like Tobes and I, and kids come along as a result of that love and commitment."

I nodded dully. "But you haven't been worn out by it all like I have. I'd be prepared, if I needed it, to have a guy on the side or maybe a monthly trip to the saunas. There's plenty of married men doing that right now."

"You sound like you already have someone in mind," he said, looking me in the eye.

"Yes," I said levelly, "I do."

CHAPTER 27
THE BIG DAY

OUTSIDE IT was a balmy autumn day with an almost cloudless sky as I paced around Toby and Macca's kitchen, adjusting my scratchy shirt collar, which had been starched stiffer than an adolescent's prick, the price I suffered for refusing point-blank to wear a fucking tie.

Women! I'd been badgered and nearly driven insane. What I should wear, what music should be played, what flowers in the chapel? All the stuff I wasn't remotely interested in. In the end I capitulated completely and told her to do what she had to do, but use the KISS principle—keep it simple, stupid.

Even that went down like a lead balloon. She just wanted everything to be perfect. "This is the most important day of your life," she'd said, "more important even than graduation."

I thought wryly to myself that it would need to be better than my graduation. I'd been pissed off my face. I hoped today just might be a little more uplifting.

Mum and Dad just laughed and poked fun at me. Good old cool-as-a-cucumber Dean, currently pacing around the place like a caged animal. In fact, I was totally frustrated because things seemed to be moving with glacial slowness. I just wished it was all over, and we could relax with some good tucker and a nice glass of red or three.

"He's here. Get your arses into gear," Macca shouted as the limo pulled into the driveway.

Keith Greenway, a fellow Rotarian and owner of a fleet of hire cars and limousines was at the wheel of his favorite vehicle, a Hummer. The big radiator grille and tractor-style tires contrasted with the slightly effeminate silver paintwork, but I knew Keith had given a wedding to another operator just so I could have this vehicle, his pride and joy. He'd dressed up too, in a uniform with gold braid everywhere, looking absolutely resplendent as he held the door open for Mum.

My eyes watered a little. She looked stunning today. Her recovery from her illness had reached a plateau, and she probably wouldn't improve much more, but she wasn't about to let that spoil her enjoyment of her eldest kid's big day.

She looked so elegant. Her crutches had been replaced by a single silver-headed cane, and she walked with just the slightest limp. Dad looked dashing in a navy blue lounge suit and burgundy tie.

Macca had scrubbed up well also. Toby had bullied and nagged him to have his hair cut properly and styled, and because he was my best man, we had sort of matching suits, although we'd agreed between ourselves they couldn't be identical—that would be too silly.

We had a fight with her over that as well, and we actually won that round.

But Macca was definitely in her corner, the inner circle as it were, and helped her make many of the "extra" arrangements, whatever they were supposed to be.

It had started to piss me off. The ceremony was to be at three o'clock, and we headed to the chapel where we would be arriving around forty-five minutes early.

"What on earth have you lot been up to?" I grouched, as Macca just smiled sweetly and handed me a glass of red from the limo's minibar.

Mum just laughed at me over her gin and tonic, and Dad's eyes twinkled as he enjoyed his first beer for the day.

"I mean," I said, "the idea of me arriving like a big sheila with everyone standing or sitting around waiting is a bit bloody crass, don't you think? I mean, I'll feel like a fool. A couple should walk in together these days."

Macca's eyes sparkled—he was really enjoying himself.

"You know better than anyone what she's like," Macca said seriously, "so go with the flow, and we'll get there. Just stay cool, Deano. We've talked about this day so often. You'll be a married man before you know what's happened, so just relax, okay?"

I knew I had to cut poor Macca some slack. He'd had my back for so long over the years I'd nearly forgotten why I'd demanded he be my best man. He understood me like no other person. No wonder he was such a good counselor.

As my thoughts unraveled, the big Hummer turned into the main driveway of Henry University, and I could feel myself begin to perspire under my shirt.

This simply wasn't me to behave like this. I was normally so calm, cool, and collected, sailing through one bloody crisis after another, but I finally recognized it was a red-letter day for me, and bugger it, I was entitled to feel a touch nervous.

"You all right, mate?" Dad asked as we swung into the forecourt of the Grand Chapel at the International Center for Human Partnerships.

"To be honest," I said to everyone in the car, "I'm as nervous as a turkey the week before Christmas."

They roared with laughter at my expense, but it was Mum who fixed me with a gimlet-like stare. "Dean, if you didn't feel like that, there would be something wrong with you and this whole scenario, but you do, and you know what you are doing is a big step but the right one. Dad and I made the same step all those years ago, and now the first of our kids is getting married. This is your day, and, speaking from experience, a few nerves will actually help you enjoy it."

I LOOKED out the window in disbelief as Macca grinned at me.

It looked like the entire contents of Simmons Park stables had assembled on either side of a bloody huge, long red carpet! Stable hands held their bridles, smartly dressed in what I recognized was the Simmons Park uniforms, usually only seen at the Melbourne or Caulfield Cups. Ray and Sharon were up front, beaming away together with their kids, Georgia and Luke, all looking pretty smug about themselves, and beside them were Clancy, Lim, and their kids, who, Macca informed me, had flown in from Hong Kong the night before.

The enormity of the organization behind the scenes just to get this far didn't escape me. I looked at the Simmons Park guard of honor and then looked at Macca. "W-w-why," I asked, "why all of this?"

"Isn't it amazing?" Macca said, "that the people who put the most into life, the people who do the most for society, are the ones most surprised when society decides to return their contribution to them in some small way."

"Well said, Robert," said Dad, and I looked at them as if they were madmen.

Then suddenly I felt both incredibly humble and even vulnerable, realizing finally the vast scope of the "extras" Macca had alluded to.

It was Mum who put it all into context for me. "What she's done, dear, is simply to demonstrate how much you've put into life in a relatively short period and how much you are appreciated by so many people. I happen to agree with her. You've been so unselfish and never looked for reward from all the animals you've helped, whether on two legs or four."

Keith opened the door, and we stepped out of the Hummer. Suddenly, behind a copse of pine trees, I glimpsed a familiar vehicle—the pub bus—and beside it the Glenfield Retirement Home bus that our club had supplied.

"What's with the retirement home bus, Keith?" I said under my breath.

"Well, they didn't need it this afternoon and offered it to the club, complete with a driver, because they knew the pub bus wouldn't hold all the members."

I laughed at last. "What a lot of pissheads."

"Yes, we are, Deano. We can smell free grog miles away."

SUDDENLY THE fog cleared in my brain. Now I understood her strategy. It was much better to arrive early so I could spend time with all these people who had obviously given their precious time and money to enhance my special day.

It would be too late to show our appreciation after we'd walked through the guard of honor, and I mentally thanked her for her thoughtfulness.

I walked over to the Simmons family first, shaking hands with everyone, then went from horse to horse. Luke had thoughtfully supplied a bag of carrots, and I had immediate equine attention as I spoke to them and they "talked" back to me, nuzzling my head and shoulders with everyone looking on. I made sure I spoke to the stable hands too. They were the engine room there, I knew that, and so did the Simmons family.

I didn't ask but assumed they were all there on their own time because they wanted to be, and I made sure they knew I was on their wavelength too. The logistics alone would have entailed a very early start for everyone.

I emerged from the other end of the honor guard of horses, and my mouth fell open again. At least ten rows of chairs stood on either side of the doorway into the chapel, every one of them filled with people young and old, and with animals of all ages and description.

"She grabbed your database from work, contacted them all by e-mail, swore them to secrecy, and invited them here with their pets," Macca said. "It's a bit like an episode from *All Creatures Great and Small*, isn't it?"

There were lambs, goats, dozens of dogs and cats, and even a snake curled around its owner's neck like a scarf. And there were birds—some of them singing their hearts out—and an aged cockatoo I knew well. I tried to scuttle away before Albert the cocky saw me, but I wasn't fast enough. I always seemed to provoke him on sight, and he let fly with some blistering language. "Jesus Fucking Christ!" Albert roared. "What a fuck-up!"

Mum, Dad, and Macca held their sides, but Albert wasn't finished yet.

"Where's my fucking tea, you asshole?" he shrieked as his owner dropped a cover over him, and he was effectively silenced.

Then my customers began loudly applauding. I wondered if the applause was for Albert or for me as I stood there with a silly look on my face, but it was obvious I had work to do. I walked around with Macca while Mum and Dad waited for me. Out of nowhere a chair was found for Mum, and she gratefully rested, watching her eldest kid progressively making a dick of himself. I spoke to each and every one, shaking hands, kissing people whose names completely escaped me, listening politely to interminable stories of pet illnesses and recoveries, but all of them focused on me and my big day.

I just had my head up, and there was bloody Adrian from 3 TripleG, grinning madly, his finger over his lips, cautioning me not to say anything nasty, because, guess what, we were on air, and those listeners who couldn't be at the chapel were breathing fucking heavily, waiting for words of wisdom from their Saturday morning veterinary surgeon.

"It's all right, Deano." He laughed. "The station and listeners wanted you to know they're on your team today and wanted to wish you all the best for a great day and a wonderful life together."

I took the microphone, said what I had to say, and Adrian embraced me. We'd done a lot of work together for the community, and he wanted me to know he cared.

Finally, we walked into the Grand Chapel together, Macca and I flanked by Mum and Dad. Immediately I heard David Canning, my old friend and celebrant, roar "everyone please stand." *Oh yes, here comes the fucking bride—this is so embarrassing.*

But it wasn't embarrassing. I forgot my nerves completely as we walked down the huge aisle together. There, on my left, were the Morgan family, Mr. and Mrs. Morgan and all their kids and grandkids as well.

"He would be really proud of you today, Dean," Mr. Morgan said, and I felt my lip quiver. He noticed and held my hands. "I didn't mean to upset you, Dean, but I can feel him around us today. You need to take those positive feelings with you. That's what he would have wanted. He would want you to be happy, that's all, and the Morgan family are here to make sure you get started in the right way."

I laughed at their Irish logic, then hugged them both, moving to the next row where Simon and Julie stood, smiling uncertainly, but smiling nonetheless. I made sure I put them at ease. How could I not do so, because between them in a capsule was the evidence of how right things had become in their world. He was only four months old, and with my permission they'd named him Daniel Dean Morgan, reminding us all that life indeed moves on for those of us that allow it to do so. I kissed them and thanked them for attending, but I couldn't help myself.

"What, no tongue today, dear? You're slipping," I said to Simon, and the three of us laughed, at peace with the world and ourselves.

Then there were the rabble-rousers, sitting together in a block on either side of the aisle. The highly salubrious members of the Western Heights Rotary Club. The moment I hove in sight, they began cheering—anyone would think they were teenagers on schoolies week instead of respected business people and leaders of our community. They'd already begun celebrating, I realized, and yes, they were on the face of it a bunch of alcoholic misfits, but seldom had they ever had such an excuse as this! They loved us, we were special to them, and they wanted us to know they stood behind us all the way. I also realized it wasn't just their love of a few drinks. Through us they could see tangible evidence of their hard work—people's lives being turned around because they had focused on community attitudes and changed perceptions.

The film and television cameras would be whirring away somewhere at the front of the chapel, I knew, and just for the record, my fellow Rotarians wanted to make sure everyone else knew they were there because they bloody well wanted to be.

As I moved toward the front, I couldn't believe my eyes. Two rows away was a face I hadn't seen for several years. Still tall, dark, slim, and still a hunk, my dear old buddy, Will! We'd kept in touch. He helped me recover after losing Danny, and we'd had several assignations no one had known about. But his loyalty to me had shone through it all, particularly since he'd been through several boyfriends himself. Recently he'd met a real keeper, Brian, a little older but with a very mature outlook to match. Sarah and I were delighted—not only were she and Will still the closest of friends, but Richard and Brian had also become mates. They were sitting together, of course. Sarah had elected to leave Matilda at home with a sitter so they could relax and have a few hours away from "kid duty."

Dearest Sarah, she had been my rock through so much of my checkered history. Never judgmental, always there to support me when I needed it, both at work and afterward. She pushed her way to the aisle and threw her arms around me. She had become the other face of West Clinic. There was no doubt she was a brilliant veterinary surgeon and, being a woman, she was probably more adept than me in managing the balance between business and pleasure. But the secret of West Clinic, we realized, was that we were a great team. There was simply nothing we couldn't do if we worked at it together, and because of our closeness, we were family to each other. There wasn't any subject that had been off-limits between us over the years. I often wondered what might have happened if other people hadn't intervened in our lives. But all bets were off when Richard came along—it was so obvious they were meant for each other.

I fell out of Sarah's arms and into Barry's, and Mum and Dad greeted him warmly. Behind him was Greg, smiling broadly, holding Samantha, their own little bundle of joy, and I thought how love had conquered all in their case.

I cuddled her for a moment, and she smiled at me. "Usually a sign that she's about to take a crap." Barry grinned. "So watch out."

How easy it could have been for Barry and me to be partners. Instead our lives had taken a totally different path, but we were still happy as individuals, and we were still friends, which was more important.

Barry and Greg were right behind the next raucous group, who were making almost as much noise as the Rotarians but being much more theatrical—Toby and Macca's friends and their families, led by Geoffy Stevenson.

Geoffy was feeling no pain. He'd clearly had a glass or two, which had made him all the more loquacious. Lisa had a death grip on him, anchoring him in place, but his excitement for me on my day was infectious, and the remainder of the group joined in like excited children. They had one thing in common—they loved a good time. But similar to the Rotarians, they put a lot more back into the community than they ever took out. Like all young people of this generation, they were absolutely nonjudgmental. I could have been marrying a kangaroo for all they cared, as long as I was happy.

They fell silent as my eyes shifted toward the end of the aisle. Mum gripped my arm tightly, as did Dad. There she stood, almost regally, in a beautiful pale lemon suit, a spray of daphne on her lapel, the kids around her feet quiet for once, as I'd put in a special request to Jack that he keep his volume lower than usual.

I grinned to myself. That would last until the exciting stuff began to happen, and then they would promptly forget and lose it. But they were kids, and this day was also about them as part of our family group, so who was I to get uptight, anyway?

She smiled her beautiful smile. No doubt about it, she was the most beautiful woman I had ever seen, and the last few months of settled family happiness had enhanced her enjoyment of life and love.

I walked up to her and kissed her on the cheek, and she kissed me back, handing me a single red rose. The kids excitedly jumping up on me, volume limitations forgotten, much to everyone's amusement. John sidled up, looking quite protective, and Mum and Dad joined the remainder of the Andrews family.

Macca led off to one side and smiled at Toby as I walked toward the old celebrant standing there with a broad grin on his face.

The figure in front of him turned toward me, and the blue splashes of light like the lake at Mount Gambier twinkled in his face above a dazzling white smile.

And my heart bloody sang.

I found myself short of breath, just as I had the first time we met, and suddenly nothing else mattered. Just Neil Andrews and me, my mind flashing back to the day when my life decided to do a U-turn and headed in the right bloody direction at last.

CHAPTER 28
THE U-TURN

I GUESS to an extent we're all creatures of habit. I for one always started my day in the office reading my e-mails, a necessary job but one that usually didn't tax my lack of early-morning cognitive powers.

Suddenly I was wide-awake. A sender and address popped up that I hadn't seen for nearly two months, and despite my negative mindset, my heart began to hammer on my bloody rib cage, because it was Neil.

I'd been doing really well, making small steps to move on with my life. Yet here was evidence that my emotions were still in lockdown because I just couldn't control my bloody breathing. And if that wasn't bad enough, Old Dick stirred and stood bolt upright, the first real performance since he'd left.

"Christ, I'm hopeless," I muttered, trying to focus on his message, which was mysteriously entitled "Unfinished Business."

I started reading again, got to the third line, and freaked out. The word I'd been skimming over *was* unfortunately still there, and I froze in horror.

Depression.

Depression had killed Danny, and my life had changed forever. Ever since that terrible time, I'd become gruesomely familiar with this aspect of men's mental health, particularly with Macca and Toby working as counselors in this specific area. And now this. Neil had been suffering from depression right under my nose, and I hadn't even picked up on it. I felt a wave of guilt sweep over me, and I cried out at the pain of what could have been another tragedy in my life.

I tried to calm myself, sitting rigidly in the chair in front of the screen as images of Neil flashed through my mind, and the more I thought, the more obvious it became that he'd been in trouble all along, probably before we even met. The mood swings, the irrational logic, the irritability, the unsmiling negativity of a gay man trying to live in a straight world. I began to understand how such sadness seemed to creep up on him from nowhere, rendering me powerless to help him.

I reached for the phone, hoping his was on global roaming.

THE BANGKOK flight landed around 7:45 p.m. at Tullamarine. I guessed the long wait thereafter was due to the sheer volume of international passengers disembarking at the same time, and I hopped from one foot to another, obsessed with the thought of seeing him alive and well. The past thirty-six hours or so had left me in a state of torment, worried sick about him, the feeling of guilt increasing rather than going away.

You fucking idiot. You didn't think about anything other than your own feelings, and because of you he could have ended his life like Danny. Yeah, just make Dean Prentice your other half and take a one-way trip to the mortuary, because he's no stranger to tragedy.

He strode through the doors, pushing a trolley loaded with luggage, his brilliant blue eyes searching for me, then finally swinging around and catching my gaze. He actually *laughed* at me!

I was shocked. Neil Andrews was essentially a serious person, and he hardly ever smiled. But there it was, a huge grin plastered all over his face. He stopped in his tracks for a moment, leaving the trolley, and we just ran at each other, totally ignoring anyone who happened to be in the way. Our lips meshed together, arms flew around each other, and I knew nothing else mattered. He was mine, and I would keep him safe.

Understandably, we'd been making quite a lot of noise, and we were, after all, standing in the middle of a busy airport arrivals hall with people streaming past in every direction. There was a polite cough from somewhere behind Neil, and he grinned again as the not unattractive face of a middle-aged security guy spoke to him.

"Sir," he said, eyes twinkling, "I realize your reunion is of a passionate nature. However, could I remind you that your *trolley* could be regarded as unattended and therefore a security risk. Why don't you show me where your car is located," he said and smiled at me. "I'll assist you in the transfer of the duty-free and all the other *goodies*?"

Not another queen. Neil grinned at me with a conspiratorial wink.

We were in the Land Cruiser on our way home, and I looked across at him. He looked amazing. He'd lost weight and was tanned and fit-looking, and I was having trouble breathing again. In the space of half an hour, he'd embraced me publicly and continued to demonstrate affection in a very open manner, which wasn't the old reserved Neil at all. And on top of everything else, he couldn't wipe the smile from his bloody face, which was rare for him, and which I suddenly found contagious and was grinning back at him.

My man now had a sense of humor, which I realized I'd never seen before. It was both marvelous and transforming all at once. He was the same person but different in the most beautiful way.

Marge was waiting for us in the kitchen with hot chocolate and a light supper, as was Millie, who nearly turned herself inside out with joy at his arrival. He knew something wasn't right and turned around, looking distressed.

"Where's Bruce?" he asked in a whisper, and I told him what and when it had happened, expecting him to lose it completely.

"Oh," he said, still sorrowful with a hint of a tear but quite in control of himself.

"It's okay, love," I said. "You can let it all out, we certainly have."

He turned to me, in front of his mother, and kissed me gently on the lips.

"Bruce was your last link with Danny, wasn't he? You must have really felt like shit, happening so soon after you and I split up." He turned to Marge. "Thanks for looking after him, Mum. You've done a great job."

THE NEXT morning felt like the best day of my life, and perhaps it was. It was a joyous occasion for the three of us to sit in the kitchen and be a real family. No lies, no dodging issues, everything was on the table now, and it was much more than bacon and eggs, because it was the future of the Andrews family. The high I'd found myself on at this early hour showed no signs of diminishing either, mainly because it was very clear that the new, confident Neil saw himself as the leader now, certainly not the follower. I breathed a sigh of relief. The stress involved in running West Clinic, then running our partnership, had evaporated, and I relaxed like never before. Not one of my previous partners had come even close to taking charge of our home life so I could concentrate on doing what I'd been trained to do—being a veterinarian.

We finished breakfast and went into the lounge room, sitting on the old club suite together, me with my head on his shoulder like a lovesick teenager, waiting for the hordes from hell to arrive.

Jack and Sophie were ahead of their mother, Jack screaming out for "Pa" before they were even out of the car, tearing through the kitchen, flying through the air, cuddling and kissing us both. Miss Sophie trotted along behind, a lovely chubby little possum creature who crawled up our legs and made herself totally indispensable by being just so cute and lovely, while her brother did it all by sheer force of personality.

I heard Justine come in, followed by John, Pam, and not-so-little-anymore Angela.

"Where did they sleep last night?" hissed Justine, and there was a muted "together" from Marge. "Oh thank Christ," Justine shouted, as she rushed inside, throwing her arms around us.

That performance was followed closely by her brother and his wife, whom I knew was about to report for work. "You're not going there yet," I said to Pam. "We'll get some backup for you. It appears there's some family business at hand."

With that, her husband burst into tears.

Christ, I meant to be helpful.

But John was focused on his dad, not me. "Dad," he said, "are you all right?"

And it was then I understood that there was a lot more to this saga than met the eye.

"I think it's time you told me the whole story," I said to Neil, who for a moment looked panic-stricken, then calmed down, because apparently the truth wasn't too bad anyway.

I'D READ his e-mail thoroughly and understood what he'd put himself through over the last months. Wendy and Peter Carmichael, out of friendship and a sense of medical duty, had included him in their holiday. Wendy, together with my GP, Darren Clarke, had diagnosed dysthymia, a depressive illness, and decided Neil needed psychotherapy, albeit on the run, so instead of relaxing on their holiday, Wendy and Peter had the case of Neil Andrews on their minds the whole time.

"Psychotherapy was basically talking it through on a one-on-one basis," Neil had said.

So the conversation at mealtimes had been predictable, going over old behavioral patterns, talking the issues through, with Peter taking over when Wendy was exhausted, or when Neil simply needed a male voice.

Wendy had been plying him with some "gentle" drugs just to slow his system down and allow him enough time "to smell the roses." She'd changed the drugs as the need changed to where he was on just one pill a day now, and he felt brand new.

Neil said he remembered when he started to feel better, because he actually laughed at something silly that happened in London, and slowly but surely he realized the awful blackness wasn't there any longer. Whenever it did come back, it wasn't for long, and the episodes were of no consequence and much easier to handle.

Neil looked around at us all, then turned his attention to me.

"I was in a mess, Dean," he said. "I'd wondered for years if I was sick, and finally all my chooks came home to roost after you told me to piss off, which I so richly deserved."

I suddenly felt like shit again, but Neil was being strong, bloody-minded, and brutally honest with himself and wouldn't allow me to feel guilty in any way.

"It was the wake-up call I needed," he said, holding my hand, and his eyes started watering again. "I thought I'd lost the love of my life, and I felt I just couldn't go on. My mother and my kids convinced me to seek help because they so believed in us as a couple. Isn't that amazing?"

I nodded, not trusting myself to say anything as he continued. "I remembered your GP's name, Darren Clarke, who helped you after Danny died, and I went to him. He was wonderful, and he referred me to Wendy Carmichael of all people, and well, I think you know the rest."

"No, there's more, isn't there, like your kids who supposedly didn't know about your other life, Neil?"

At least he had the decency to blush as Justine said drily, "Well, that's a joke, Joyce," and we all exploded, the mood decidedly lighter.

"Mum told us about two months before she passed on," John said seriously, "but we already knew anyway. We just didn't mention it because we knew Dad wanted it kept private."

"Mum explained it in the most loving way," Justine said, smiling at her father and me cuddled up on the couch together with her kids spread all over us. "She said that when she fell pregnant with me, Dad had insisted they get married even though he'd admitted to her that he was gay and because they did love each other in their own way. And then, of course, they had Johnny very soon afterward. But when she wasn't around anymore, she wanted Dad to have a partnership with a man as nature intended him to. She told all of us that she'd come back to haunt us all if Dad ever married a woman."

I must have looked like an imbecile with my mouth hanging open, causing Pam to laugh at me.

"What's wrong, princess?" she asked. "The Andrews family secrets too much for you to handle?"

I shook my head as the fog cleared. Now it made sense. Ever since Neil and I split, there had always been a member of the Andrews family close by. In my days off and spare time, I found myself obligated to be with one or all of them, but I knew I also enjoyed that obligation, particularly helping raise Jack and Sophie.

"So what would've happened if I'd suddenly developed an attraction for a tall, dark, handsome stranger while your father was overseas?" I said, not terribly serious, more interested in what the response would be.

"Oh," said John, "we had contingency plans in place but never had to use 'em."

"Shotgun?" I smirked.

"Oh no, nothing as crass as that. Just castration." John grinned. "We really meant business."

TWO HOURS later we were in the Merc and headed south toward the coast. We simply craved some time together, and I'd booked the same B&B where Paul and Dougie had their week of healing. Millie's inclusion was "mandatory," my now bossy other half said, and she knew she was the favored one, sitting up in the back seat of the SUV like a princess, complete with her harness.

The two lovely owners, Esther and Rhonda, and their spaniels were waiting for us, and Millie deserted us immediately, fascinated by the sights and smells of new territory. We had a comfortable room at the head of the stairs with sliding doors onto a little balcony looking out to sea—and total privacy.

Singing Pines was so named because of the row of pines across the road. It was lovely to lie in bed at night with the window open just enough for ventilation and listen to the symphony of nature playing outside through the trees.

Every day we walked along the beach, hand in hand, doing the things that lovers do, allowing ourselves the luxury of time for healing and loving, understanding we were reconnecting for the remainder of our lives and knowing this was our opportunity to get it right.

Neil *was* different, and he actually said the same about the new relaxed me, which was pretty much like the old relaxed me, except that during our previous relationship it hadn't time to emerge as it had now. Now I had the confidence to say exactly what was on my mind when and where I wanted to without worrying about his reaction. I felt myself actually *blooming*, I was so bloody happy.

All the things that had pissed me off in the past were magically gone. In fact, Neil was almost embarrassing in his outward display of affection—except that affection was directed fairly and squarely at me, and I sucked it all up like a drowning man being fed a lifeline of oxygen.

Our optimism appeared contagious. We seemed to feed each other with the excitement of the future. Any misgivings I'd had about his transformation were dispelled a few hours into our little holiday by Neil himself. He made no secret of the fact that his depression could return in part in the future, but with the two of us working "with medication and dedication," he felt confident we could conquer anything, and I agreed.

"It was only when I began to recover in London that I realized how long my mind had been in the wrong place," Neil said softly as we cuddled up on the bed on the only wet day. "To be honest, I nearly dropped my bundle there and then because of the task ahead, just getting my mind right. That's where Peter was marvelous. Wendy had kick-started the process with medication and talking the issues through, but Peter put it into perspective, reminding me not to take my eye off the goal I'd set myself."

"Which was?" I asked, a bit stupidly.

"Why, to get you back, of course," he said. "You were always the incentive all through my recovery. I knew I was hopeless the way I was, and I had to fix my mindset and rid myself of all these silly demons that haunted me. I had to be the partner you could be proud of, not one who was worried about what everyone else thought."

He paused, smiling at my face, which must have been a study of concentration.

"It wasn't until we arrived in Thailand that everything came together. I'd always thought that the old men chasing after young boys and girls there was disgusting, and I wasn't a happy camper for the first day or so until Wendy and Peter introduced me to an Australian friend of theirs, Stanley. Stan was seventy-two, a tremendously fit specimen with a great outlook on life. He'd been married twice, and his family closely resembled mine in many ways. They'd told the second wife to piss off and sent Stan to Thailand to enjoy himself. A few months later, Stan met this guy, Cert, a masseur on the beach at Jomtien, near Pattaya. Cert is late thirties, so he's half Stan's age, and they are the most beautiful couple." Neil smiled, his eyes becoming misty. "They were so kind to me. They spent endless hours talking it all through just as Wendy had, and I really started to feel optimistic again. It had never occurred to me to question the seventeen years age difference with us," he said, "and, well, I know I'm a dirty old man, and I know I'm ready. That's when I borrowed Stan's desktop and spent hours writing that e-mail."

"Don't worry." I smiled at my bloke. "I've printed it off on some nice paper, and I intend to have it framed."

LESS THAN a week ago, on the car phone and on my way to the airport, I'd explained briefly to Mum and Dad that Neil had basically suffered from the same illness that had taken Danny from us, and asked them to be their normal supportive selves while Neil and I sorted ourselves out. I could only imagine what was going through their minds. With Danny, the prognosis came too late. With Neil, they must have worried themselves sick. When I rang them again two days later with the best possible news, they were ecstatic and demanded we call in after our little holiday, which we'd intended anyway.

We drove into my parents' driveway just after 5:00 p.m. It was Friday night, and they were both there as the Merc slid to a gentle stop on the loose gravel, Millie watching with surprise as my parents, making lots of noise, hugged Neil, making sure he was safe and well. I thought they'd react this way. Neil's situation must have seemed like a nightmare revisited, but I watched the pair of them with pride as they continued to fuss over my other half. I suddenly realized how happy we'd made them by committing permanently to each other over the last few days, and I felt really good about myself for the first time in a very long time.

THIS WAS Neil's first visit home with me. I showed him the things that had been important in my life—the rock Dad had rolled under my window for Danny, which we'd placed on the edge of the lawn as a sort of memorial; the battered stile over the fence; and the pathway beyond, now overgrown with trees and grass, which led to the Morgan household. I pointed out Bruce's old kennel, which was farther along the fence, and Neil was just a little tearful. Mum had thoughtfully put new bedding in there, and Millie was busily rooting around inside making it comfortable.

"You see," I said and smiled at him, "it's the cycle of life. You knew all about that stuff long before you met me. I can't afford to get upset with all the dogs I have to euthanize."

"But Bruce wasn't a dog, Deano." He smiled at me, holding my hand, the tears really flowing by now. "Bruce was more like a human. He knew things, and he loved me. I'm just so sorry I wasn't around when he went."

I wasn't surprised at his reaction, as there'd been an undeniable bond between the two of them. Millie would never fill the gap. She was a lovely dog but only fleetingly showed the sort of understanding Bruce had. No doubt about it, he'd been one in a million.

We slept in my old room and in my old double bed. It had seen ex-lovers that had been through the sheets, including Danny and Barry, yet it didn't faze him at all. He just made the comment, "The future has overtaken the past," which I thought was pretty cool.

But even better was the affection and the *respect* I enjoyed from Neil, and Mum and Dad picked up on it immediately. So did my sisters and their boyfriends, who arrived for breakfast the next morning. The conversation flowed along, and there was laughter in the Prentice kitchen because Neil Andrews had a gentle sense of humor, and they loved him for it and for himself. He told the boys how proud he was of them for standing up against homophobia at the local football club and what an example they had made in the local district.

"The cycle of violent behavior has been broken," he said, "and generations to come will thank you for it."

He also spent time, I noticed, with Dad. I watched them through the kitchen window as Dad shook his finger at Neil, no doubt telling him what to expect if he didn't treat me properly, and I watched Neil laugh back at him, their bodies bending toward each other in mirth. It was a pleasant change for me to have Mum mostly to myself, and we talked some lovely rubbish. Neil and Dad would've been horrified if they'd overheard us, but it had been such a long time since we'd spent quality time with each other, and it was like a new beginning for me.

That night, Mum, Dad, Neil, and I trooped through the trees to Uncle Ted and Aunt Helga. Uncle Ted was a gentle, kind, and caring bloke who also happened to be a bloody good farmer and loved what he did for a living. Aunt Helga was her normal polite but reserved self, probably fulminating about this man who'd pissed off overseas, leaving her poor nephew to fend for himself. I knew she'd work it all out in time. I'd even warned Neil what she was like and not to hold his breath waiting for an endorsement, because it wouldn't happen.

We had a lovely meal. They enjoyed visitors because Aunt Helga had an excuse to cook. I realized, like Mum and Dad, they'd become empty nesters and missed the hurly-burly of full-on family life. Neil seemed to develop a similar relationship with Uncle Ted as he had with Dad. There was common ground through farming and also the friendship with Toby. I saw a flicker of interest in Aunt Helga's eyes as we talked about Toby and Macca and their extended family circle.

We'd just finished the main course when Uncle Ted suggested we take a short walk. Mum grabbed her walking stick, and Aunt Helga led the way outside to another world. For anyone not interested in animals it would have been boring, but for those so involved it was fascinating. Uncle Ted and Aunt Helga had been breeding Kelpies for over thirty years, and their stud was probably the best known and most respected in Australia.

The pens and surroundings were immaculate. Aunt Helga used the same cleaning discipline as if it were the lounge room in the house. As the years moved on and Mum's health improved, Aunt Helga found more time on her hands than she needed, and to everyone's amazement, including her husband's, she began competing at sheepdog trials. I remembered Toby telling me how she stunned the Working Sheep Dog Association—a woman winning the state title was unusual enough but winning with Kelpies up against Border collies was considered extraordinary. I wondered what she and Uncle Ted were planning, and we didn't have long to find out.

"Wait here," she barked, sounding like a KGB general doing a tour of the Kremlin.

Neil grinned at me but didn't dare speak. He obviously thought he might well lose his baby-makers if he did.

She reappeared with a dog on a lead, which I judged around twelve months old, unclipping the lead and telling him to sit. I looked at my parents, who smiled uncertainly but obviously knew what was going on.

Then I looked at the dog, and I froze—it was as if the clock had been turned back fifteen years, because there, looking at me, was Bruce.

Bruce reincarnated, certainly, but Bruce nonetheless.

"The same bloodlines," Uncle Ted said. "He not only looks the same, but I think he might have the same affinity for horses."

"What did you call him?" Neil asked.

"Donald," snapped Aunt Helga.

"Oh, Donny," Neil whispered, "what a beautiful boy you are." And he held out his arms.

In a flash, Donny had catapulted himself through the air, with Neil catching him, and twisted around in Neil's grip, with his head on his shoulder, making little squeaks of delight.

"Well, thank you for your lovely thought," I said to my aunt and uncle, "but it looks like Donny has chosen his new owner already."

Just as she'd done all those years ago, when Aunt Helga was dealing with the issue of having a gay son, she clearly had made up her mind about Neil Andrews.

"You are a good man," she said, looking Neil in the eye. "Animals tell us everything if we listen."

And Neil was lost to us in a blur of licking dog and kissing Aunt Helga. She was on the Neil team, and nothing now or in the future would persuade her otherwise.

ARRIVING HOME, I watched with amusement as Millie showed Donny "the ropes" around the yard and at the clinic. In other words, what they were allowed to get away with, and that wasn't much at all, particularly as a curious mob of Hereford vealers were in the paddock next to our building. I started to worry about the consequences, but it was totally unnecessary. Neil just handled all that stuff, and everything ran like clockwork.

I felt great. Being in love and, importantly, having that love returned just put a rosy hue on everything that happened on my first day back at work. Jobs that were normally full of pressure and stress just seemed to happen by themselves, and when Neil arrived with morning tea for all of us, I nearly burst with bloody pride. Now I wasn't struggling by myself anymore. He was in my corner looking out for me, helping me get through the day, and waiting at night with a big glass of red and a cuddle. It was overwhelming, yet it was lovely, and I realized this is what most couples did for each other. And finally, after all this time, it was happening to me.

The following week went by at breakneck speed. If I'd been asked where the time went there was no way I could have accounted for it, but Neil seemed to guide us through troubled waters as if they didn't even exist—at the clinic, at home, on the farm—and still pointedly left time just for us. The old Neil seemed to have sunk without trace—there was no sign of the behavior that caused the split. In fact, he was now an open book to everyone, and that both pleased and worried the shit out of me. Neil seemed to think that because he'd radically changed his attitudes, so the rest of the world would automatically follow, which obviously wasn't the case.

The irony of my fears didn't escape me. After insisting he go public with our relationship for so long and refusing to compromise, reality and common sense took center stage. I saw a need to be protective of him because of his naïveté. I knew we'd survive as a couple regardless, but I didn't want Neil hurt by either homophobia or the stigma of mental health issues from busybodies who had nothing better to do, and sadly our town still had plenty of those.

I discussed my concerns with him, but my lovely bloke was adamant.

"Fuck 'em," he said. "I was part of that mindset once. Not anymore, thank you, and I know you're worried about my feelings, but I really think public opinion has moved on, and frankly I don't give a shit as long as you're around."

After work the following Monday evening, I locked up the clinic and walked up the driveway toward the homestead. Suddenly my bloody sixth sense kicked in, because something wasn't right. I strode into the lounge room where Neil and Marge were sitting, and immediately I could see things were far from okay.

"What's wrong?" I said as gently as I could, noting all the while that Marge looked almost terrified.

"Um, just an anxiety attack," he said apologetically. "Wendy said they'd happen from time to time."

"You take your medication?"

He nodded. "About an hour ago. I do feel a bit better actually."

I'd spoken to Wendy and Peter at great length and knew what to expect, and this was just textbook stuff.

"It's okay, Marge." I said. "We'll have a few of these as time progresses. Nothing to worry about, is there, darl?" I said to him, and he bloody grinned at me, and we all relaxed.

"So what brought this on?" I said carefully, trying not to undo the fix the medication was providing. "You worried about the presentation at Rotary tomorrow night? You want to call in sick and let Wendy and Peter do it?"

His response was immediate and forthright.

"No, no, no," he said. "I'm fine, thanks, it's just we have to expect a few of these from time to time."

WENDY AND Peter had finally arrived home from Thailand a week ago, and together with Neil, they were to present the Rotary banners exchanged with each club they'd visited throughout Europe and Asia, creating a degree of expectation among members because this was like visiting another country through the eyes of a fellow Rotarian.

Mum and Dad arrived during the afternoon because Neil thought they would enjoy the show. The Andrews clan minus the kids was there as well—a table of eight of us.

President Valerie welcomed everyone. She said the night should focus on the three members who had quite studiously gathered information on no less than fifteen clubs and had returned safely home.

"Tonight," she said, "we'll be treated to a first-class presentation from our inveterate travelers, which will cover much more than the normal swapping of banners, patting people on the back, and shaking hands. Wendy, Peter, and Neil have gathered information on member profiles, local industries, even the local food of every club they've visited. So in recognition of their efforts I think it's appropriate that we shorten up the normal business items on our agenda and cover them next week. In addition, after that presentation, Neil has an important address to members and a presentation in his own right, which will hopefully encourage this club to take a leadership position in the community on these very same issues."

"But what about the reports?" said Jim Smythe, the secretary.

"Jim," said Valerie, "you're a lovely man and probably the best secretary this club has seen in recent years, but you weren't listening to what I had to say. I made the point that Neil Andrews, through his address to the club, will issue a challenge to us all for the future. So with all due respect, Jim, fuck the reports."

Jesus, what is my other half up to? He rose to his feet to help Wendy and Peter.

He was about to walk off when he turned, smiled at me, and kissed me full on the lips in the full glare of the Rotary spotlight. I felt pretty good as everyone at our table smiled in appreciation, so I relaxed a little. Around the room there seemed to be smiles from every corner, so I relaxed further and tuned in to Peter Carmichael, who was leading the presentation.

I had to admit it was a stellar job. They'd captured the lifeblood of every club they visited, with the facts spelled out clearly and with the minimum amount of bullshit. They presented fifteen little banners to

President Valerie, one at a time, pinning them to a display board for viewing after the meeting.

There was generous applause for a job well done. Wendy and Peter sat down, and Neil walked to the center of the stage. The conversation immediately ceased as members and friends gave him the courtesy of a good hearing.

My heart was in my mouth, and I was just a little bit pissed off. We were supposed to be a couple, for Christ's sake, and here I was with absolutely no idea what he was going to say or do.

Fuck.

He looked at me, and those amazing blue puddles called eyes drew me in, and I forgot about everyone else in the room. *It's bloody hypnosis, and he knows how to get me under his spell—he only has to glance at me.*

He began speaking, completely without notes, and rather gently told the story of the last few months, how it wasn't much of a holiday for Wendy and Peter because of his illness, how they'd persisted until he recovered, and as a result of his experience he realized depression was far more widespread within humanity than he'd ever expected.

"I want to publicly thank Wendy and Peter for their devotion to me as a patient and as a person." He continued. "I also want to thank my family for standing by me and supporting me through what was a process of healing and self-discovery. But above all, I want to thank my partner, Dean, because without him I wouldn't be standing here now speaking to you."

I must have looked stupid. Suddenly I was the center of attention. I could feel around sixty pairs of eyes focused on me, and my mouth felt as dry as buggery—probably because I just couldn't close it.

"Dean," Neil said, "would you come up here, please?"

He beckoned with his finger, and I stood up, moving through the tables toward him. I watched where I was putting my big feet, and when I looked up, he seemed to be on the floor to one side of the lectern. *Christ, he's hurt or he's fainted.*

But when I got closer, I could see he was okay and maybe he was tying up his shoelace, but then I remembered he was wearing his nice black slip-on shoes.

I was within cooee when I saw he was on one knee with the top of the little box cracked open and jewelry glinting inside… and I froze.

"Dean," he said. "I love you. Will you marry me?"

IT WAS the very last thing on my mind. I'd been focusing on our partnership—correctly, I thought—and really hadn't considered marriage at all, and for someone who had a sixth sense for an ambush, I'd been cut off at the pass completely. I was really taken by surprise.

I suppose my stunned silence probably seemed like half an hour to everyone gathered there—family, friends, and fellow Rotarians. It did cross my mind that being proposed to at a Rotary meeting would probably create some sort of record for Rotary International.

I glanced over at President Valerie, who was grinning like a maniac. *The master strategist.* But she was absolutely on our side, and somehow I reckoned our fellow members who might be even slightly homophobic wouldn't dare cross her. Then I glanced at our family group, and my father was totally overcome, which was amazing, and Mum was just smiling beautifully, holding Marge's hand. My soon-to-be stepchildren had forgotten I could lip-read, and "wicked stepmother" was certainly on their lips. I'd catch up with them later, but I realized Neil deserved an answer after all the trouble he'd gone to.

I reached down and pulled him to his feet, and I whispered "Yes" in his ear, and his face broke into a beautiful smile as he pressed a magnificent, heavy ring onto my finger. I was about to tell him his good taste hadn't failed him when there was an explosion of sound.

He and I watched transfixed as a room full of middle Australia erupted in jubilation, cheering, yelling, and applauding, and I think we both wondered what on earth we'd ever been scared of.

CHAPTER 29
THE BIG DAY GETS BETTER

HIS GAZE held me in an almost hypnotic state as I turned and faced the bloke who was about to become my husband, as I was to become his.

We joined hands together just in front of David Canning, who was the absolute model of patience and understanding.

"Please be seated," he roared at the guests, who wisely did as they were told, but David sensed we needed just a little more time before he actually began.

I knew Neil felt the same as I did. It was one of the comforting things about our lovely partnership. We just knew our way around each other's heads. Today, for us, was looking forward, not back. In six weeks we would be parents. Our surrogate was doing really well, considering she was bearing not one child, but twins. Twin boys in fact, which—despite dire warnings from other parents—didn't faze us at all. Jack, Sophie, and Angela were all being raised by the Andrews "village," and they were thriving, to say the least. Two more kids wouldn't be a problem.

Both of us turned at the same time and smiled at the family group immediately behind us, then looked lovingly at each other. He leaned into me, and I did the same, and we managed the most passionate kiss possible that seemed to go on for ages, but we were bloody enjoying it anyway. There was a smattering of applause and a few raucous laughs, but it was little Jack with the big voice who suddenly had the floor.

"Haw, haw, haw, haw," he chortled, and I realized Justine was trying to shut him up but to no avail, the microphones picking up every sound. He didn't need them anyway. "I think Pa loves Dean," he roared, and his sister, quite insulted, decided she had to have her say as well.

"Well, Dean loves Pa too," she shrilled, if anything, louder than her brother.

The response was immediate. The tension we felt as participants abated, and we all remembered our sense of humor at the same time as the guests held their sides, applauding wildly.

And somewhere in Outer Mongolia, as the herdsmen sat around sipping their yak milk, they, too, were nodding in agreement.

"Yes, Dean loves Pa, and Pa loves Dean too."

JOHN TERRY MOORE lives with his partner Russell in Geelong, Victoria's largest regional center, one hour from Melbourne, Australia. He completed his education at Hobart Matriculation College, and held a number of senior positions in the automotive industry over a thirty-five year period.

He has been a civil marriage celebrant and funeral celebrant since 1995 (now retired), and together with his partner were successful flower growers, raised stud sheep and bred Kelpies, Australia's working dogs. Born into a farming family; his empathy and understanding of country people has allowed him to focus on rural issues in his writing.

Geographical and social isolation through the worry and stress of poor seasons, fluctuating prices, and in particular, sexual orientation in men has fuelled depression across regional and rural Australia in epidemic proportions. Driven by his experiences as a funeral celebrant, he understands full well the ultimate penalty paid by men of all age groups when they feel marginalized by homophobic attitudes and actions in rural and regional communities in particular.

Over the years, John has become an increasingly strident and persistent voice with politicians, community groups, and the general public, encouraging, supporting, and driving the push for gay marriage and equal rights for same sex parents and their children. Black Dog reminds us that gay kids should never be allowed to feel that they aren't as good as straight kids. That only when everyone is treated exactly the same under law will society begin to heal itself.

http://www.dreamspinnerpress.com

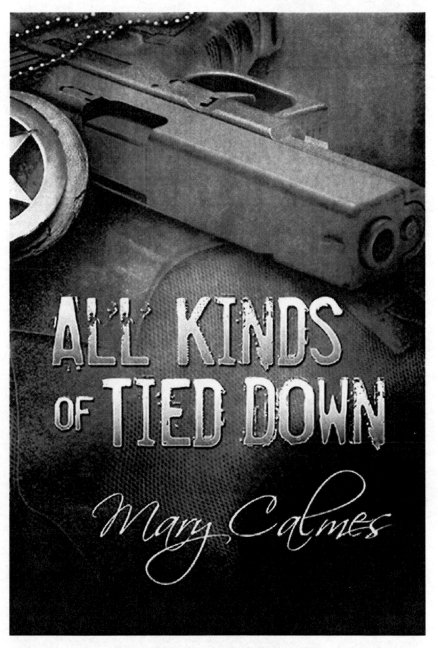

ALL KINDS OF TIED DOWN

Mary Calmes

http://www.dreamspinnerpress.com

RAINBOW BLUES

KC Burn

http://www.dreamspinnerpress.com

http://www.dreamspinnerpress.com

CPSIA information can be obtained
at www.ICGtesting.com
Printed in the USA
FFOW02n1230040914
7138FF